The
First
Few Friends

The First Few Friends

a novel by

Marilyn Singer

HARPER & ROW, PUBLISHERS

NEW YORK

Cambridge   London
Hagerstown   Mexico City
Philadelphia   São Paulo
San Francisco   Sydney

1817

F
S6176 4F
B2

THE FIRST FEW FRIENDS

FIRST EDITION

Library of Congress Cataloging in Publication Data
Singer, Marilyn.
  The first few friends.

  Summary: Nina returns to New York City in August 1968 after a year at an English university and finds the times have changed drastically.
  I. Title.
PZ7.S6172Fi 1981   [Fic]   80–8938
ISBN 0-06-025728-8   AACR2
ISBN 0-06-025729-6 (lib. bdg.)

Acknowledgments

Special thanks to the following people:
Steve Aronson
Jane Levine, esq.
Donn Livingston, esq.
Michael Mushlin, esq.
Wilson Ortiz
James Woods
And to Liz Gordon and Terry Moogan for their incredible patience.

To All of My Friends, wherever they are,
and to the spirit of John Lennon

While riding on a train goin' west
I fell asleep for to take my rest,
I dreamed a dream that made me sad
Concerning myself and the first few friends I had.

"Bob Dylan's Dream"
Bob Dylan

PART ONE

August 1968

Chapter 1

My ass really hurts.

I've been on this damn plane for nearly fourteen hours. It's almost midnight. Five a.m. in London. We were supposed to have arrived at five p.m. Eastern Daylight Time. It figures that just when I'm coming home after being in England for a year, there'd be an airport strike. We circled Kennedy Airport for three hours, flew to Toronto to refuel, flew back to New York and have been circling for almost three hours again. Any more circling and I'll have permanent vertigo.

Oh God, there goes another poor slob staggering to the loo. That's toilet in English.

Come to think of it, I'm not feeling so well myself. I don't think that Scotch and soda helped. I hope my parents don't smell it on my breath. I can hear the comments already—"You went to England a teetotaler and came back a wino," "Our daughter a boozer!" et al.

Was it really just yesterday Gwyn kissed me good-bye in Victoria Station?

"Don't see me off at the airport," I'd begged. "I couldn't bear it. It's too final."

3

"Nothing's final. I'll come to the States within a year. I promise you I will," he answered seriously. Then he got that mischievous glint in his eye that I love so much. "And I'll thrill your friends with my British charm and perfect manners," he said and pinched my bum—or ass, as Americans call it.

Oh Gwyn. Oh God.

Why do I have to come back to New York?

"Please fasten your etceteras."

I must have dozed off. I wonder who's waiting for me at the terminal. My parents, of course. What will they think about me now? I've changed a lot in a year, a year spent at Reading University learning about literature and life. A hefty hunk of life. I'm twenty (almost). A grown-up. So my parents can't pretend I'm their little girl anymore, can they? Things have to be different A.E. (After England).

Will the Whole Sick Crew be waiting too? I hope so—at least then I'll have some people to talk to. We had a lot of good times before I left—Aviva, Dorrie, Nancy and me, the Whole Sick Crew. I remember how Aviva dubbed us that. We were going out to Nathan's on Long Island to consume large quantities of hot dogs and Cokes and to show off Dorrie's bike to the Rebels, a motorcycle gang we heard hung out there. That was Avi's latest craze—motorcycles. Avi had lots of crazes—poker, blues clubs (for which we made trips to strange corners of Manhattan), learning and riding the entire New York City subway system, and Tolkien. And we went through all of the crazes with her. After all, they were fun. The one thing she'd always stuck with was singing (even though the type of music changed), just as I stuck with my writing, Dorrie with her sculpture and Nancy with her violin. Anyway, this time Avi's craze was motorcycles. She was too young to own a bike, so Dorrie bought one instead, a used BMW that

4

ate up most of her savings. Dorrie looked great on that cycle, with her strong, hard-muscled arms, crash helmet and dark shades. And Avi looked good too, sitting on the back. Sometimes Dorrie let her practice driving it. Nancy and I couldn't afford motorcycles—or drive them for that matter—so we just followed along in my old Chevy. When we reached Nathan's there were the Rebels and their girls in their jeans and black leather jackets with the chains and the studs and the name *Rebels* written in bold red letters.

The Rebels were knocked out by Dorrie and Avi and offered us beer and rides on their bikes. One of them, Tiny, who was 6'5" and 280 pounds or so, as a supreme compliment lifted up Dorrie and Avi together as if they were two little birds, set them on his bike and told them to take it for a spin. Dorrie and Avi loved it. We all did—even though rounding those sharp corners and heading through those dark streets made me and Nancy a little nervous. When we finally left, beer bloated, exhilarated and slightly woozy, a silent gloating passed between us. We were tough, it said. We were any man's equal.

Then, back in Dorrie's room, we shared some leftover rice pudding and exchanged imitations of the Rebels' pungent speech until we collapsed laughing.

"Look at us. The Whole Sick Crew!" Aviva said.

"The Whole Sick Crew? Did you make that up?" I asked.

"No, I got it from this weird book called *V.* The Crew is a bunch of lethargic, decadent romantics."

"That's us, all right," Dorrie said.

"There's a character in it, Benny Profane, who hunts alligators in the sewers of New York."

"Are there really alligators in the sewers of New York?" Nancy asked.

"Sure, but they're disguised as rats," Dorrie answered.

"The Whole Sick Crew. I like that," I said.

And so that's who we became.

The Crew made life at Queens College bearable. Maybe they can make this year bearable too. If anyone can. Anyone besides Gwyn.

"We are now descending. On your left is Manhattan. . . ."

It sure is. Lights and all. I don't know whether I feel like laughing or crying. I wish Gwyn were here. I wish he were stroking my breasts. Blimey, I don't think that's the kind of thought one is supposed to have when one is about to see one's parents once again.

Oh England!

The plane has miraculously landed. Behind the glare of lights there are faces looking for their disembarking loved ones.

Baggage. Pushing through the mob. Customs. "Anything to declare . . ."

Yes. My freedom, my independence, my love for Gwyn. "No, nothing," I say.

Through the swinging doors. There they are. Mom's face, bright, moon-shaped. Dad, smiling, but still managing to look dour.

"There she is!"

"Here I am."

Hugs. Kisses.

"You gained weight, Nina."

"I guess I did."

"What's this you're wearing?" Dad asks, disdainfully surveying the dashiki I have on, gift from a Nigerian friend.

"It's . . . Aviva! Nancy! Dorrie!"

The Whole Sick Crew made it after all. More hugs, kisses.

"We've been waiting for . . ."

"How was the . . ."

"Are you glad to . . ."

We go into a huddle.

6

And Aviva asks the question everyone really wants the answer to: "So, Nina, did you get laid?"

Should I expose what was so private between Gwyn and me to the hot New York air and my friends' eager ears? Of course. "Yup," I say. "Did you?" I ask teasingly.

Her answer surprises me—maybe because sex never seemed very important to Aviva. "Yeah," she says. "And it was terrific. How about for you?"

Terrific? It was so many things. But I can't talk about them now.

"It was terrific!" I exclaim.

"Great! Listen, I've got a lot to tell you. I'm auditioning for a rock group on Monday. The Rabbit's Foot. Name stinks, but the group's good."

Rock. A new craze. But that was Avi.

"Can you come with me to the audition?" she asks.

How to tell her right now I just want to go to sleep? Dorrie rescues me, as she's always done.

"How about letting her get over jet lag first, Avi?"

"Okay. I'll remind you again so you don't forget."

"I won't," I say. And I couldn't even if I wanted to—that's the way things always are with Aviva.

Then Nancy says, "Here's a present," and she slips a joint into my bag. "You do get stoned, don't you?"

Yet another vice acquired in the Mother Country. "You do too, I see." We grin at each other. It looks as though the Crew is expanding its horizons.

"Nina, time to go home," my parents say.

Hugs and kisses again. "See you when you recover," the Crew says.

Sitting in the Chevy watching the landmarks that were so familiar a year ago and now seem so strange. The Chevy's especially strange—I haven't been in a big car for a long time.

7

"You must have lots of photos," Dad says.

"Uh-huh."

"Lots of scenic spots, huh?"

"No. Just people," I answer, thinking of the photos of Gwyn. Gwyn in a purple shirt holding a purple candle. Gwyn at Caerphilly Castle when I visited him in Wales. Gwyn reading Chaucer. And one photo of me in my dashiki—a special photo that Gwyn took right after we made love. Would my parents be able to tell from looking at it what I'd just done? Maybe I won't show them that one.

"Just people? We sent you a couple of dozen rolls and all you shot were people? What about all those places you went to?"

"I didn't want to take a lot of tourist shots," I say. But what I mean is I didn't want to seem a goggle-eyed American.

Dad wants to continue this discussion, but Mom steps in.

"So many people have asked about you," she says.

"Oh, like who?"

"Your Aunt Betty. Uncle Harry. My friend Charlotte. Lots of people."

"I'm surprised you didn't get them to come to the airport."

"Well, dear, they're busy people," Mom explains, misunderstanding my remark.

I laugh. Nothing changes after all.

"What's funny?" Dad asks.

"Nothing. I'm just shagged."

"Shagged?"

"Sorry. Tired. Pooped."

"Well, you sound like a real Englishman now," Mom says.

I hope so, I think.

And then, there's quiet. I watch the road move along and feel myself standing still. I wonder if Gwyn is doing the same thing. I wonder if it's raining in Wales. In Barry, where Gwyn must be by now.

Somewhere in the rain
The road moves
And the figure stands still,
Looks into a bush of broom.

The poem starts forming in my head magically, as the poems always do. And I can even smell the broom, see the brilliant yellow flowers. A sprig in my hair. And Gwyn and me under the bush, his shirt unbuttoned, his hand on my thigh.

Somewhere
The girl with broomed hair
Remembers,
Feels the rain.

It was such a soft rain. It carried Gwyn's scent. It made us laugh. But right now, the memory of it makes me cry. Softly.

It is not as damp as her eyes.

I will write down the poem and send it to Gwyn tomorrow. He will understand.

Finally in bed. Mom and Dad didn't press me to chitchat. "There's plenty of time for that now that you're home," Dad said. Mom had my room painted. Baby blue. With new curtains, flowered bedspread. A surprise. She was so excited. I had to tell her I love it. I don't. I miss the old faded wallpaper with the garish roses, and I miss the moth-eaten pink chenille bedspread. I even miss all the art postcards and pictures of the Beatles stuck on my wall. This room doesn't feel real. Home doesn't feel real. Nothing feels real. I thought home would always feel like home, but I guess that's not true. God, I don't know where I am!

And I'm too exhausted to sleep. Music might help. All my new albums are in my trunk, not yet arrived. Except one. *Disraeli Gears* by Cream. I couldn't wait even one extra day for that one.

I turn on my old stereo, low, put the record on and lie, listening, in the dark.

I'll stay with you, darling, now.
I'll stay with you 'til my seas are dried uh-up.
I've been waiting so long
To be where I'm going
In the sunshine of your love.

St. George's Hall. Gwyn and I, fearing a visit from the warden or the cleaning woman, moving together to "The Sunshine of Your Love" blasting out of the little hi-fi, moving in pain and embarrassment and ecstasy and music.

I touch myself and I can feel Gwyn's hands, his lips, his breath. Love me, Gwyn. Love me. Love me. Now. Now. Oh yes. Now.

But there's no Gwyn. No sunshine of your love. Only Nina alone, having sex with herself. And feeling worse than before. I guess I'll cry myself to sleep.

Chapter 2

I went to England because I was in love with Paul McCartney. Oh, I didn't write that in my essay or say it in my interview for the Study Abroad program, but it was true all the same. I even went to his house in St. John's Wood and sat outside writing poetry which I slipped into his postal slot along with my name and address. I'm afraid he didn't write back.

I tried to maintain my crush on my unattainable idol. But England was really swinging. Short skirts, tight pants, hard rock, good dope, super conversation and all of us living in one place—a mini city of wit, wisdom and lust. And so Paul was soon usurped by a host of very attainable and very handsome Reading University students. I had never dated much at Queens College, so this was new and fun, but also a little frustrating. All these gorgeous men and I didn't know what to do. Some of my English girl friends were still virgins, and some of them were having sex all over the place. I wanted to be somewhere in between. So I finally settled on Colin. Sensitive, dramatic, handsome-in-a-pink-and-gold-English-way Colin. A talented actor who was studying to be a farmer, he was getting over a rotten love affair, the gory details of which

11

he told me. We necked and fooled around some, and one day, he asked me if I'd care to let him deflower me. "Yes," I answered, surprising us both, "but first let me go on the Pill." I was determined—no messy condoms or clumsy diaphragms would mar my first lovemaking. So on the Pill I went, and during the time it took to "work," Colin reunited with his girl friend and I got dumped.

Feeling miserable and horny, as well as nauseous from contraceptives, I asked my friend Rhys what to do.

"You know my chum Gwyn," he said, "the one you met at Christmas?"

Oh yes. I remembered. Gwyn was one of the most striking men I'd ever seen, replete with high cheekbones, bright blue eyes and a husky, sexy voice that sounded particularly seductive when he spoke Welsh. I nodded.

"Well," said Rhys, "I know you rather fancied him. Why don't you go up to East Anglia and pay him a visit."

"Oh Rhys, I couldn't do that. I hardly know him."

"England's a friendly country. And besides, I'll write you a letter of introduction."

And so, maybe it was the full moon or maybe just the Pill, but, throwing my proverbial caution to the proverbial winds, I said Yes. Oh my God did I say Yes.

Next to Gwyn, poor Paul McCartney became for me a mere shadow of his former self. But you know, somehow, now, I wish I still had my crush on Paul. After all, waiting for a word from Paul McCartney, which, deep down inside, you know you're never going to get, is not as painful as waiting for a letter from a person with whom you've actually had an affair.

But Gwyn's letter did finally come—today, in time to allow me to be at least somewhat gracious to my college friends arriving for the Welcome-Home-Barbecue, to be held this afternoon in my backyard.

The letter is residing in my pocket. I will not move it. It is beautiful.

Dearest Nina,

A celibate am I in Barry-by-the-Sea. Standing pebble deep at the Cold Knap sending ripple messages across the Atlantic. Sworn off anything alcoholic for a week (at least) in mourning for the loss of. Also sworn off looking at other women, although one (Rhys' Vanessa) came beating at the door this very morning. A talk, she said she wanted. A talk was all she got. Then there was Gaye. You remember my mentioning her? She called and said she was going to throw herself into the sea if I didn't come see her. So I had to trot over to her house and listen to her for an hour or two while she proposed to me, among other things, marriage, suicide, murder, friendship and communal living. I listened politely and told her to sleep it off. See how good I'm being.

Listening to the new Moody Blues l.p. Must send to you when, if, money is at hand. Must save some so I can own a new pair of boots for Welsh climb-ate.

Rhys will not communicate with me. I fear he fears his lady-love fancies me. Perhaps I will speak with her again. What secrets may be uncovered?

Ah, Nina, are you being love out there to those who need you? And you are needed, you know.

Remember—

License my roving hands, and let them go,
Before, behind, between, above, below.
Oh my America, my new-found-land,
My Kingdom, safeliest when with one man man'd,
My Mine of precious stones, My Emperie,

13

How blest am I in this discovering thee!
Good old John Donne.
Nina, Nina, my bed is so cold.

Au récrire.

Love,

Gwyn

I read it over at least ten times.

My mother came into my room once. "Who's it from?" she asked.

"A bloke I'm going with."

She looked at me strangely, trying to read all that that sentence meant, no doubt. "Andy Gertz and Stan Wasserman are both coming today," she said, too brightly.

I had to smile. Andy and Stan. Two guys I fancied what seems eons ago. My mother is so obvious sometimes.

"I see that makes you happy," she said cheerily.

I smiled again. Why spoil her fantasy, I thought.

"What are you wearing?" she asked.

"I haven't thought about it, but I guess this." I took out a blue dress with a miniskirt that I'd bought my first day in London at a fashionable boutique. I could see my mother's disapproval immediately.

"Nina, isn't it a little short?"

"Actually, it's a lot short," I said, "but I do have nice legs. At least, that's what everybody at Reading said."

My mother clucked her tongue and left the room.

And I took out Gwyn's letter once again.

This barbecue is really cooking. Ugh, what a pun! Dad is grilling the franks and burgers and avoiding talking to people. Mom is bustling about, making sure everyone is eating and talking. Most of my college friends are here. And the lines are drawn just as they were before I left. On one side are the Andy Gertzes, Stan Wassermans, Lisa Scherbers and Didi Hinkels of my life—the high-achieving, propriety-conscious young collegiates I am ashamed to admit I wanted desperately to be a part of when I was an anxious freshman and even a slightly jaded sophomore. I had always been something of a misfit in high school—studious, awkward, with oddball tastes like Renaissance poetry and classical music. So, when I got to college, I really wanted to be part of the "in" crowd for a change. And I did a pretty good job of worming my way into it. Joined a "house plan," Queens' slightly less elite version of a sorority, with the insipid name of Dew Drop Inn. Took part in social teas, dances with male house plans, performed in the Follies, etc. But the boys—and they were indeed boys— turned out to belong to the old grope-and-gripe school; and the girls, with their talk of makeup and hairdos and "getting pinned," bored me to distraction. So I eventually gave up on the idea of ever really fitting in.

However, my parents, who invited the guests, obviously think these people are still my friends.

"You sure look groovy," Andy Gertz says, patting me on my bum.

I restrain myself from smashing a hot dog in his face and pass him the relish.

On the other side of the line is the Whole Sick Crew. Aviva looks outrageous as usual—big sunglasses and some old dress she found in an antique shop.

I first met Aviva in English 3, The History of Drama. She sauntered in, in granny glasses and a military jacket—ages before John Lennon made them popular in *Sergeant Pepper's Lonely Hearts Club Band*—and took the seat next to mine.

"Hey." A guy behind us tapped her shoulder. "Army, Navy or Marines?"

"Women's Christian Temperance Union, Fifth Division," she said, deadpan.

15

I giggled.

The guy didn't know what she was talking about, so he made a cuckoo sign with his finger and went back to talking to his neighbor.

"Smash up many saloons lately?" I asked.

Her face lit up. "Ah, a kindred spirit," she said. "How about joining me after class so we can sharpen our axes."

"For God, Glory and Carrie Nation," I answered.

"L'chaim!" she responded.

We smiled at each other in approval.

Then our professor, Dr. McCracken, walked in, and Avi and I immediately fell in love with her. She was one of those dynamic older women whose wit and enthusiasm just sweep you up. Instantly, she had us waving our hands frantically to answer her questions. Aviva and I spent the term competing to see who answered more of them.We also spent our lunch hours acting out plays and goofing around. I found out she had gone to the High School of Performing Arts and could act, paint, sing, write, play piano and speak four languages with perfect ease. At three, she was able to read *Hamlet.* At five, she was able to understand it. She set her own style and didn't give a damn who liked it. And unlike the other girls I'd met at Q.C., she gave almost no thought to boys, who most often were scared of her anyway. But she also could betray a touching vulnerability that made me want to protect her. Eventually, she attracted a few other misfits to the fold— Nancy and Dorrie and some others who drifted in and out of favor. But for a while, it was just me and Avi. I was so grateful to her for rescuing me from the house-plan set. I liked and admired and was intimidated by her a lot. And I realize I still feel the same way.

Bringing over a burger to Aviva, I see that Didi is there, attempting to cross the line.

"Where did you get those fabulous sunglasses? Blooming-dale's?" she asks.

"No. The Salvation Army," Aviva cracks.

Didi tries again. "What are you studying at college?"

"I'm an Ursa Major," Aviva answers, straight faced.

Didi looks puzzled. "Isn't that the Big Dipper?"

"Isn't that a great ice cream place?"

Didi gives up and rejoins her safe and sane friends.

"Did you have to?" I ask Aviva.

"Yes, I had to."

At that moment, Lisa Scherber sidles over and puts her elegantly manicured hand on my arm.

"Nina, will you settle a vital question for us?" she asks loudly, glancing at Stan Wasserman.

I wait, not very patiently, for the vital question.

"Well," says Lisa, "you must tell us if English guys are really cuter than American ones."

Stan and company incline their heads eagerly.

"No," I say flutteringly, "the Welsh ones are."

Everyone laughs. And I suddenly feel very tired.

I turn to Aviva, who is not laughing. "Listen, Neen," she says. "This is a drag. We're going to split now. How about you coming over later after this soirée is over?"

"I don't think my parents will appreciate that."

"Jesus, you did fine without their appreciation for a year, didn't you?"

I am annoyed—at Aviva and at myself. Four days at home and already I was slipping into a timeworn groove. Old patterns do not die, they just fade away—temporarily.

"I'll be there," I said firmly. "Your place?"

"No, Dorrie's. More privacy. We can. . ." She holds an imaginary joint to her mouth and sucks in the imaginary smoke.

17

"Hash or grass?" I say knowledgeably.

"Grass. Did you smoke hash in Merry Old?"

"But of course," I say.

Aviva looks at me briefly with admiration. "Do tell."

"Later." And I notice Lisa trotting off briskly to spread the word to Didi and friends that upright, law-abiding Nina Ritter has irredeemably become a head.

I drive with all the windows open and the radio blasting. The car handles surprisingly well—or rather I handle the car surprisingly well. I thought I might have forgotten how.

In my head I am composing and rejecting various openings to a letter to Gwyn.

Dear Gwyn,
     Tell all women to cease and desist from door beating.

Too threatened?

Dear Gwyn,
     O them dirty poems!

Too jokey?

Dear Gwyn,
     I love you.

Too bald. I have not told him. He has not told me. All the feelings, the lovemaking, but not the words.

I love you.

I know I will not be able to write it. Not yet.

I feel sad. Horribly sad. After the elation over Gwyn's letter, I now feel even more lost from him.

And then that barbecue. How can I face my last year of college? Those people! Thank heavens for the Crew. And yet,

I wonder what Aviva will lead us to. And if I will be able to handle it as well as I can this car.

I pull up to the curb in front of Dorrie's flat. She lives in the furnished basement of a split-level house in Queens. Her job as a bus driver for the Happy Bunny Nursery School allows her the enviable position of having her own place. Because of this, she should be accorded the deference shown to the more worldly, but since she's from Ashtabula, Ohio, we decided her worldliness leaves something to be desired.

Dorrie is three years older than the rest of us. She was "discovered" by Shoshanna, Aviva's older sister, when they were camp counselors together. Dorrie quickly learned to appreciate the wit and wisdom of Aviva over that of Shoshanna.

When I push open Dorrie's door, I am greeted by the familiar smell of grass and the not-so-familiar sight of Nancy, grinning maniacally, her hair a mad frizz all over her head, wearing a long purple robe and fiddling antically on her violin. I have never seen her look so crazy before. Dorrie is photographing her, and Aviva is rolling a joint. In the background is a weird assemblage of cans and twine and wood—obviously Dorrie's latest creation.

"Enter, enter, O Homecoming Queen," Aviva greets me.

"Shut up and pass the pot," I retort.

"Yes, O Prodigal Daughter." She hands me the joint.

I take a long toke and hold the smoke until my lungs give out.

"Ahhh," I exhale. "I needed that."

"Tsk. Tsk. What nasty habits our Nina has acquired."

I take another toke. Nancy's violin playing suddenly seems sharper. "What the hell is she doing?" I ask.

"She's being photographed for her entry as the next Miss Subways," Dorrie says.

"Yeah. And it's going to read: 'This month's Miss Subways

19

is Nancy Gold. Her hobbies are screwing, smoking dope and playing the violin. And she's built like a brick shithouse.' Can you see it?" Nancy announces.

Brain clearing under the influence, I can see it. And I crack up.

Then Aviva starts to sing, "Boom-boom-boom-boom. She's built like a brick shithouse. Boom-boom-boom-boom. She's built like a brick shithouse."

Nancy chimes in with high harmony, "She's built like a . . . She's built like a . . ."

I join in with bass, "Boom-boom-boom-boom. Boom-boom-boom-boom."

Dorrie adds a falsetto, "Ooo-wee-ooo-waaa."

Standing close, heads together, we keep it up until Dorrie's voice breaks. Then we collapse in a heap on the floor, sputtering and hiccuping.

"Jesus," I finally gasp. "What happened to Nice Nancy?"

"Dirty Laundry," the Crew choruses.

"Huh?"

"Aviva's last group," Nancy explains.

"Dirty Laundry?"

"Yeah. Organized by Bill Darrow, the filmmaker. We sang gems such as 'Baby, Let Me Beat Your Buns' and 'Up Yours, Forever,' " Aviva says.

"Oh shit. You're kidding, no?"

"No."

"How'd you get involved with them?"

"Through a friend of Shoshanna's."

"How come you're not still with them?"

"Got kicked out of one too many clubs for singing 'Thunder Thighs.' "

"I won't even ask," I say.

"You'll meet the rest of Dirty Laundry one of these days and receive your initiation." Aviva leers.

Dorrie and Nancy giggle.

"Mark will especially dig you. He's a tits-and-ass man."

Even stoned, I wince and then ask, "Who's Mark?"

"The drummer."

"And he certainly knows how to use his sticks," Nancy says with a wink.

The Crew all laugh suggestively.

I look from one to the other. "All of you?" I finally ask.

"All of us," Aviva answers. "It'll be your turn next."

"I can hardly wait," I say, trying for levity but feeling heavily uncomfortable. I see Gwyn's head on my breasts and shudder at the image of another head in its stead. Also, I am surprised by this new taste of Aviva's and the Crew's. I mean, we were all bawdy on occasion, but not gross. And I used to think when Aviva got interested, really interested in the opposite sex, she'd probably be something of a romantic like me. I'm not sure what she's into now. Maybe she thinks a rock musician has to act this way. Or maybe—God forbid—this is another craze. Well, damn it, if it is, it's not one I'll go along with.

Dorrie alone seems to sense my discomfort. "See any hookahs in England?" she asks me.

I recover quickly. "Sure, you could tell them by their lack of handbags."

"Whoa-ho-ho, pun time," Aviva chortles. "Get out the old water pipe, Dorrie my dear, and let us begin."

Dorrie brings out an ornate green glass hookah with wooden-tipped, multi-colored pipes.

"What a beauty!" I exclaim. "You have any wine?"

"Wine?"

"Yep. You fill it with wine instead of water—a smoother taste."

"Leave it to the British," Dorrie says, fetching a bottle of souring burgundy.

"I'm surprised they don't put beer in it instead," Nancy remarks.

"That would taste un-beer-able," Aviva says.

"There she goes again." Dorrie shakes her head and burbles the hookah.

"She's always been an outrageous punster. She handed in an English paper with the opening sentence: 'Hamlet was a great Dane,' " I say.

Dorrie snorts and begins to choke on the smoke and wine. Nancy lets loose with her high-pitched whinny.

"Didn't you give in a paper called 'Easier Said Than Donne'?" Aviva rejoins.

Dorrie and Nancy pound each other's backs.

"Yeah, but it took me all day to come up with that title."

"Well, I was always faster than you."

"Duel! Duel!" Nancy yells, waving the hookah.

"Okay." Aviva looks mischievous. "Here are the rules. You give us each a word and we have one minute to make a pun on it. On a scale of one to ten a perfect pun is a five—not too simpleminded, not too esoteric. Let's go."

"Wait a second. I didn't accept any challenge," I say.

"You chicken?"

I pause, take a drag on the hookah and exhale slowly. "Okay, shoot." I nod at Dorrie.

Aviva grins.

Dorrie closes her reddened eyes and purses her full lips, empurpled from the swig of wine she has just taken. Then she looks at me. "Interior," she says and starts timing me.

"Interior, interior." My brain wants to play different games. I try to force it to pun. Inter. In. Terior. In. Terrier. In. Ter. Ior. In. Ter. Your. That's it. In Ter. Your.

I clear my dry throat. "Let me whisper sweet nothings in ter your ear," I say seductively.

Aviva groans. Nancy laughs. "A three," Dorrie says.
I salaam and reach for the wine bottle.
Aviva releases her latest dope-soaked breath. "Ready, Nancy."
"Opera," Nancy says promptly.
"Are you going opera down?" Aviva replies immediately.
We all groan.
"Also a three," Nancy says.
"Score tied. Nina, how about this one: expectations."
"Toughie, toughie," Nancy shouts.
I sigh and slump onto Dorrie's bed pillows, my brain a blank.
"Thirty seconds," Dorrie announces.
It's like a test. An English exam, I think. A quiz on Charles Dickens. Jesus, why'd I think of Charles Dickens?
"Forty-five seconds."
Then, a slow smile spreads across my face. Charles Dickens. Of course. *Great Expectations. Great Expectorations,* I called it in Professor Huntley's course.
I sit up and recite, "A summary of a work by Charles Dickens entitled *Great Expectorations,* by Nina Ritter. *Great Expectorations*—you spit out the Pips."
Aviva breaks up instantly. Nancy does after a minute. But Dorrie just looks puzzled.
"I don't get it," she says.
I am not in the mood for explanations, but I say, with forced patience, "Do you know what to expectorate means?"
Dorrie is offended. "I'm not stupid. It means to spit, as in spitting out apple pips or seeds."
"Well then, have you ever read *Great Expectations*?"
"No."
"That's why you don't get it. The main character's name is Pip."

23

"Ohhhh." Then Dorrie starts to laugh too.

"Clever girl," says Aviva to me, "But that rates an eight or nine—too esoteric."

"Thank you and fuck you," I say. "Here's a word for you—yesterday."

"Hey, I'm supposed to give her the word," Nancy yells.

"Fiddle while my dome burns, Nan, and don't worry about it," Aviva answers. "There was a veterinarian who carefully labeled all stool samples . . ."

"*Stool* samples?" Dorrie interrupts.

"Shit, you dope," Aviva says. "There was a veterinarian who carefully labeled all stool samples Turd A, Turd B and so forth. One day as he was about to perform a test, he requested his assistant to bring him a sample.

" 'Are you working on Turd A today?' his assistant asked.

" 'Yes Turd A,' he replied."

The laughter is instantaneous.

"A veritable five, if I do say so myself." Aviva puffs up her chest.

"I quit," I respond.

And Nancy, who is by now sprawled flat on the rug, says, "Let's get some food. I've got the munchies."

One hour and two buckets of Chicken Delite (with french fries, coleslaw, buttered rolls and Coke) later, we have all slipped inside ourselves, listening to the Jefferson Airplane, Aviva singing along, pushing, twisting, stroking, twining her own voice with lead singer Grace Slick. I have never heard her sing rock before. She is not working hard now, but the sound is beautiful.

It makes me want to be held by someone. One someone. Gwyn. Out of my mind most of the evening, but coming in strong now.

I look around the room. Dorrie is drawing on the huge

white graffiti sheet tacked to the wall next to her bed. Nancy is lying down on the floor, eyes closed, probably hearing a violin accompaniment to Aviva's singing in her head.

Suddenly, I do not want to be here.

I rise and step outside. No one seems to notice. The yellow roses smell strong. The air is cooler tonight; a breeze ruffles the rose petals and tightens my breasts.

I sit on the low wall bordering the roses. The moon is nearly full and it makes my hands silver.

The pain is in my veins. Suffusive.

From my pocket I pull out the small notebook I always carry.

I begin to write, trying to pour the pain through my fingers to my pen and onto paper. I am not outside. I am in a small cell, terribly alone.

> When my breasts are hard
> Only with the cold
> And the moon
>   drips
> Into the room like wax
>   from dead candles
> And I lie so still
> The bed doesn't creak
> I will
>   Suddenly
>   Remember
> And the wind will be as warm
> As your hands.

I read it over by moonlight and begin to cry. Harsh tears that hurt my already dry throat.

Inside, Aviva is still singing, wailing notes that seem to parody my tears.

And then, the phone rings. Twice. Thrice. Four times. Until someone finally picks it up.

Dorrie comes out to me. "It's your mother," she says. "She wants to know when you're coming home."

"Oh God," I say, wiping my eyes. "Tell her . . . Never mind. I'll tell her."

I go in, pick up the phone.

"Why didn't you call me?" my mother begins.

"I'm sorry," I interrupt, "we got to talking. About my year abroad." I realize that curiously we have not talked about England at all.

"When are you coming home?"

"Soon," I say. "Don't wait up."

"Don't tell me what I should or shouldn't do. You come home now."

"Soon," I repeat. "Sleep well." I hang up.

"Jesus. I've heard of protective mothers . . ." Aviva says.

I cut her off. "Dorrie, where's your coffee? I want a strong cup."

"I'll make it," she says, and she puts her arm around me and walks me to the kitchen.

We are silent while she brews the coffee. Aviva doesn't come in, and Nancy is already asleep.

Dorrie sets a cup before me.

"Bad?" she asks.

"Bad," I nod.

She pauses and then asks, "Love?"

I smile wanly. "Love."

"Tell me about him."

"He has gentle hands," I say. Nothing else will come out. The coffee makes me feel better. I want conversation.

"Does Aviva really want to be a rock singer? I mean, do you think it's serious, or another one of her crazes?"

"Oh, it's serious all right, and her parents are furious about it."

I remember Avi's parents—her handsome, immensely talented architect father, her caustic, immensely talented painter mother. They had made me feel in somewhat bad taste, and so I visited infrequently.

"There are different types of overprotective," Dorrie says. It is a wise remark and it makes me look differently at Dorrie.

"I'd better go," I say.

She nods.

When I walk into the other room, Aviva is leaning back in her chair, eyes closed, straight, short strawberry-blond hair framing her small face. She looks very young.

And suddenly I want to say something kind. I touch her arm. "Night, Avi. Your singing sounds terrific."

Aviva opens her eyes. "Do you really think so?"

"Yes."

"Will you come tomorrow—to the audition?"

"Will Mark the drummer be there?"

"No." She is puzzled.

"Then I'll come."

She gets it and regains her sarcasm. "Don't want any, huh?"

"Oh yes I do, but not from rock musicians."

"We'll see about that."

We smile at each other.

And I make my way, quite soberly, to my car.

Chapter 3

"Hold your butt, baby, hold your butt." The voice bellows out the grimy window, over the traffic blare of the West Side Highway, over the whining jukebox and bleary voices of the West Side Bar.

Having found the doorbell broken, we—Aviva, Dorrie, Nancy and I—stand outside the old brick building, yelling up at the window until a sleepy, bearded face finally appears and issues his above charming greeting.

The face materializes at the door and lets us in. It belongs to a flabby bloke who has got to be at least thirty-five.

We trek up a narrow, badly lit staircase and are ushered into a huge, surprisingly sunny (and mercifully air-conditioned) room.

"All you chicks auditioning?" he asks.

"No, I am," Aviva answers.

He looks her up and down, slowly.

"You sing rock?"

"If I don't, what the hell do you think I'm doing here?" she retorts.

He grins. "Yeah. I guess so. Well, park your carcasses somewhere. The rest of the cats will be here soon. Oh yeah—I'm Sam."

"You play horn?"

"Sax. You know me?"

"Just your chops, man, just your chops," Aviva says.

Sam chuckles. "Smart thing."

He sits on the one bed in the room, takes his saxophone from its case and begins to blow.

Aviva immediately sits down next to him and starts doo-wahing along.

A brief glance around and Dorrie, Nancy and I all choose spots on the floor, sit down and wait. I stare out the window. So strange not to see sky. So strange. I wonder what I am doing here—in this studio, this city, this country. But wondering will not take me back to England.

An hour later—we might have known rock musicians have their own sense of time—the rest of the band begins to straggle in. First, a big, fair-haired guitarist with pockmarked skin who leers at us and says, "Well, well. Who'd like to be first? Or how about four in one blow?"

Aviva laughs. Dorrie and Nancy snicker. I grimace.

"Chester, man, put away your dick and take out your axe," Sam says, so good-naturedly that everyone laughs.

Chester is followed by the trombone player, balding, big nosed and wry. He wears glasses and his name is Murray. Then, the organist, David, tall, dark, mustachioed and apologetic.

"Sorry I'm late," he says to Aviva. "Had a lesson that ran overtime."

The drummer and bass player are the last to arrive. The bass player is tall and slender, with long, tangled blond hair nearly reaching his waist. His expression is so mild I can't help but think of some painting of Jesus I once saw. By contrast, the drummer is short and muscular, with close-cropped curly hair, a tattoo of a heart on his arm and a pair of clenched fists.

"Shit, man," he says, kicking the door closed.

"What's the matter, your old lady pregnant again?" Chester hoots.

The drummer's face turns a particularly ugly red. He rushes at Chester and grabs him by the collar.

"Shut up, chickenshit, if you want to stay able to play the guitar."

"Okay, okay. Cut the fun and games," Sam yells.

"Yeah, we got ladies present," Murray says and winks broadly at us.

I see the drummer's muscles relax, but he doesn't let go of Chester.

I'm still watching the two of them when a voice says, "Hello." I look up. It's the bass player, his long white guitar in his hands.

"Hello. Do they often fight?" I ask.

"Yeah. But they don't hurt each other." His voice is as mild as his looks. "What's your name?"

"Nina. Yours?" I look into his extremely blue eyes.

"John," he says and plucks at his guitar.

I glance beyond him. The drummer has relinquished his hold on Chester and both are tuning up. From across the room, Aviva is staring at me. There is something challenging in her stare—the same expression she had last night when we dueled with puns, only more intense. I am startled and uneasy. Then, abruptly, she smiles and winks.

And, as though that were a signal, the band begins to play Jefferson Airplane's "White Rabbit."

And Aviva stands up slowly and saunters over to them.

The intro finished, she starts to sing, low, seductive.

"One pill makes you larger,
And one pill makes you small.
And the ones that Mother gives you
Don't do anything at all.
Go ask Alice
When she's ten feet tall."

Into the second verse, Aviva's voice still gloved, insinuating.
I find I am gripping my hands.

"And if you go chasing rabbits,
And you know you're going to fall,
Tell 'em a hookah-smoking caterpillar
Has given you the call.
Call Alice
When she was just small."

Then the bridge and suddenly, steel, unsheathed, ringing
loud and clear.

"When the men on the chessboard
Get up and tell you where to go,
And you've just had some kind of mushroom
And your mind is movin' low,
Go ask Alice,
I think she'll know."

She slashes out the final verse, the band embellishing the
words, the melody she etches.

"When logic and proportion
Have fallen so I'll be dead,
And the White Knight's talkin' backwards
And the Red Queen's off with her head,
Remember what the dormouse said,
'Feed your head.
Feed your he-ad.'"

31

Silence, save for the last note, hanging, burning in air. The room is quivering. No one looks at anyone else.

Then, finally, someone exhales and Sam breathes one long "Je-sus," and everyone, released, sighs.

"You sure can sing. Can't she, Pete?" Chester says.

"You got yourself a gig, girl," Pete the drummer affirms.

Dorrie, Nancy and I look at each other and grin, pridefully acknowledging ourselves as the possessors of a full-fledged rock singer in our midst.

"Now, let's hear what you can do with our material," David says, handing Aviva a sheet of what appear to be lyrics.

He begins to play the melody on his organ, Avi nodding in time.

The mood shatters. Next to the pulse and dazzle of "White Rabbit," this tune is flat and trite. Boop-boop-be-doop time.

Aviva starts singing dutifully from the sheet.

"I'm a Super Chick.
You gotta catch me quick
'Cause here I go.
Whoaaaaaaaaaaaaaaa!"

I lower my face down on my arms and pretend I'm concentrating. Actually, I feel like barfing.

When the song is over, the band nods approvingly.

"Try this next one," Sam says.

I decide it is time for me to take my leave and I politely bid ta-ta, promising I'll be back in time to meet the Crew for dinner.

As I make my way to the door, Chester grabs my bum. "Ripe and juicy," he says.

I smile sweetly. "Go get stuffed," I say.

It is a genuine exit line.

I walk rapidly to clear my head of "Super Chick" and also the fact that Aviva really wants to be a member of this raggedy-assed band. She's so damn good, what does she need them for? I wonder. I think about music and sex and the vacant-faced bass player. Oh Gwyn, help. Lead me unto the path of righteousness . . .

I get on a bus, allowing it to take me anywhere.

I am so oblivious to space and time that before I know it, I am in the Village.

Shit, I think, I better just sit for a while. So I head for trees, benches and Washington Square Park.

There is a large crowd gathered in the park. Larger than I've ever seen. Several people are shouting.

Oh God, not Jesus freaks again, I think.

Someone grabs my arm.

"Did you hear? Now they're busting heads. Busting heads," a girl with long blond hair shouts at me.

I think she means the police are arresting pot smokers, and I thank heaven I'm not carrying any weed on me.

But it turns out she means something else.

"Now they're cracking skulls. Tomorrow they'll be murdering all of us."

"What are you talking about?" I ask.

"Don't you know? In Chicago. The Democratic Convention. The cops are beating up on the demonstrators!"

The Democratic Convention. I haven't read an American newspaper in a year.

"Jesus. Really?" I ask.

She grabs my arm again and begins to drag me through the crowds.

I don't bother to ask where we're going.

We enter a dingy bar called something like The Kettle of Fish. But it stinks more like Scotch than salmon.

"Look," she points to the TV.

33

I look.

A commentator's voice drones on about what atrocities we are seeing on the screen, while the men in uniform are indeed busting heads right and left. There is black-and-white blood everywhere.

"Let 'em have it," a roaring boy on the bar stool bellows. "Give it to them rotten hippies good!"

I feel quite ill.

"Hey, sweetie," another drunk calls, shambling over to us.

I turn to my companion.

She is gone.

"Jesus," I say once again. It is certainly a day for taking His name in vain.

And then I run.

Out of the bar, into the street, on until I reach Sixth Avenue.

Please, God, don't let me be sick, I pray, and keep running.

When I reach 25th Street, I slow down.

Fuck it, I say, and hail a cab.

On the way up to the studio and my car, I pray again that Aviva is still there—but ready to split. I want to get the hell out of this city, back to suburbia as fast as I can. I think up restaurants near home to suggest, dark movie theaters to sit in, anything, so long as it's not here.

"We're here, girlie," the cabbie says.

I give him a huge tip, take a large breath and ring the bell.

No answer, of course. I remember it's broken.

I lean against the door.

It opens and I stumble in and rush up the decaying stairs.

I pound at the door.

"Okay, okay," I hear faintly.

The door opens. It is Sam, disheveled, in his jockey shorts.

"Yeah. What do you want?" he asks.

But before I can answer, he says, "Oh yeah. You're the

friend." And he opens the door wider to let me in.

The room is empty of people and instruments. The Crew has obviously sailed away.

But then I see the pile of sheets on the bed rise and a tousled head grin triumphantly at me.

"Hi, Nina," it says.

I answer slowly, "Hi, Aviva. See you around."

I spin on my heel and march out.

When I reach my car, damp, bent, I climb inside, throw my head back and scream.

And in a wrenching moment, I know the first line of my letter to Gwyn.

"Dear Gwyn," it reads. "Dear Gwyn. Apocalypse is come. Armageddon is now."

September 23, 1968

Dear Gwyn,

Sorry my letters have been so down lately. It's all so damn hard. Last year at this time, I arrived in England, naive, expectant. And everything was so wonderful—the sunshine was more brilliant, the leaves more red and gold, the air more sparkling. I was never homesick, not once.

Crisp
    Things are just turning
Crisp—
There
    Leaves and things,
    All along warm, red brick walls.
And mellow
    Things are just turning

35

Mellow.

> All apples and pears,
> This time of year—
> There
> They call it Autumn
> And it's strange to be back
> Here
> In the fall.

There's another sad poem for you. Oh Gwyn, it's as though I've forgotten how to be happy. Maybe you could reteach me.

Speaking of celibacy (who was?), what did you mean "you don't have to remain celibate on my account"? On who else's account would I remain celibate? I know you're being generous, but you don't have to be. There isn't anyone I'd want to "break my vows" with anyway. By the way, how is Gaye? Out of your hair for good? And Vanessa? Still phoning you every day? I don't think you should have spent the night with her even if nothing did happen. No wonder she keeps calling. I hope Rhys will not stay angry.

I haven't seen much of Aviva lately. I am busy with university; she is busy with the band. She hardly shows up for classes and I guess she's thinking of dropping out. Can't say I wouldn't like to join her, but all I have, she has, is this last year to go, and, as Mother says, "It would be a shame . . ."

I have seen some of Dorrie and Nancy lately. I went sailing with Nancy, an excursion which might have been restful except that it included her overbearing papa-doc(tor) and her nervous mama. Also went to a recital of hers that was pretty good. I saw a couple of movies with Dorrie, who has an idea for a new sculpture made of bicycle wheels and wax (a D.K.—Dorrie Kopkind—original). But I haven't yet met the current light of her life, Billy, who is a dancer and who, according to Nancy, doesn't seem to burn with mutual passion. He studies at Queens College too, so I expect I'll meet him soon.

Queens College is weird—not the same place I left at all, even though some of the old collegiate types are still around. Stoned-out people mingle with the grass on the lawns. Very long male hair abounds. And an organization called SDS—Students for a Democratic Society—is big. It's an interesting change from shaving cream fights and beer chugalugging—yesteryear's entertainments. Maybe I'll end up just hanging out too, but I doubt it; the scholar in me won't allow it during school hours. People keep asking me what I think about the war in Vietnam and I can't waffle the way I did in England (remember at that pub when I told that bloke I was an anarchist and he seemed to think that was wonderful? I don't think that would go down so well here and now). I wish I didn't feel so out of it.

I go to the beach a lot and picture you on the pebbles at the Cold Knap. Strange to be separated by so much water. But at least the beach is a constant in my life in its ebb and flow. I need that constancy. I need to know that on the other side of all that gray-green is you as you always were and are.

Dear Gwyn, kiss the soil of Norwich for me and don't forget to study hard. And please, if you talk to Rhys and stay away from Vanessa, I promise to try to cheer up.

Love,
Nina

October 1968

Chapter 4

"You did what?" I say, my voice taut.

"He's in just for the weekend, Nina. From M.I.T. And Charlotte thought . . ."

"I know what Charlotte thought. And I know what you thought. But I'm twenty years old . . ."

"Nineteen."

"I'll be twenty tomorrow, Mother. And the point is not my age but the fact that you're trying to arrange my life for me."

"I am not trying to arrange your life for you."

"I call fixing me up with a blind date I expressed no interest in arranging my life for me."

"So phone Charlotte and tell her you don't want to date her son."

"It's a little late for that, don't you think—he's coming over in two hours."

"I don't know what you're so upset about—you didn't have any plans for this evening and you've been moping around so much . . ."

"I have not been moping."

"No? You spend half your time hidden away in your room writing letters and the other half sitting outside staring at the mailbox."

"That is a ridiculous exaggeration."

My mother's voice softens. And the softness makes me angrier than anything else she's done. "Nina, honey, he's thousands of miles away. You can't waste yourself over some boy you'll never see."

"You don't understand a thing," I shout. "He's not just *some* boy, damn it!"

"Nina, there is no need to scream at me. I'm sure you have strong feelings for him, but you'll get over him."

"I love him, Mother, love him," I bellow. "Do you know what that means?"

Her mouth sets in a thin line. "All you girls today think it's love," she says tightly.

Instantly, I know what she is thinking. I say nothing, afraid shocking revelations will tumble from my lips and scare my mother into catatonia.

There is an extended silence. And then my mother says, "So, are you going out with Charlotte's boy tonight?"

I exhale heavily. "Yes, Mother," I answer, defeated, "I will go out tonight with Charlotte's boy."

"Engineering must be very interesting," I say to Jeff Zlotnick (Charlotte's boy) over underdone hamburgers in the Sip'N'Sup restaurant. There is something about Jeff Zlotnick himself that reminds me of an underdone hamburger.

"Yes, it is interesting," he answers.

Dead silence. "You must be awfully good at math," I say, attempting to keep this drowning conversation afloat.

"Yes, I'm good at math. I've always been good at math. Are you good at math?"

"Oh no, I'm lousy at it," I answer, cheerfully. "I'm studying English."

"Oh," says Jeff Zlotnick.

And then he furrows his brow and stares hard into his Coke.

What have I said, I wonder, and am just about to begin on the topic of how pleasant the weather has been lately when his brow clears and he looks up and recites: " 'To follow knowledge like a sinking star, Beyond the utmost bound of human thought.' "

The effect of this pathetic, pimply engineering student reciting Alfred, Lord Tennyson to me in the Sip'N'Sup is more than I can handle. I begin to giggle and quickly alter it to a cough.

Jeff Zlotnick slaps my back heartily. "Are you all right?" he asks solicitously.

"Fine, fine," I squeak.

When I finally stop coughing, he says proudly, "That was from 'Ulysses.' "

"Uh-huh." I nod.

"Lord Tennyson," he insists.

"Right. Very good."

"I used to know the whole poem."

I smile. He is so eager I almost regret giggling. But then I remember something—a joke between Gwyn and me. We were sitting under a big oak in Norwich, eating a picnic lunch.

"I'll come to New York and stay with you and your parents," he said, his head in my lap.

"Wouldn't they love that!" I answered sarcastically.

"Oh, they will. You see, I'll be very, very good. I'll court you properly: I'll ask your mother to chaperone us to the cinema. I'll read you Alfred, Lord Tennyson in the evenings in the parlor. . . ."

I began to laugh. He sat up.

41

"And on Sundays, we'll all go to temple," he finished with a flourish.

Then I really roared.

"It wasn't quite that funny," he said.

"Oh yes it was," I sputtered. "I don't k-know w-what the Jews you k-know do, but the ones I k-know d-don't go to temple on Sundays."

Then he started to laugh too until we tumbled against each other and slid down among the Stilton and biscuits and wine and stopped the cackles with kisses.

"Are you sure you're okay?"

I look up at Jeff Zlotnick peering anxiously into my face.

"I'm fine, fine," I repeat.

"You drifted away or something. And then your face went red."

"No, really. I'm okay. I'll just go to the rest room and wash my face."

He nods, relieved.

I hurry to the john and into a stall and bang the door shut. Then I whip out my notebook and begin to write.

"Dearest Gwyn. Dearest, dearest Gwyn. Come to me and read Alfred, Lord Tennyson, O fire of my loins. I need. I ache . . ."

Three pages later, I stop writing and leave the stall.

A woman running a comb through her teased hair gives me a funny look.

I splash water on my face and make my way back to my blind date.

"Are you all right?" he asks once again.

"On my word of honor, I am fine."

"That's good. Well, we'll have to hurry if we want to make the movie."

I finish the last of my Coke quickly. If we don't make the movie, I will have to spend the rest of the evening making (or forcing) conversation with Jeff Zlotnick, and I just don't feel that stoic.

"Ready!" I bubble.

And we are off to the home of popcorn and furtive feels.

Furtive feels is right. It's amazing how fast even shy guys become beasts. Throughout the whole movie, Charlotte's boy tried successively to: 1) Blow in my ear; 2) Nibble my neck; 3) Fondle my thigh; 4) French kiss me; 5) Squeeze my breasts. I spent the whole damn movie (which seemed to be a good one, as much as I managed to see of it) fending off Jeff Zlotnick's hands, legs and mouth.

When we finally exited, I hadn't a shred of kind feeling left toward him and no inclination to carry on any further conversation. We sat in the car in the proverbial stony silence until we pulled up to my house. Then, he leaned over for the big good-night smooch. Fortunately for me I saw him coming and moved my head. Unfortunately for him, having missed my face, he ended up nearly falling through the open car-door window.

When he pulled himself up, he glared at me and said, with all the spite he could muster, "Frigid bitch!"

I laughed and let myself out of his car.

I was still laughing when I entered my house, saw my mother, fully dressed, waiting for me.

"Well, why didn't you ask him in?" she said

I ha-haed so loudly she gave me an "Are you nuts?" look. That made me laugh even harder, so I just waved good night and staggered to my bedroom.

Then I flopped on my bed and buried my face in my pillow until I could stop laughing.

That was a half hour ago. Now, I feel drained and sad. I read the letter I wrote to Gwyn in the toilet tonight. It is

43

terrible—gushing and rambling and I will never send it. God, what an October this is turning out to be—no Gwyn, no Aviva, and some jerk calls me a frigid bitch.

Frigid bitch, my ass.

Being turned off by someone is not frigidity, Jeff Zlotnick! Not jumping into bed with some two-bit rock musician is not frigidity, Aviva!

"Did you hear that, Aviva? Did you?" I say to my ceiling. "Oh Aviva, how could you?"

It's been over a month since I stumbled in on you and Sam. A month of evasions. What did I write to Gwyn? "I haven't seen much of Aviva lately. I'm busy with university—she is busy with the band . . ." Come off it, Nina. You want to reduce it all to that—pretend you weren't repelled when you found her in bed with Sam. Pretend you didn't feel sullied in some way and let down, no, more than let down, *betrayed* in some way—by the intrusion of men or sex or change or something in Aviva's life. Pretend you haven't ignored her phone calls, her invitations. Worst of all, do you want to pretend that somewhere inside you, you weren't hoping to have a swell time with Charlotte's respectable boy and then wave him in Aviva's face as a sign of your intrinsic respectability. You are a frigid bitch, Nina—you have a heart of ice.

I lie quietly for a while, then sigh and pick up the phone and dial.

"Hello."

"Avi, it's Nina. I know it's been . . ."

"Nina! I tried calling earlier . . ."

"Sorry. I was out on a blind date—and I do mean blind. Look, I want to apologize . . ."

"For your blind date? Forget it. Listen, be ready tomorrow at noon for a Magical Mystery Tour, courtesy of the Crew."

"Huh?"

"Birthday time."

"You remembered!"

"A rock singer never forgets."

"But Aviva, I have a term paper . . ."

"Oh come on, Nina. It's the one and only time you're leaving your teens."

There is a pause.

"Okay, Aviva, you win," I finally say.

"I'm a born winner."

I laugh. "You know something? I've missed you."

"I've missed you too, Neen."

Another pause.

"How's Sam?" I say.

Aviva chortles. "Lousy in bed."

"Oh." I can't think of anything else to say.

"Toots, I've got to go. See you tomorrow at noon, okay?"

"Okay. Night."

"Night."

I hang up. There is a knock at the door.

"Come in," I call out.

"Are you all right?" my mother asks, entering.

I smile at her.

"Better than I've been for a while," I say.

"What was so funny before?"

"Me. I was funny."

She looks puzzled. "I don't understand, did Charlotte's boy do something . . ." She stops.

"No, Ma. He didn't do anything. He just tried to a lot. Don't worry about it. He's fine. I'm fine. Everybody's fine."

She still appears confused, but she says, "Well, good night then—and an early happy birthday."

"Thanks . . . Oh that reminds me. I'm going out with Aviva and the Crew tomorrow."

"With Aviva?" Her voice gets strained. "But I thought you weren't seeing her anymore."

"Whatever gave you that idea?" I ask firmly.

She doesn't reply. Then, she asks, "Where are you going?"

"It's a surprise."

"Oh . . . well, be careful not to . . . overdo it."

"Don't worry, Mother, I'm always careful," I say. "Always."

Chapter 5

The thing has big red light bulbs for nipples, two enormous steel claws for hands and a bicycle tire filled with shards of plates to represent a teeth-filled vagina.

It speaks: "Hello, honey. Would you do me a favor?"

It says the same thing over and over in a syrupy voice.

I try to get into its artistic statement, its use of materials, its explosion of sexual restraint. But all I feel is nauseated. I start to turn away.

"Hello, honey. Happy birthday," it says.

I gasp and jump.

Then Aviva grabs my arm. "That was me, dodo."

"Damn it, don't do that again! You scared the shit out of me!"

Aviva laughs.

"Let's get out of here," I say.

"But we haven't seen the whole show." Nancy frowns.

"I've seen enough." I'm being "difficult," and I know it. This horrendous erotic art exhibit is not the Crew's fault. In fact, at another time, I might have, if not exactly enjoyed it, at least laughed at it. And the earlier part of this "Magical

Mystery Tour" the Crew took me on was pretty good—pickles and knishes on the Lower East Side; a ride on the Staten Island Ferry; *gelati* at the Trattoria in the Pan Am building. But I didn't, can't enjoy any of it. I feel dull, benumbed. I know I must be angry, but I can't touch the anger.

"Hey, look at this," Dorrie calls.

We join her.

"It's an empty stall shower. What's so erotic about that?" Nancy asks.

"What's so erotic about this whole show?" I mutter.

"Watch," Dorrie says.

And, presto, there's a naked woman in the shower, soaping her armpits and having a whale of a time.

"It's a film," Nancy gasps.

"Nope," Aviva says, "a hologram."

"It's a naked woman." I yawn. "Now can we go."

"Party pooper," Aviva says.

"It's my party and I can poop if I want to," I rejoin.

"How come there aren't any naked men in this show?" Dorrie asks.

"Good question," I say.

"Women have better bodies," Aviva says. "Can you imagine Sam standing naked in this shower?"

Dorrie and Nancy snicker.

"Or Murray," Aviva adds.

"Murray!" I yell.

The Crew cackles.

Murray. The balding trombonist. Him too? Who next? The organ player (no pun intended). Or the Jesus-faced bassist. No, not him, I hope, and then wonder why I feel that way. Then I get this tightness in my stomach. Sex is overwhelmingly everywhere—pervasive, evasive, obvious, oblivious. But not for me.

"Of course, maybe Gwyn would look good . . ." Aviva says.

And the tightness snaps; the anger roils up and over like lava. "Shut up!" I growl. "Shut up!"

"God, aren't we sour today," Aviva says. "And priggish," she adds.

"SHUT UP!" I shout.

Heads turn, and it grows so quiet all we hear is the syrupy voice asking, "Hello, honey. Would you do me a favor?"

"Let's get out of here," whispers Nancy.

I turn to go.

"I wouldn't step backward if I were you," Aviva says, an impish expression abruptly flashing across her face.

I whirl around.

A man is standing behind me, his raincoat held wide open, revealing that he wears garters to hold up his socks and nothing else.

"Oh Jesus!" I yell. "Put that away!"

The man closes his coat, bows and walks off.

"Put that away." Dorrie snorts. And everyone cracks up. Everyone but me.

"I have to come to an art gallery for this? I can get it on the street!" I shout.

Then, in a refined English dowager voice, Aviva says, "But not with the garters."

We look at each other.

And then I have to laugh.

When we hit the street, Dorrie asks, "What's really bugging you today?"

What's really bugging me? Why am I so upset? A good question. But the answer is so mundane I'm embarrassed to tell the Crew.

"Aren't you glad to be twenty?"

Twenty. When I woke up this morning, it took me a few confused minutes to remember that today I, Nina Carolyn Ritter, have left the age of adolescence, the years of change, the puberty and pimples parade. That I have turned twenty big ones. But then I got excited, waiting for the post. And when it arrived, in a frenzy I rifled through the envelopes, flinging cards from aunts, uncles, English friends, Grandma and Grandpa, Didi Hinkel, Stan Wasserman, etc., etc., madly on the floor, searching for the birthday missive from Gwyn.

There wasn't any. Not even a postcard.

"Happy birthday, Nina. It's sure great to be twenty," I say sarcastically.

And Dorrie misunderstands. "Oh, come on, it's not so old. I'm twenty-three," she says soothingly.

"A woman doesn't even reach her sexual peak until she's forty," Nancy adds.

"Methinks Nina is reaching her sexual pique right now," Avi says.

We all look quizzically at her.

"P-i-q-u-e, dimwits."

We all groan.

"How about calling Mark?" Nancy suggests.

I feel the tightness coming on once again.

"How about going to Central Park and smoking some dope?" Aviva says. "And then Dorrie can row us around the lake."

"Who me?" Dorrie asks.

"Sure, you've got the muscles," says Avi, and puts her arm around my shoulders.

And off we go to the grass and the trees and the cool, dirty water.

"This is the life," Avi says languidly, trying to stretch out on the floor of the rowboat.

"Hey, watch out for the oar," Dorrie warns.

50

"Hey, watch out for your ass—you're going to get it very wet," I say.

"Oh so what. It's hot today anyway—especially for October," Avi says.

"Don't you like it being just the four of us together?" Nancy says dreamily, passing me a joint. "Like it was before you left, Nina."

I take a drag. "Yeah, it is nice," I say, starting to feel pretty good. After all, it *is* my birthday and I've got good friends and good grass.

We row around the lake for a while. Dorrie complains about what a lazy lot we all are, but I can see she's proud of being so skillful with an oar. She does have great muscles. In fact, on her dresser is a picture of herself she proudly shows everyone—ten pounds heavier, but most of it muscle, in shorts and a straw hat, wielding a machete in front of a banana tree on a kibbutz in Israel—the only place she's been besides New York and Ohio.

When we—or she—get tired, we return the boat and decide to check out the Bethesda Fountain.

The fountain is a huge, white stone baroque affair with cherubs and an angel on the top. But it isn't nearly as strange as the freaks gathered around it. A girl in a flowing tie-dyed robe is drawing a pentagram on a wall. A boy in a kaftan is juggling. A man with a beard down to his stomach is meditating. Others are playing instruments, playing ball or just playing. And everyone seems high on something.

"Wow!" I exclaim, watching an elfin figure of indeterminate sex in green shorts and a peaked cap like Robin Hood's dance to a band of conga players. "Welcome to Wonderland!"

A girl all in white hands us a jay.

"Give it to the birthday girl first," Avi says.

"Ooh, your birthday!" The girl squeals. "Hey everybody, it's her birthday!" she shouts.

"Happy birthday!" a shirtless boy in what looks like pajama bottoms sings out to Nancy.

"It's not my birthday. It's hers," she says.

But the boy ignores her correction. "Today is the first day of the rest of your life," he says. "You should cleanse yourself of the old. That's good karma."

Nancy takes a hit of the jay. It's strong stuff. I watch her eyes grow wide. She turns and stares straight at the boy. "Yeah? How do I do that?"

Avi answers, "He means you should jump in the fountain."

"Oooh," says the girl in white. "The fountain! The fountain! Come on! Come on!" She grabs Nancy's hand.

By this time, there's a little crowd around her and Nancy. They all start to yell, "The fountain! The fountain!"

"Go ahead, Nance. You can be Nina's proxy. It'll be good for your soul."

Nancy looks like she's trying to decide what to do.

"Oh come on, Nancy," Avi says, somewhat impatiently. "For the honor of the Crew and Miss Subways. You don't want to let your fans down, do you?"

Nancy is still thinking. But one more toke and she's decided. "My fans, here comes Miss Subways!" she yells, and, with a shriek, splashes into the shallow water. Five people follow.

Dorrie, Avi and I are practically hysterical. "Oh . . . my . . . God . . . what . . . happened . . . to . . . the . . . nice . . . Jewish . . . girl . . . next . . . door?" I gasp between giggles.

"She went to pot," Avi and Dorrie say simultaneously.

And we crack up all over again.

Later, with Nancy drying out and all of us a little more sober, we lie on the grass and watch a golden sun setting. I'm starting to feel kind of low again, as though everything's kind of pointless.

A girl in a fringed vest studded with buttons reading "McCarthy," "Peace Now" and "Make love, not war" strides over. She looks so purposeful. She hands me a wad of leaflets and marches on. I glance at one. Peace march. Washington. Get out of Vietnam now! Names of speakers I don't know. Names of singers I do know. Pete Seeger. Phil Ochs. Joan Baez. Peter, Paul and Mary.

"Hey, this looks interesting," I say, perking up a little. "Look."

Avi looks. And yawns. "Shit," she says. "Folk music is dead. Rock lives!"

"And Paganini," adds Nancy. "Paganini lives."

"So does Frodo," says Dorrie.

"No, look, this is interesting. There are going to be speakers who've fought in Vietnam and are opposed . . ."

Avi groans. "No politics, Neen, please. It's boring."

I am silenced. The War has kind of been disturbing me lately—maybe because I'm beginning to find out more about it. But it's not one of the Crew's favorite subjects. Oh, it's not that the Crew is pro-war. It's just that the War is a heavy topic and Aviva likes to stay away from heavy topics. Maybe she feels she can't do anything really, so why talk about it?

"I hope Billy sticks it out at Queens. God, it would be awful if he got drafted," Dorrie says.

"Good grief, enough!" Aviva says, standing up.

After a pause, I ask, "When am I going to meet this hunk?"

"Tonight at the . . ." Dorrie begins.

"Shhh," Aviva hisses. "It's a surprise."

"For me?" I ask.

"Of course. You're the birthday girl. . . . Hey, let's grab some Chinese food."

"Another excellent idea from our Rising Rock Star," Nancy says.

And we totter out of the trees and into Dorrie's Volkswagen, which she bought when she sold the motorcycle. I have a feeling tonight's surprise is going to be a special one, so I make a new resolution—to enjoy it if it kills me.

We roll up in front of a small disco-bar with a black facade and a big pink neon wheel in the window. The place is called Wheels, of course.

"A legal parking space!" Dorrie exults.

We stumble out of the car.

"We're going here?" I say stupidly.

"Yep," answers Aviva and jerks open the big, black metal door.

Inside, more neon. Over the bar. Around the dance floor. Behind the stage. And all in the shape of, you guessed it, wheels! The rest of the place is dark as an abandoned car.

On the small stage a band is setting up. It takes me a minute to realize who the band is.

"Aviva!" I shout. "Your first gig!"

She grins.

"Hey, Aviva, baby!" Sam sings. "Ready for some ac-tion?"

"I'm always ready, baby. Always," Avi calls.

Murray chortles.

"Aviva. Why don't you get ready to perform?" David the organ player asks querulously.

"My dear man, first things first," Aviva replies. "This is a birthday party for my good friend Nina." She waves my hand. "Nina, what would you like to drink? A daiquiri?"

"A daiquiri? Ich! I'll have a gin and orange," I say.

"Well, well. The girl's a hard drinker. Murray, will you get Nina a gin and orange?"

"Sure," he says, laying down his trombone.

"And make mine a cognac," she calls.

"Cognac?" I ask.

"Yeah. Good for my pipes. Come on, let's find you a table."

"Hi," I hear behind me.

I turn. It's the bass player.

"Hi to you." I smile.

"Happy birthday."

"Thanks."

"Can I get you anything?" he asks.

"No, th—" I start to say, but Aviva interrupts with "A trip to England."

"What?" he asks.

"She's pining for the 'sceptered isle.' "

He looks at her confusedly.

"Murray's getting me a drink, er . . . ?" I say quickly.

"John," he says.

"Yes. I remember."

We look at each other for a moment.

Then Avi grabs my arm and escorts me over to a table where Dorrie and Nancy are already sitting. There are three other women there as well.

"I'm going to change. Enjoy the set," Aviva says and exits.

"Break a leg," calls Nancy.

I glance around, wondering about these women. It's dark, but I can tell that one of them is pregnant and one of them is strange.

The third, who is neither pregnant nor strange, inclines her long, probably brown hair toward me and says, "Hi. I'm Pat. Murray's old lady."

I must have misheard. "You go with Murray?" I ask.

"Yeah. You know. The trombonist."

"Someone call me?" Murray appears and hands me my drink. Pat pinches his butt.

"Just introducing myself, lover," she says.

Murray pats her cheek. "Good girl," he says and saunters back to the platform.

But Aviva said . . . She and Murray . . . And ordering

him to get drinks . . . I am stunned. Silently, I sip my gin and orange and watch the band tune up.

"Doesn't Sam look just like a pirate?" the weird bird says. Her voice is queer, breathy—with elongated syllables. She has scarves floating from her head and shoulders, dripping off her arms.

"Naw," answers the pregnant one, "more like a doped-up rock musician."

The weird bird doesn't appear to have heard her. She just laughs huskily and repeats, "Like a pirate."

"This is Lolly." Pat motions to the pregnant woman. "Pete's chick. And this is Terry. Sam's her man."

Before or after Aviva, I wonder.

"Amelia Theresa. But you can call me Terry," she breathes. "Are you John's girl?"

"N-no," I stammer. "I'm Aviva's friend."

Dorrie and Nancy giggle. I notice the empty glasses in front of them.

"Don't you want to go with John?" Amelia Theresa asks.

"I never thought about it," I answer, even more confused.

Dorrie and Nancy laugh harder. I give them a dirty look, but they're laughing too hard to notice.

"What sign are you?"

"Libra. Today's my birthday."

"That's perfect. John's an Aquarius."

"What are you?" I ask, trying to get away from the topic of John.

"A Scorpio, of course. Couldn't you tell?"

"Hey, here comes Avi!" Nancy shouts.

A spotlight hits. And Avi it is in a slinky orange velvet blouse with butterfly sleeves and black satin pants. She shakes her shoulders, and I can see she's not wearing a bra.

I take another sip of my drink. "Nineteen sixty-eight," I murmur.

"What?" asks Lolly.

"Nothing."

"You wanna know when my baby's due?" she asks.

I don't really; I want to watch the band's intro, but I say, "When?"

"In four months. Pretty good, huh?"

I'm not sure what's so good about it, but I nod.

"I'm gonna call it Sasha if it's a boy and Janis if it's a girl—after Janis Joplin, you know."

"Oh. That's nice." I take a big gulp of my drink.

Suddenly, a second circle of neon rings the stage, then a third. And the Rabbit's Foot strikes its opening chord.

"Shit, it's that damn 'Super Chick' tune," I grunt.

"Shhhh," Nancy shushes.

Then Aviva begins to wail. She's singing good, but the song really sucks.

As she finishes the song, I finish my drink. The small crowd in the discotheque applauds politely, except for the Ladies at our table.

"Yeah, Pete," shouts Lolly.

"You show them, baby," Amelia Theresa calls.

The next number is just as mediocre, lyrically and musically.

It's not that the band doesn't play well—they're damn good musicians—but they can't write songs worth a damn. Sam is singing the first verse in a raspy baritone:

"Better watch it, baby
Gimme none of your jive.
I'm like a fiery furnace—
Gonna burn you alive.
Now, watch it, watch it, watch it."

Then Aviva sings back at him something similar. Her voice is harsher than I've ever heard it, harsher and bigger. Almost overblown, but not quite. And it almost works. But not quite.

"Is she trying to sound like Joplin?" I whisper to Dorrie, but Nancy shushes me.

When "Watch It, Baby," or whatever it's called, finishes and the band segues into an instrumental with Avi playing the tambourine, I head for the bar and order another gin and orange. The bartender spills a little when he sets it down. I "tsk" him. But he's watching the band. His eyes are a cool blue. Like Gwyn's. I turn and see Aviva doing a slow shimmy in front of John. He plays a riff and smiles at her. I swallow my drink and turn back to the bartender. Then, from the corner of my eye, I see a tall, muscular bloke come in, pass the bar and head for the Crew and the Ladies. I swing around on my stool and watch. Dorrie jumps up and hugs him. Aha, the famous Billy, I think. I order another drink and stroll back to the table.

"Nina," Dorrie practically sings, "meet Billy."

"Hi," I say, for the millionth time this evening.

"Hi. I've heard a lot about you. Happy birthday!" He smiles. Handsome white teeth under a bushy mustache. A dancer, Dorrie said. I look over his body. No wonder Dorrie has the hots.

"Shhh." Nancy's familiar remark.

Aviva has stepped to the mike. She begins to sing in a gentle voice—unlike the Joplin one. The lyrics are lovely, evocative:

"On an island hung with jewels
None are princes; all are fools
Wise with wonder
Bright as Mars
And their eyes are sea-changed
And they watch the stars.

"When the wind begins to rhyme
Tempest dreams and tales of time
Skeins of memory

Ancient lore
And their thoughts are sea-filled
On a different shore."

Avi's voice rises like a flute.

"Oooh—ooh—lada-lada-loday
Oooh—ooh—lada-lada-loday
Oooh—ooh—lada-lada-loday
Oooh—ooh—ooh—sail away."

The whole table is swaying, clapping in rhythm. Avi smiles
ecstatically as the organ goes into a lovely riff. And then we
all know. Avi has written this tune. And the band has deigned
to perform it. And suddenly I love her. For being so good,
for being this Avi.

"On an island hung with jewels
None are princes; all are fools
Brave new people
Oh magic scene
And they shine like seaweed
And they're evergreen."

The song ends. I feel drunk. There are tears running down
my cheeks. A pause. Then everyone applauds enthusiastically.
And without giving us a chance to hold on to the feel-
ing, Sam immediately plunges the band into some raucous
song.
"Hey!" Nancy yells.
But the band doesn't hear. And once again, Aviva starts
to sing in her new harsh voice, then to dance, grinding her
hips and jiggling her boobs.
I down my drink and keep crying.
"Want to dance?" Billy taps my shoulder.
Blurry. Things are blurry. I hear Dorrie saying, "Go ahead,
Nina, it's your birthday."

Fast. The music. Bump and shake and shimmy. Gwyn loves it. Loved it.

But Billy is not impressed. "No, no," he is saying. "You're pushing too hard and shaking too much. Relax. Relax." He puts my hands on his hips. And his on mine.

"Hey. Cha cha cha."

"No. No. Slow down," he says.

And suddenly, we're moving together real good.

"Yeah!" I yell.

I'm stoned and drunk and I know the whole room is watching me. But I'm flying, flying.

"Yeah!"

The music goes slow and Billy pulls me to him. Pelvis against pelvis. Round and round. Oh Gwyn. Ohhhhhh Gwyn.

Music stops. Gwyn is looking at me with ardor. Not Gwyn. Billy. Billy. "Got to sit," I mumble and stumble to my seat. Dorrie gives me a black look.

"Good dancer. Billy," I say.

Fuzzy. Fuzzier.

"Drink?" someone says.

Somebody waving something orange. "Compliments from Aviva."

"Condiments to you, too."

Drink. Belch.

"Hey, Birthday Girl, I think you've had enough," Billy, I think, says. "Want to go home?"

"Nope. Nope, nope, nope, nope."

My head. Can't hold it up. Where am I?

And then some jerk turns out the lights.

Ringing. Ringing. Shut it off. Ooh, my head.

Something heavy on my chest. An arm.

"Hello."

Shut up. Oh, my head!

"Yes, she's here."

Shut up. Sleep. Need sleep.

"Just a minute. Nina, wake up. Wake up!"

Groan. Sleep. Oh, my gut. Mouth tastes like inside of my shoe.

"Nina! Wake up!"

Who's talking? Where am I?

"It's for you. From England."

What's for me? Sleep. I need to . . .

"NINA! It's Gwyn!"

Gwyn. Here? In bed?

"Stop hugging me. I'm Dorrie. Gwyn's on the phone."

Did I hear right? "Gwyn? On the phone?" I peer at the clock. 3:30. "Now? He's calling now?"

"Yes. Here."

The phone is pressed into my hand. Wish my head didn't ache so.

"Hello," I say.

The voice on the other end coughs and then says, "Transatlantic call for Miss Nina Ritter. Is this she?"

I grab at my heart.

"Yes."

"Your party is on the line. Go ahead, sir."

"Nina?"

"Gwyn?"

"Yes."

"My God, Gwyn."

"Nina. Happy birthday."

"Oh Gwyn."

"I called your home first and your mother told me where to reach you."

Where am I? Oh yes. Dorrie's. "I think I got drunk . . . pissed," I say.

"Was it fun?"

"I'm not sure . . . Oh Gwyn, I miss you so." I begin to cry.

"I know. But Nina, listen. I have good news. I'm coming to the U.S. in January."

"Wh-what did you say?"

"An American fellowship. In Colorado."

"Oh my lord. But Colorado? That's practically as far as England."

"But it is in the U.S. and I get vacations. Besides, I'm arriving in New York."

"Oh Gwyn." I can't seem to say anything else.

"I want to touch you," he says. "I want to put flowers in the curly hair that covers . . ."

"Don't," I moan, "I can't take it."

Dorrie pokes me. "What's he saying?"

"Then, take me."

"I want you," I whisper.

"January."

"Yes."

Silence.

"I have to go now, luv."

"Gwyn, I . . ."

"Yes?"

"I . . ." But I can't say it.

"Send me a lock of your hair," he says.

I smile, the tears still running down my cheeks. "All right. Send me a lock of yours."

"A lock and a key. Good night, my new-found world."

New-found world. Sea-changed.

"Good night, Gwyn."

The phone clicks. I stare at the dark receiver, wondering if I dreamed the conversation. I touch my breasts and shut my eyes tightly. How could I ever have doubted him?

"Well, what did he say?"

62

I start and sit bolt upright. Dorrie. I forgot she is here, or rather I am here. But then, it wasn't a dream. "He's coming here. In January." Then, my stomach spasms. And I realize I'm going to vomit.

I stagger up, into Dorrie's toilet, banging into one of the bicycle wheels from Dorrie's sculpture on the way. Groaning, I hang over the bowl and feel like my guts have dropped into it. I rinse my mouth, but it's useless. I only have to barf again.

Finally, I curl up on the cold tiles. No use going back to bed.

January. Three months.

I'll have to live on rock and roll and hope.

Chapter 6

"Go on, eat a little." Dorrie pushes a container of yoghurt in front of me and then turns off a pot of wax she has melting on the stove.

"Umph," I grunt.

"It'll help your stomach. You were really bombed."

"Yeah," I say soberly. "I made an awful ass of myself, didn't I? With Billy."

"Oh, forget it. I'm not angry now. You were so out of it you didn't know what you were doing."

"Yeah," I say again. But, truth to tell, I wasn't so out of it I didn't know that it was fun and rather sexy.

"He's sexy, isn't he?" Dorrie asks.

"Yeah, he's sexy," I answer.

She's waiting for me to ask something, I think. I take a spoonful of yoghurt and make a face.

Dorrie gives up waiting and says, "I haven't slept with him, yet."

"No?"

"No." She ruffles her short, curly hair. "Soon, though. My New Year's resolution."

I watch her carefully pour some of the wax over the bicycle wheel that gave me a black-and-blue mark last night. "You need a studio," I say.

"I can't afford one."

"Why don't you have a show and sell some of your stuff instead of carting it off to Ohio and storing it in your parents' basement?"

"It's not so easy to get a show. Besides, my stuff isn't good enough yet."

"It's better than that supposedly erotic junk we saw yesterday."

Dorrie just smiles.

A pause. Then she says, "So Gwyn's really coming here in January."

My heart jumps as it always does when Gwyn's name is mentioned.

"I still can't believe it," I say.

"Aviva and Nancy will be really excited."

"Yeah," I say. "I can't wait to tell them."

Dorrie smiles. Just as she finishes pouring the wax, the phone rings. She sets down the pot, straightens her short, black kimono around her plump thighs and goes to answer it. In a minute, she returns. "It's Avi. Her parents are leaving this evening for a long vacation and they want to see you before they go. So you're invited to lunch. Me, too."

"Lunch. Ugh. What do they want to see me for anyway?"

"Probably to find out if England has made you cultured."

"Double ugh."

"Yeah, but after they leave, we get the whole house to ourselves."

"How long are they going to be gone?"

"Three weeks."

"Whew! Oh, the dope-filled evenings!"

65

"Oh, the dope-filled days!"

"All right. Tell them okay for lunch."

I am having trouble with my quiche lorraine. I mean, it's perfectly baked—the cheese firm, but creamy, the crust beautifully fluted and tender-crisp. But my stomach is still rebelling. And the conversation isn't helping.

"Oh, Nina, I just can't get over how wonderful you look. Older. You look older. You look a lot older than Aviva," Shoshanna is saying.

"She is older," Aviva retorts.

Shoshanna throws her a look. "And poised. That's it. Poised. I better keep Carter away from you. You're just his type."

Mr. Marcus wrinkles his nose. My guess is that Carter is Shoshanna's latest non-Jewish boyfriend. She had racked up quite a few of them before I left for England.

"Doesn't she look poised, Mother?" beautiful, poised, talented Shoshanna asks.

"Yes, but she's not eating," Mrs. Marcus says. "Haven't you ever had quiche before?" she asks me.

"Oh yes." I smile and struggle with another bite. "This is delicious."

"Oh, I'm glad you like it," Shoshanna says. "I made it especially for you."

"I think you put too much scallion in it this time," Aviva says.

"Really?" Shoshanna says with too broad a smile.

"Please pass me the salad." "Where's Nancy today?" Dorrie and Mrs. Marcus say simultaneously.

I hand Dorrie the salad.

"Nancy has a lesson," Avi says.

"A talented girl with a taste for fine music," Mr. Marcus says, looking coldly at Aviva.

But Aviva seems to ignore his look. "The gig went pretty well, last night," she says.

"Don't say 'pretty,' Aviva. You know that such a usage is sloppy."

I think she's going to thumb her nose at her father or something, but she just nods.

"However, I am glad to hear that it went well." He turns to me. "Well, Nina. How did you find the English university experience?"

Sexually stimulating, I think. But I merely say, "Lively."

"A much better system than ours, I've always thought. Seminars. Supervisions. And a deep foundation in the great critical writers and thinkers of modern and contemporary times."

Only he would make a distinction between modern and contemporary.

"How about the English Zionist movement?" asks Aviva's mother. "Did you find it lively?"

"I didn't really get involved with it," I say slowly.

"You didn't? Did you know that there are well over three hundred thousand Jews in England? And that English history has been one long persecution of them. Oh, I'll grant you often a subtle persecution, but still a persecution nonetheless."

"No, I . . ."

"Not very well-informed, are you?"

"Would anyone like more quiche?" Shoshanna says brightly.

"I would," answers Dorrie.

"You don't need any more," says Aviva's mother.

Dorrie blushes.

"What did you think of my song?" Aviva asks me. "Or were you too drunk to notice?"

I blush.

"You got drunk?" Shoshanna says. "What fun!"

"Only if you create great poetic works—as Dylan Thomas did," Aviva's father interjects.

67

"Yes, but Dylan Thomas was always looking for lost youth. And he finally drank himself to death," answers Shoshanna.

"But what fun he had doing it," Aviva says.

There is a silence.

"I liked it—your song," I say.

Aviva looks at me. "Oh—good," she says.

"Come on, Mother, I'll help you pack," Shoshanna says.

"Oh, fine. Aviva. You and your friends clear the table." She pauses, then, looking at Dorrie and me, says, "I have the most talented, beautiful daughters in the world, don't I?"

Dorrie and I mumble our extracted consensus.

Shoshanna smiles.

Then she and her mother leave, arm in arm.

"I have a wonderful recording of Dylan Thomas reading some of his works. Would anyone care to hear it?" asks Mr. Marcus.

"After we clear the table," Aviva responds promptly.

"Couldn't we have some Jimi Hendrix instead?" Dorrie mutters.

"Don't be such a philistine, Dorrie," Aviva says.

Dorrie and I look at each other and shake our heads and wish we could light up a joint.

Aviva is brushing my hair. Long, even strokes. Everyone's left—Avi's parents, Shoshanna (gone to see her boyfriend), Dorrie and Nancy, who was here this evening. It was a strange evening. After Avi's parents and sister split and we got properly zonked, Dorrie said, "Hey Crew, Nina's got an announcement."

"Speech! Speech!" Nancy yelled.

"I feel like I should give this a big buildup," I said. "But, to keep it short and very sweet, Gwyn's coming to New York in January."

"Wow!" Nancy squealed. "I guess you won't need Mark after all."

"Is he coming here to live?" asked Aviva.

"No. He'll be teaching at the University of Colorado and he's going to stop here on his way there."

"That's nice," Avi said.

I was a little disappointed in her reaction, but then she insisted that to celebrate we go to the Blue Dolphin diner for their great onion rings and then to Baskin-Robbins for the Jamoca ice cream. So we did. And by then, it was dark.

"Hey, let's go to that peaceful place we discovered last weekend," she said to Dorrie.

"Oh, that one," Dorrie answered.

"What did you find? Another Cold Spring Harbor?" I asked, referring to a favorite Long Island hideaway of ours.

"No, much more peaceful than that," Aviva said.

And soon we were zipping along the Expressway. Off at Maurice Avenue and down the service road. A turn.

"Close your eyes," Avi said to me and Nancy. "And don't open them until I tell you to."

I obeyed. Nancy probably peeked.

Another turn. The car slowed, stopped.

"Okay. Now."

I opened my eyes. Before them was an immense pair of gates. Wrought iron. Gothic. Curlicued. Massive. Forbidding. And topped with huge iron crosses. And beyond them, glowing indistinctly in the weird moonlight, stood row after row of tombstones and mausoleums.

I gasped.

Nancy shrieked.

Dorrie and Aviva cracked up.

"Jesus Christ!" I yelled when I had caught my breath.

"Oh, he's here all right," Dorrie said.

"See, I told you it's more peaceful than Cold Spring Harbor," Aviva said.

"We're not going in, are we?" Nancy asked.

"What's the matter, Nancy? Afraid of ghosts?"

"No. I just don't like cemeteries after dark. That's all."

"Don't worry. We're not going in. These gates are locked at sundown," Dorrie said.

"But I bet there's a way to get in. Next time, I'm going to find it," Aviva announced.

"Next time, I'll stay home," Nancy said.

"But you'll come, won't you, Nina?" Avi asked.

"Oh sure. The dead don't scare me. Only the living do," I answered, thinking about Avi's parents and Shoshanna.

"Let's go back and listen to some music," Nancy said.

"All right, nervous Nancy." Then Avi stuck her head out the window and sang "Dem Bones, Dem Bones, Dem Dry Bones" all the way home.

Actually, Avi didn't seem to want to go home. She kept suggesting places to visit, but we said, Forget it. Then, once we got back, she was still restless—playing record after record, noodling at the piano, sketching Nancy and, finally, cleaning the living room. Dorrie and Nancy soon left, but I agreed to stay over.

"You really have lovely hair," Avi says.

"Thanks."

"Hey, you want to stay here while my parents are gone?"

"All three weeks?"

"Sure."

"I'd love to. But my parents would get pissed off. They claim they've hardly seen me as it is since I came home."

"Oh, screw your parents!"

"What a disgusting thought!"

Avi laughs.

"Maybe for a week or so, though," I say.

70

She nods.

"Hey Avi," I say carefully. "Is something bugging you tonight?"

"Bugging me? No, why do you think that?"

"Well, you seem kind of agitated."

"Agitated? No, I'm okay. Just a little excited, having this place to myself."

"And nervous, maybe," I prod gently.

She smiles an embarrassed smile. "Well, yeah. I guess maybe a little. Sometimes I get nervous being alone. I like having people around me."

I smile back. Then I say, "Listen, there's something I've been meaning to ask you. I hope you don't mind. Aviva, I think you've got a lot of talent. You know that. I think you're more talented than anyone in the Rabbit's Foot . . ."

"No," she interrupts. "They really are super musicians."

"Okay, they do play well and anyway you know best. But *you* are a better songwriter and you're also the focal point of the group. So what I want to know is, why do you take such shit from them?"

"What do you mean?"

"The way they stomped all over your song last night, which they seemed to think they were doing you a favor by performing."

Avi just shrugs. "Aw, they're not used to a new style. But I'll break them in."

"And also the . . . um . . . style they seem to want you to sing in."

"The style?"

"That Joplin voice. It's not really yours."

"Yeah, well, I have to fumble around for a while until I find my rock voice. Is it really bad?"

"No. It's just not you."

"It will be. Listen, Nina, the Rabbit's Foot really *is* good.

71

And they're going to make it. *We're* going to make it," she says fiercely.

"I hope you do," I respond. "I know it means a lot to you."

"Yeah. It does." Then she frowns. "Hey . . . Neen . . . Now can I . . . ask you something?" Her tone is surprisingly timid.

"Sure," I say.

"I trust you a lot, Neen. You always seem to know what you're doing."

I blink. Me? Confused Nina, the original yo-yo?

"Sometimes it irritates me—how much you seem to know what you're doing." Avi smiles.

"I think you must have the wrong number," I say, shaking my head.

She laughs. "Oh no, I know I'm right."

"Well, you can believe what you care to. But tell me, what did you want to ask me?"

"Oh." Her face flushes slightly and she takes a breath. "Well . . . when you . . . got . . . laid, did you . . . uh . . . come?"

This is so different from the bawdy Aviva I thought I knew I just repeat, "Come?"

"You know . . . have an orgasm?"

"I know what 'to come' means. I'm trying to think how to answer your question. Gwyn and I—we actually only had intercourse three times. And I didn't come then. But when he would touch me, yes, then I always came." I feel sort of half embarrassed, half pleased telling her this. And also womanly. Grown-up and sophisticated.

"Uh-huh. Do you think something's wrong if you don't come?"

"Wrong? No. It's supposed to take a while sometimes until you relax enough to. Why?"

"Oh . . . nothing." She pauses.

I wait.

"Well, last night Pete called me frigid."

"Pete!" I shout. "What about Lolly!"

She stiffens. "Yeah, Pete. Lolly didn't stick around," she says snidely.

I swallow my prudishness and try another tack. "Avi, I'm sorry I freaked out. Let me ask you something. Do you really dig Pete?"

"Sure . . . why not?"

"Well, I don't know. I mean, do you want to have a long-term relationship with him?"

"Oh, Nina. Come off it. This is nineteen sixty-eight! Nobody gets involved in a 'long-term relationship' now."

I do, I want to yell, but instead I murmur, "Yeah. Nineteen sixty-eight. I seem to recall saying something about it to Lolly the night before." Then I think of something. "Look," I ask, "do you come when you masturbate?"

"I don't masturbate," she says.

I fight another urge to yell "You *don't?*" and instead say, "Well, you could try that and see how you . . . uh . . . react."

"Yeah," she says dubiously. "Maybe . . ."

Suddenly I feel exhausted. "Let's go to sleep," I say.

"Yeah, good idea. Hey, you want to sleep in my parents' bed? It's king-sized."

"Sure. Why not?"

Brush teeth. Rinse mouth. Slip into bed.

I lie on my side. Aviva's on her back. I hear her breathing quietly.

"Nina," she says. "So you don't think I'm frigid?"

Charlotte's boy wafts in and out of view mouthing "Frigid bitch!" I puff out a breath and gently lay a hand on Avi's shoulder. "No Avi, I don't think you're frigid. I think that's a word some man made up. But maybe you should stay away from Pete." And Murray. And Sam. And John. Especially John. "Maybe you should do it just with someone you really dig a lot."

"Yeah. Maybe you're right." Then she sighs and shudders slightly under my hand.

"Avi, are you okay?"

"Yeah, I'm okay." After a minute, she says, "Hey Neen, that's really *great* about Gwyn coming to New York . . ."

"Yeah. Thanks, Avi."

"But are you really going to wait three months for a good lay?" she finishes.

"Oh you." I laugh.

"Turn around and I'll tickle your back."

"Ooh, lovely," I say, and, feeling warm and sleepy, I turn over onto my other side and let Aviva's magic fingers do their stuff.

Chapter 7

Aviva is making one of her increasingly infrequent appearances at Queens College. "Let's go get some smoke," she says.

"No," I answer, "I have a class."

"Shit, haven't you ever gone to class wrecked?"

"No. I wouldn't be able to concentrate."

"Look, what's your next class?"

"Social dancing."

"Social dancing? Are you kidding?"

"No. I have to fill my phys. ed. requirement somehow."

"So why didn't you take modern dance or folk dance? I mean, social dancing! Come on!"

"I signed up for what I thought was modern dance, but when I got to the gym, boy, was I surprised. And so were my classmates."

"Why?"

"I had registered for men's weight lifting."

"No shit?"

"No shit. I read the bulletin wrong."

We crack up.

Still chuckling, I wipe my eyes and say, "The only

thing . . . hee-hee . . . still available . . . ho-ho . . . was social dancing. So, that's why . . . ha-ha . . . I'm taking it."

"Gotcha. But, listen, you don't have to concentrate to dance. So let's get stoned."

"What about your next class?"

"Russian literature."

"Avi, you can't be stoned for that!"

"Why not? Dostoevski was. Come on, let's go to the Union and grab a reefer."

"Reefer. Reefer. Reefer. Is that all you mamas ever think about?"

Avi and I turn our heads simultaneously.

"Floyd!" Avi yells. "What are you doing here? I thought you were quitting school."

"I was going to, baby, but I decided to fight instead." He pauses and looks at me. "Hello. As you gathered, the name's Floyd." He is tall, dark skinned and handsome, with a big Afro and a wide smile.

"I'm Nina."

"You a musician too?"

"No. A friend."

"Floyd plays great flute," Avi says.

He bows.

"What do you mean you decided to fight instead?" she asks.

"Well, you know we're starting a Black Students Alliance here? We're gonna push for an Afro-American history course, a Swahili course and a tutoring program. And that's just for starters."

"Floyd, what the hell do you want with a Swahili course? You were born in Queens and you're strictly middle class."

"Shit, Aviva. That isn't the point. Look at the useless crap they teach here! Russian literature! What the hell do *you* need with Russian literature? You're a white middle-class Jew from Queens!"

76

Avi laughs. "Touché!" she says.

Timidly, I ask, "Ummm, why *are* you pushing for these courses? I mean, we don't have courses in Hindi, for example. Or in Jewish-American history."

Floyd looks at me. Hard. Then, satisfied that I'm really waiting for a serious answer and not dumping on him, he says quietly, "You ever look at an American history book? Blacks don't exist in it—except as them undifferentiated darkies Massa Lincoln rescued from the big bad South. Blacks don't exist in literature courses either—except as them same darkies Harriet Beecher Stowe wrote about. You won't find us in Music 101 or in Art 500. And yet we write books, we make art, we *are* music, and we helped build this fucking country from scratch. We got a long history the university, the state, the goddamn government would like to forget about. But here we are. And here we're staying. And if we gotta fight to be recognized, to let us *have* our history, to let our children have it, we will." He finishes as quietly as he began.

I am very moved by what he has said, but I don't know how to respond. So I just smile again.

"As for courses in Hindi and Jewish-American history, sure, why not, let's have them too. But, sugar, I'm not Hindi and I'm not Jewish, and those courses just ain't my concern."

"Okay, Floyd, I've had enough heavy rap. You wanna have a toke with us?"

"No, I got a meeting. You want to come?"

"What's the meeting?" I ask.

"To discuss the idea of open admissions."

Avi snorts.

"Open admissions! Floyd, you gotta be nuts! Stick to the flute."

He turns to me. "How about you?"

"I've got a class."

"Yeah, she's gotta mambo her way into the hearts of millions . . ."

"Huh?"

"Social dancing, y'all."

Floyd grunts. "Shit. What did I say about useless crap?"

"Phys. ed. requirement," I say lamely.

"Right. And what for? So you can attend the debutante ball?"

I recoil and feel myself turn red.

Floyd instantly picks up my hand. "I'm sorry. I'm lashing out at you and I don't even know you. I just get so damn mad at all this shit. Look, you seem interested. Maybe we can talk sometime. Okay?"

I nod. "Okay."

"Well, I gotta go. And you better go mambo."

"First, she's gonna get stoned," Avi says. "Right?"

I sigh. "Okay. You win."

"Hippies," Floyd says, shaking his head. But then he grins and winks. "See you, now."

"Next time, bring your flute," Avi replies.

He laughs and strides toward the amphitheater.

Avi watches his retreating back and says, "Wonder what he's like in bed?"

"Jesus, Avi" is all I can say. "Jesus."

In the Student Union, it's very easy to score. So soon we're inhaling the weed and listening to some dude play the guitar.

"Not bad," Avi says. She begins to sing along, spinning out a nice tune.

I close my eyes. Memory begins to seep into my brain.

It was April when I went to visit Gwyn. Rhys had written to him as promised. Then Gwyn wrote to me, enclosing a pressed flower and an invitation to come up to East Anglia University in Norwich. I'd be delighted to, I wrote back. Signed out for the weekend. Took a train and fidgeted the whole ride. Thumbed a lift to the university. Found Gwyn's dorm, but no Gwyn. Bloke invited me to wait in his room while he went to find him. I waited, thinking, This is pretty damn bold of me, visiting a man I hardly know. I didn't dare admit to myself the worse truth—that this was no chaste visit. I was hoping for SEX, in capital letters.

Gwyn hopped through the open French windows like some strange sparrow, pecked my cheek, and, hopping back out again with me in tow, introduced me to his girl friend, Elspeth. Elspeth was, is, of some different realm. Beautiful. Ethereal. Spiritual. She looked like Glinda the Good. But nothing much escaped her notice. Rhys had said she and Gwyn were on the rocks. So I was surprised when Gwyn told me I'd be sharing her room that night.

"And then . . . ?" I asked quizzically.

"And then my roommate leaves and you can share my room." This in front of Elspeth.

"Oh" was all I could say. My entire position taken for granted—or perhaps clearly perceived and accepted.

Elspeth did not even look miffed, let alone furious. What a chummy breakup, I thought. "Here, let me help you with your things," she said. And she, Gwyn and I walked to her hall and room.

"Nice," I commented on the huge flower prints on her wall.

"Georgia O'Keeffe. One of your artists."

"Oh. A woman," I said stupidly.

"There are more women artists than you think. Few are written about. Quintessential male chauvinism," she said.

"Male what?"

"Chauvinism. Excessive patriotism—in this case to their own sex."

"Oh. Sounds terrible. Can someone be a female chauvinist?"

"No. I don't think so. It's a question of political power.

Only those who have it can be chauvinists. Women don't have political power."

"Women have other kinds of power, though," Gwyn said, looking at me.

I blushed.

"Yes. Often developed in self-defense." Elspeth laughed. "I'll make some tea." She left.

Gwyn immediately flung his arms around me and looked into my eyes.

I felt as though I should say, "Oh, Mr. Davies, this is so sudden," but instead, I said something equally ridiculous like, "Oh, hello."

"Hello," he answered back. And he kissed me. A slow, lingering kiss. "Yum. I'm glad you've come," he said.

"I don't want you to think . . ." I began breathlessly.

"Don't worry. I'm not thinking," he interrupted with a grin.

Then Elspeth came back in, and Gwyn spun away, took the tray from her and poured tea. All as if nothing had happened.

That night in Elspeth's room she and I stayed up talking about poetry. She showed me some of her poems. I showed her some of mine. I was liking her more and more and feeling a bit guilty about Gwyn.

"I'm glad you've come here," she said.

Are you sure? I wanted to say. Instead I said, "Thanks." And she answered my unspoken question for me.

"I don't mind, you know. About Gwyn."

"We haven't . . ." I began and stopped, acutely embarrassed.

"No, but you will. Just be careful."

"I will," I answered without knowing what she meant I should be careful about.

We spent the next day alone, Gwyn and I. Picnicking. Punting. Cathedral cruising. It was all lovely. And we talked and talked, pouring out whole portions of our lives. I cried about Colin. He consoled me, saying "Colin must be a dunce to throw away someone as precious as you are." When we finally returned to his room late that night, we felt we had known each other for a year instead of just a day.

"Time to go to bed," he said.

"Yes."

"The ladies' bathroom is straight down the corridor, if you wish to use it."

"There's only a men's loo in my hall—no baths or showers."

"Men are not supposed to spend the evening in ladies' halls. But the reverse is expected, if not perfectly acceptable. Yer British double standard."

I washed luxuriously and returned in my nightgown and robe. Gwyn was sitting in his p.j.'s on his bed writing in a journal. He raised his head. "You look beautiful."

"Thank you."

He got up, came over and kissed me. "I'll tuck you in," he said.

I slid under the covers, my heart thumping like mad.

He kissed me again and stroked my cheek. "Good night, luv."

I was surprised, to say the least. And I must have shown it.

He caressed my cheek again. "Not yet, *cariad.* It wouldn't be right. We should know each other better."

I know you well enough, I thought. But I smiled and said, "Good night, then."

The next morning, I glanced at his journal, lying face up on a table near his bed. "How could I have been so blind about Nina when we first met?" it read. "Didn't see the beauty, the intelligence, the vulnerability. At least, I am clear-eyed enough to see it now. But I must be gentle, patient, and let time play out its hours . . ."

Guiltily, I stopped reading.

We kissed good-bye, and I returned to Reading, pure and chaste as ever.

But two weeks later, Gwyn came down to visit and returned to Norwich with my maidenhead.

And I was certainly glad he took it. . . .

My eyes snap open.

Aviva is still sitting next to me. She offers me more grass. I inhale. Hold. Exhale slowly.

"What were you thinking about?" Avi asks.

"Gwyn and sex." I grin.

"For you the two are apparently synonymous. . . . So, what's he like in the hay?"

"Dunno. Never did it in the hay."

"Ha ha. Where did you do it?"

"In bed. And once in a meadow."

"Yeah? Was it nice or itchy?"

"Oh, it was nice. The grass was very soft and it smelled good."

"Hmmm. Maybe I'll suggest that to Pete."

I feel my smile tighten. "Did you say Pete? But I thought you . . . And I said . . . " I stutter.

She just shrugs.

"Jesus, Avi. Sometimes I don't understand you at all!"

"Well, you don't have to shout about it."

"Yeah. Okay." But just don't ask me for advice anymore, I want to say, but I don't. Then something dings in my head and I look at my watch. "Shit, I'm late. See you later."

"Aw, why don't you cut?"

"Nope. See you later."

"Here, finish this joint on the way."

As I puff the weed and hurry to my class, I say to myself, Man, lately I really don't understand Aviva. I thought I did the other night. I felt really close to her. But now, I don't know. I mean, how can a person who writes something so delicate as "On an Island" be so crass. How can a person dig sex without romance? And does she even dig sex? I hope she knows what she's doing, that's all. But I wonder if she does.

"One-two-and three. Ba-de-da-de-da. One-two-and three. Ba-de-da-de-da. One-two-and three. Ba-de-da-de-da. One and two and three and stop." Mr. Russo smooths back his thick gray hair and flicks off the record. "And that's the tango. Did everybody get it? I'll do it once more."

I look at Janice, who is my partner. She's short and fat, but, blimey, can she dance. The guys in our class are all spastics—except for Mr. Russo, of course. Janice and I are, by far, the best dancers—at least for Latin dances; we tend to screw up the waltz somehow—so we gravitate toward each other.

"All right," says Mr. Russo. "Now you try it." He flicks the record back on.

Janice and I try it and succeed beautifully. Giggling, she dips me into a gorgeous back glide. I put one hand, palm up, against my forehead in a tango vamp gesture. She giggles again.

"Hey, are you stoned too?" I ask.

"No. Are you?"

"Yeah."

"Oh wow."

"Yeah . . . Hey, help me up."

She does.

"That was very good, girls," Mr. Russo says, fox-trotting our way.

"Uh-oh," Janice mutters.

"Miss Ritter." He proffers his arm. "You will be my partner for the umbrella step."

"Whee," I say.

Mr. Russo raises one eyebrow at me and steers me to the center of the floor.

"The step is simple," he says. "Gentlemen, clasp your partner firmly at the waist. Like so."

I am clasped firmly.

"Take her right hand and raise it above her head. Like so."

My right hand is raised above my head.

"Now. You will spin your partner as if twirling an upside-down umbrella. Like so."

I am twirled like an upside-down umbrella. Faster and faster. "Wheee," I yell. "Whoopeeeee!"

The class begins to giggle. Maybe they're stoned too.

"Miss Ritter, you're getting a bit overenthused," Mr. Russo says, dipping me low to the ground.

I hang limp in his arms.

The class applauds.

Mr. Russo helps me up.

"Perhaps we should return to the waltz step we worked on last week."

I blow a raspberry.

Mr. Russo pretends not to notice. He fiddles with the record player. A scratchy version of "The Blue Danube Waltz" blares out.

Janice and I start to dance. One-two-three. One-two-three.

"You're crazy," she says.

"Why?"

"Coming to class stoned."

"Didn't know he'd pick me for his partner."

"That doesn't matter. How can you concentrate?"

"I'm doing okay, aren't I?" With those words, I step on her toe.

"Owwwww," she yells, picking up her foot.

"Will you allow me?" says a voice behind me.

I turn.

It's Billy.

"What are you doing here?" I ask.

"Practicing. There's no class here after yours, so dance majors can use this gym. Shall we?" He offers me his arm.

I take it and he leads me to the center of the floor.

"Is this déjà vu?" I ask.

"What?"

"Didn't this happen the other night?"

"Shhh. Don't talk. Dance."

And then we're in a movie. I'm in an ice-blue dress covered with feathers. He's in top hat and tails. We whirl effortlessly. He lifts me high in the air, sets me down gently; and we never miss a beat. And it's divine.

Applause. "You see, Miss Ritter, you *can* do the waltz," says Mr. Russo.

A look passes between Billy and me—of stars and bird wings and neon.

"Class dismissed," says Mr. Russo.

Janice waves good-bye. The class shuffles out. Billy and I sit down on a rolled-up gym mat.

"Did that really happen?" I ask.

Billy grins. "I like dancing with you," he says.

"I like dancing with you, too." I'm not so stoned now, so I decide not to mention the other evening again. But I wonder if Billy thinks I'm perpetually wrecked.

"I wish I could just dance," he says wistfully.

"What do you mean?"

"Not bother with Math and Eng. Comp. 22 and all that crap."

85

"Why are you here then? I mean, couldn't you study at a dance school or something?"

"Yeah, I could. But there's a little something called The Draft."

"I hope Billy sticks it out at Q.C.," Dorrie had said. "Do you think you'll be able to stick it out here?" I ask.

"I don't know. It's getting harder to every day."

I nod sympathetically.

"Nina. Will you go out with me?"

"Out? Like on a date?"

He grins again. A lovely warm grin. "Yeah. Like on a date."

I smile back ruefully. "Billy, I can't. For two reasons: One, I'm in love with a bloke—guy—named Gwyn. He's coming to New York in three months. Two, Dorrie."

"Dorrie," he repeats.

"She really likes you. Maybe I shouldn't ask this, but how do you feel about her?"

He thinks for a minute. "I like her, but it's a friend thing."

"That's too bad. Do you think you'll ever feel differently?"

He shrugs. "Who knows?"

"Do you think we can be friends?"

"As in no sex, please?"

"As in no sex, please."

"We can try."

We smile at each other.

"Can I take you dancing—as a friend?" he asks.

I laugh. "I'll have to ask my mother."

Then he laughs.

Soon, I head for the Union, thinking, well, I did something right today—for Billy, for Dorrie, for Gwyn, for me.

Chapter 8

"Barber's *Adagio for Strings*, please," I say, handing in my call slip.

"Right-o," answers the lanky guy at the desk. "So you're a Barber fan?"

"Yes," I say. Actually, I only know this one piece by Barber. Aviva once played it for me and I immediately fell in love with it. I used to listen to it all the time in the music lab before I went to England, whenever I needed something to soothe my brain. But I didn't feel like striking up a conversation with this guy—or, for that matter, revealing my ignorance.

"I'm a Barber fan myself. Have you heard 'Toccata Festiva'? Fantastic. That section where . . ."

I sigh and turn to look at the listeners. And there, eyes shut, head tilted back, fingers tapping lightly on the desk, is Floyd.

"Excuse me," I say to the librarian and slide into the seat next to Floyd.

He opens his eyes and smiles. "Nina. Right?"

"Right." I nod. "What are you listening to?"

He doesn't answer—just picks up my earphones, puts them on my head and turns on Channel 8 for me.

A mellow saxophone is playing something that sounds familiar. I listen for a while and realize it's "My Favorite Things" from *The Sound of Music*, a song I always found rather dumb. But I never heard it sound like this before, so rich and exciting. I find myself tapping along too, the way Floyd had been and I'm sorry when it ends.

"Who was that?" I whisper, pulling off one side of the earphone.

"The 'Trane," he whispers back.

"Who?"

"John Coltrane. Haven't you ever heard him before?"

I shake my head. "I haven't listened to much jazz. Some blues, but not much jazz."

"That's too bad. It's the best music there is."

"Shhh," a girl sitting in front of us says.

I take out a note pad and scribble, "But you play rock."

"For money," Floyd writes back. "I play jazz too—for joy," he whispers.

"Jazz for Joy. Sounds like a record title," I say.

"Will you please be quiet," the girl says.

"Take it easy, madam," Floyd tells her. "We'll let you listen in peace." He motions with his eyes toward the door.

I nod.

"Hey, aren't you going to listen to Barber?" the lanky librarian asks as we pass him.

"Later," I say. "Keep the turntable warm for me."

Floyd snorts. "I'll have to remember that one."

We walk to the amphitheater—my favorite spot on the whole campus, a cool, grassy slope with a small stage at the bottom. Once, the Drama department put on a production of *Oedipus Rex* here. I don't remember if the acting was good or not, but the setting was perfect. Floyd sprawls on the grass. I sit next to him.

"So you play rock just for money," I say.

He grins. "No, I was just bullshitting. I like rock, all right, but jazz really is my favorite. Jazz is essentially Black. Popular rock is just watered-down stuff white folks stole from R & B and soul."

"What about Jimi Hendrix?" I protest.

"What about him?"

"He's black."

"Yeah, so?"

"He's popular with everybody and his stuff certainly isn't watered down."

"He's an exception. And he's more popular with honkies anyway."

I feel myself bristle. "Does that mean I am or I'm not supposed to like his music?" I retort.

Floyd laughs. Then he reaches for my hand and looks at my palm. "You got a strong head line, you know that?"

"Where?"

"Here." He traces the line.

"You read palms?"

"No. I just know about the head line 'cause my grandma told me I got a strong one, too. And I also know where the heart line is."

"What's that?"

"Your love nature. Ah, yours is deep." He grins again.

"Oh." Embarrassed, I take my hand away.

After a pause, I say, "Are you majoring in music?"

"No. History. You?"

"English."

"Oh yeah. When I played a gig with Aviva, she said she got a letter from a friend of hers who was studying in England. Was that you?"

89

"Yes."

"Were you part of any sit-ins there?"

His question takes me aback. Sit-ins. I didn't even know there had been any in England. "No. I . . ." I begin, but Floyd isn't listening.

"That pig Enoch Powell and that speech he gave about racial quotas! Shit, what a country. England still wants to hold on to its goddamn empire. Fucking fascist state!"

I wince. England, that green, quiet place a fascist state?

Floyd looks at me, gauging my reaction to his words.

"There weren't any protests at the university I went to," I say slowly, "except about curfews."

"Curfews?"

"Yes. Men had none, but women had to be in hall—dormitory—by midnight. And men had to leave women's halls by ten."

"You protested that?"

"Yes—I helped circulate a petition."

"You protested that and not the policies that keep Blacks, Indians, working-class people, and women too out of the university. Shit, Nina! What'd you do after 'circulating' your petition. Drink sherry with the professors?"

I stand up. "I have a paper to write," I say shortly.

"On what?"

"What do you care?"

"Because I don't think we're finished talking," he says quietly.

"You call this talking?"

He smiles ruefully. "I'm yelling at you again, aren't I?"

I don't answer.

"Let's start over. You tell me about what the university was like and I'll tell you what's wrong with it."

I laugh. "Should I take notes?" I ask wryly.

"Yeah. Revolution 101. Come on, I'll buy you coffee—unless you want to buy me coffee."

"Let's go Dutch."

"Yes, ma'am," he says.

And we head for the cafeteria.

October 15, 1968

Dear Nina,
Your voice over wires
Crackles electric
In the humming air
Currents over currents
Waves over waves
Awakening all my him-pulses.

Sorry for that, but we cannot all be John Donne (or even Mother Goose). Ah, dearest Nina, to lie with you again. To talk of poetry and peanut butter. To explore the realm of the senses . . .

Rhys came to visit. No longer angry with me since he has thrust Vanessa from his heart. He seemed happy. Unfortunately, that is when his writing suffers. Meaning—he can only create when in the throes of something or other. Anyway, he introduced his new Beatrice—Diana. At the pub, she got tiddly and, embracing me heartily, invited me to spend a weekend with her in Reading. Rhys saw and heard. Now he's angry with me again.

Spent this past weekend in Paris—city of lights and flights. Met a couple of luverly French dollies who took me for a tour of the Champs-Élysées (I've seen it at least a dozen times, but I played along). As we walked *bras dessus*, a little bald-headed chap passed by, stopped, turned back, said, *"Égoïste!"* and winked.

Ah, Nina. Can I help being irresistible? Margaret says I can. Perhaps I should get married. Lead a productive life.

Happy birthday again. Will scribble more upon awakening after sleeping.

Love,
Gwyn

From an unsent letter—

Dear Gwyn,
Who the hell is Margaret?
Love,
Nina

December 1968

Chapter 9

Glittering skeins of red and green lights alternately spelling trees, wreaths, Happy Holidays. Rotating reindeer. Multiple Saint Nicks wearing red acrylic suits (flameproof) stuffed with pillows (stuffed in turn with foam chips). Christmastime in New York.

I miss the plum pudding, holly decorated; the candlelight processional through arched cloisters; "The Boar's Head Carol." I miss the mugs of hot mulled wine; the Christmas crackers exploding, with a poof, tiny whistles and rings into our hands; the Jantaculum with its hokey Victorian melodramas and twinkling madrigals.

I miss England.

But New York in December, rotating reindeer and all, still manages to make my eyes sparkle. The streets smell of balsam and the air crackles with the promise of snow, snow, snow. Shop windows, sadly neglected the rest of the year, suddenly burst with color and even spectacle. People *actually* bustle. And then there are all those gifts to buy and to wrap, and all those parties. . . .

And this December is even better than most. Because it's

only one month away from January. And January means Gwyn. Because my mother has stopped pestering me about blind dates. And because the Crew has really been together. Almost like we were before I went to England. Long bull sessions in Dorrie's yellow kitchen—pot and tapioca at hand. Frequent trips to Baskin-Robbins. Forgetful games of Botticelli. Avi seems less interested in sex and more interested, once again, in crazy escapades. And I do mean crazy.

Like, for instance, the stop-sign caper.

Dorrie, Avi and I were hanging around Dorrie's flat looking at her waxed bicycle wheel piece.

"Do you like it, Avi?" Dorrie was asking.

"Yes, I do. But I think it needs something more—a finishing touch."

"I agree," I said. "Something to add color."

"And to set off the shapes," Avi said.

"Hmmm," Dorrie mused.

And then Nancy banged on the door.

"It's open," Dorrie called.

"Well, Crew," Nancy said. "I've brought us an early Christmas present—or maybe a late Thanksgiving present."

"Shush, we're working," Avi said.

"Huh?" Nancy looked dumbfounded.

"Never mind," Dorrie said. "What's your present?"

"Well, after my lesson, it was so nice out, I decided to take a walk. And, after a while, I realized I was being followed . . ."

"What!" I exclaimed.

"Listen, listen, it's okay. I was scared too, but when the guy came alongside me, I could tell he was just another card-carrying freak like the rest of us. He held something out to me and mumbled something and . . ."

"Nancy, get to the point," Avi interrupted.

"Well, he asked me if I wanted to buy some hash . . ."

"Hash! I haven't had that since England!" I said.

"Only ten dollars he said for a big chunk. So I bought it. And here it is!" Dramatically she flourished a foil-wrapped piece the size of a Chunky candy bar.

"Wow!" Dorrie shouted. "I'll get the pipe."

But Avi said calmly, "Give it here." Deftly, she unwrapped the stuff and held the thick, black lump to her nose. "You'd be better off using this to pave the streets," she said.

"What?" Nancy said.

Avi tossed me the chunk and I sniffed it and then said gently. "She's right, Nance. This is tar."

"Oh no!" Poor Nancy looked utterly crestfallen. For weeks Avi had been teasing her about smoking everyone else's dope and not contributing any of her own.

"It's okay, Nancy," Dorrie said. "I've got some dope."

But Nancy slumped down into a chair and shook her head despondently.

"Hey, look, everyone gets ripped off sometime," Avi said.

"Yeah . . . forget it," I offered. "Listen, maybe you have a bright idea. Just before you came in, we were looking at Dorrie's sculpture and trying to decide what it needed for a finishing touch. What do you think?"

Nancy barely raised her head to look at the piece and then she mumbled, "I don't know. Maybe a stop sign or something."

"A stop sign!" Dorrie shouted. "Nancy, you're a genius!"

"I am?" Nancy said.

"Fantastic!" Avi agreed. "Let's go."

"Go where?" I asked.

"To steal us a stop sign."

"You're kidding." "Oh, man." "Holy shit!" we said simultaneously.

But, giggling, we bundled into our coats and, grabbing Dorrie's dope, piled into her car for yet another adventure.

Slowly, we drove the smoke-filled Volkswagen through the streets.

"There's one," Nancy said, pointing to a stop sign near an elementary school.

"Not near a school, dummy!" Avi said.

"There's another!" Nancy shouted.

"You don't have to point them out. We see them," Avi said.

"We should take one from a place where it won't be missed," I said. "I mean, you know, a place where everyone stops anyway. You know what I mean."

"The El Dorado Shopping Center." Dorrie snapped her fingers.

"Don't take your hands off the wheel," Avi said. "And take us to El Dorado immediately."

I quoted, " 'Gaily bedight, a gallant knight/in sunshine and in shadow/had journeyed long, singing a song/in search of . . .' "

"Mia Farrow," Nancy finished.

We cracked up.

"Boy, are you stoned!" I said.

"Here it is," Dorrie said, and we entered the parking lot of a little shopping center that consisted of a grocery store, a hardware store, a pharmacy and a deli. Everything was dark and deserted. But there, gleaming dully in the lamplight, was our prized octagon.

"Drumroll, please," I announced.

"That's for executions," Avi said.

"Well, we're gonna decapitate the sign, aren't we?" I retorted.

"How are we gonna do this?" Dorrie whispered.

"I'll climb on your shoulders and unscrew it. You got a wrench?" Avi asked.

"Yeah."

"Okay." Avi, as usual, took charge. "Nancy, you stand guard. Nina, you be ready to catch the sign."

"You mean be crushed by the sign."

"Nancy will help you."

Dorrie got out the wrench and handed it to me. Then she squatted down and Avi got on her shoulders. She stood up and I gave Avi the wrench.

"Man, these bolts are on tight," Avi said, through gritted teeth. "Shit. Okay, there's one."

"Hurry up," Dorrie said. "You're not so light, you know."

"There's another."

"Hey, someone's coming!" Nancy yelled, too loudly.

Then we became a scene from a Laurel and Hardy movie. Dorrie jumped and Avi banged her arm with the wrench. "Oow," she shouted and fell off Dorrie with a dull thud. "Oow!" Dorrie landed on her rear. I tripped over Avi's leg and grabbed the stop-sign pole to keep myself from falling. That shook the pole and the sign swung off and hung tipsily upside down.

"Oh God, let's get out of here," Dorrie whimpered, trying to scramble to her feet.

"It's okay, it's okay!" Nancy called. "I was wrong. Nobody's coming."

"You stupid idiot," Aviva hissed.

"Are you okay?" I asked, bending down to her.

"Leave me and get that sign."

"Maybe we really ought to forget it."

"Get the sign!"

"Right, chief," I said sarcastically and climbed onto Dorrie's sore shoulders. "Nancy, come here and grab this." I struggled with the final bolts and the sign slid heavily into Nancy's arms.

97

She sat down with a thump. "Ugh," she grunted.

I clambered down and grasped an end of the sign. Nancy staggered up with the other end.

"Get it into the car, quick," Avi commanded, rising and wiggling her foot.

"Man, this weighs a ton," I panted.

"Watch it, you're shoving me off balance!" Nancy warned.

Finally, we got to the Volkswagen.

"A car!" Avi called. "A cop car!"

"Oh shit," Dorrie groaned and dropped her keys.

"Nancy, shove the sign under the car," I yelled.

We did, while Dorrie searched the ground for her keys.

The cop car pulled into the lot. A short cop got out. The other one stayed in the car. The short cop sauntered over. "Something wrong here, girls?" he asked.

"No, er, officer. We just changed a flat," Avi said.

The cop gave us a suspicious look.

Dorrie finally found her keys.

"Well, good night," Avi said jauntily.

But the cop just stood there.

We looked at each other and got into the car.

"What do we do?" Nancy wailed. "We can't drive off. They'll see the sign."

Dorrie moaned.

"No kidding," Avi snapped.

"Well, chief, what do we do?" I asked.

"We pretend the car won't start," Avi said.

Dorrie moaned again, pulled out the choke, stepped on the gas pedal a few times too many and flooded the engine.

The cop came over again. "*Now* what seems to be the trouble?"

"I think I . . . er . . . flooded the carburetor," Dorrie said.

"Miss, let me see your license."

Dorrie reached for her bag.

"Frank. Got an emergency on Jewel Avenue. Let's go," called his partner.

Dorrie extended the license and the cop barely looked at it.

"Okay. But you look like you need driving lessons," he said. Then he got into his car and he and his partner sped off.

For a minute, we just sat there; then we got out, dragged out the sign and shoved it into Dorrie's trunk. Then, we drove off. Halfway back to Dorrie's house, we all cracked up.

"Whew, that was a good one!" Avi said.

"And a close one," I added.

"It sure was." Dorrie shook her head.

"I'm proud of us all," said Avi.

"All for one and one for all!" Nancy sang. "And the Crew forever!"

The next day, Dorrie nailed the sign to a plank and placed it under one of the bicycle wheels. It really did add the finishing touch.

Some things haven't been as much fun as our escapades. Like school, for example. College is still strange—and it keeps getting stranger. More and more meetings. Rallies. Calls for action. It's hard to study. Vietnam is on everyone's lips. Lists of the dead or missing appear daily. Of the American dead, that is. How many Vietnamese men, women and children have been killed is anybody's guess. Actually, there are reports that the lists of American casualties have been doctored too. Someone drew a picture of the Vietcong choking an Uncle Sam-dressed pig on the side of the Social Science building. People booed when the painters came and whitewashed it. Floyd says all black men should be exempt from military service because they should not be forced to fight and kill other Third World people who are being victimized by the white racist government of America. I asked why not exempt *all* people from the draft?

He smiled and said I was getting the right idea. Oh, Floyd. Now there's another problem. I don't understand our relationship at all. It's so . . . prickly. There are times when he's, I don't know, nice. Like the time two weeks ago.

There was another rally. I stopped to listen because Floyd was one of the speakers scheduled to talk about the need for a Black Studies program.

"The Black Panther Party put it concisely in their platform and program: 'We believe in an educational system that will give to our people a knowledge of self. If a man does not have knowledge of himself and his position in society and the world, then he has little chance to relate to anything else.' In the City University of New York, there are over 16,000 Black students. In the City University of New York, there is not one Black History course. Not one Black Literature course. Not one Black Music course. We Black students ask whose history are we studying? Whose literature? Whose music? How are we to gain a knowledge of our people, ourselves, when the Shitty University of New York will not teach us?" Floyd was saying.

"Right on!"

"Power to the People!"

"You tell it, brother!"

People shouted and applauded.

I stayed until the end of his speech and when he finished I cheered along with everyone else.

Then, I went to the amphitheater. It was kind of cold, but I felt like sitting outside anyway—soon it would be too cold to sit out at all. I wanted to think about Floyd's speech. The things he'd said sounded right—most of what he says to me sounds right, once he explains it. I thought about all the English courses I'd taken and how we read few—if any—works by black writers. But there are other things Floyd said that are not so clear to me. Like will a Black Studies program educate white students, make them aware? And will black students study other history and literature and music besides their own?

Too bad the Crew doesn't want to talk about this stuff. Damn, I got so confused and weary thinking that after a bit I gave up and started to read a copy of John Donne's poems Gwyn had sent me—along with a lovely letter telling me how much he missed me and how Margaret was looking forward to meeting me. Margaret, by the way, turns out to be a fellow student who might also be coming to Colorado. Seems Gwyn spends a fair amount of time with her because they have the same major. I guess he's told her a lot about me, which is good in case she has any romantic inclinations. Anyway, there I was reading divine Donne when Floyd appeared.

"I thought I'd find you here." He smiled. "Saw you out there. What'd you think?"

"You're a good speaker."

"Thanks. That all you got to say?"

"Oh Floyd. I can't talk about it right now. My head's all muddled. I need time to think."

"I can dig it." He picked up the book I'd laid aside and flipped it open. " 'To teach thee I am naked first, why than/ What needst thou have more covering than a man.' "

"Not that one," I rapped out, involuntarily, and then turned red.

He grinned. "What's the matter? Too risqué?"

"No . . . it's just . . . my boyfriend used to read that to me."

He stopped grinning. "Your boyfriend? Where's he when he's at home?"

"England."

"Shee-it. No wonder you're so hung up on that place."

"Don't. Please," I warned.

He smiled again. "Okay, mama, I won't. I'm feeling too good to fight. That was a good speech I gave if I do say so myself." After a quiet minute, he reached out and pulled a withered leaf from my hair. "What do you want out of life, Nina girl?" he asked softly.

I knew the answer. Gwyn. I want Gwyn. And I want to be with my friends. But somehow I couldn't say that. I couldn't say anything, so I just shrugged. "I'm not sure. Do you know what you want?" I finally asked.

"Freedom. Power. Pride. Love. I want to live in a place where I—and my people—don't have to worry about getting shot in the back by some cop or being beaten to death in some cell or starving in some rat-infested dump. I want to teach my brothers and sisters about ourselves. I want us—and all oppressed people—to have freedom and food too. And I want to make music because we always need music."

Then I felt ashamed of myself and my paltry wishes. And suddenly I felt like bursting into tears. I bit my lip.

"What is it?" he asked.

"Nothing. I . . . . admire you."

"Don't admire me. That's like making me some kind of thing. I may be a little exotic—provocative—to you because I'm Black and I talk politics. But I'm still just another human, that's all. And I have been known in the past to piss, to get drunk occasionally and even to cheat on exams."

I laughed, then shivered. It was cold out there and an icy wind had suddenly sprung up, making it even colder.

"Whew, time to split before they find us frozen in place like vanilla and chocolate popsicles."

"Ugh!" I said.

"Yeah, that *was* pretty bad. *Vamanos*!"

After that, we sat in the Union and talked some more and I felt pretty comfortable with him, as though maybe our relationship was improving.

But that's not how I felt the last time I saw him—about a week ago.

I had asked Billy if I could watch one of his dance classes. Billy and I have gotten to be pretty good friends. We met a lot at Q.C., sometimes for lunch, sometimes to dance in the Union, sometimes to see some film being shown or some play or concert being performed during an afternoon. It's all been light and casual and undemanding, with a friendly platonic physicality I've never had with a guy before. But I haven't bothered to tell Dorrie about our relationship because as she and Billy still haven't gotten it together, I thought she'd misunderstand. Anyway, now Billy has dropped out to take dance classes at the Joffrey. I really miss our meetings and excursions at Queens, so that's why I asked if I could attend one of his classes. He said, "Sure. Come to a class." So I did. And it was fascinating.

His teacher, a thin, elegant woman one would hesitate to call so vulgar a phrase as middle-aged, in black leotard and pink tights, surveyed the class with a practiced eye, correcting and complimenting and forcing the students to push past what they once thought were their limits.

"Rita, turn out your left foot. Gillian—bend the arms. Billy, straighten your leg."

Billy's leg already looked pretty straight to me, but he strained his hamstrings a bit more to achieve that perfect line.

I found the whole thing paradoxically awesome and human. Awesome because of those gorgeous, strong bodies and their sublime grace. Human because of their prodigious sweat and their tired faces.

"God, that was wonderful," I said to Billy when he plunked down beside me and massaged his left foot.

"I've got to work on that arabesque. It's still not right," he said, frowning at his reddened big toe.

"Can I help?" I asked.

"My arabesque?"

103

"No, your toe. Here, I'll rub it," I said, gently kneading the knuckle.

"Oooh, that feels good. You're a born toe rubber."

"Thank God! I've found my station in life. . . . There. Better?"

"Yep." He shook his foot, then stretched his legs straight up in the air.

I watched in admiration. "Boy, you have terrific legs," I said.

"Why thank you, Miss Ritter. No one's ever complimented me on my legs before," he said, lowering them to the floor.

"No? Well, the rest of you ain't bad either," I said, patting his flat hard stomach.

"You're pretty good yourself." He conspicuously ran his eyes over my body.

"Nah, my hips are too big."

"I like big hips. They're womanly. Those skinny things in my class don't turn me on at all. Give me fl-esh!" he growled and, in one motion, pushed me down, flipped himself over on me and nuzzled my neck.

"Get off, you loony." I feebly smacked his bum.

He sighed and rolled off. "Oh Nina, you're so cruel."

"And you're so sweaty," I said, scrambling to my feet.

"Do I smell?" He sniffed his armpit. "Ugh. I'm going to change. You want to go someplace?"

"Yes, the Eighth Street Bookstore. Okay?"

"Sure. I'll be back in a few minutes. Wait for me downstairs."

On the way to Eighth Street, we talked about how Billy had wanted to be a dancer since he was eight and how he didn't want to tell anyone because they'd call him a fruit.

"But you are a fruit," I said. "You're completely bananas."

"So are you—so I guess we're quite a pear. Thank you. Thank you." He applauds himself and bows.

"Blah! We've been around Aviva too long."

"Aviva. She's a real trip. One of a kind. But you know, I wouldn't trust her with any personal confidence."

I was puzzled. "What do you mean? You think she'd tell everybody or something?"

"No, it's not that. But I get the feeling that she'd store it and use it against me somehow."

"Billy, what a strange thing to say. I thought you liked her."

"I do. But . . . I . . . don't trust her."

"Well, I do. She may be freaky and self-centered and demanding and sometimes she annoys the hell out of me, but I trust her."

He shrugs. "Maybe I'm just paranoid."

"Maybe," I said. But his remark left me thinking. Aviva had done some thoughtless things. She was fully capable of the stinging retort or the supercilious put-down—like the time she read a poem of mine and pronounced it worthy of a Hallmark greeting card—or even of the unwitting insult, such as when she admired my parents' antique sewing table and proclaimed, "That's wonderful—the first really nice piece of furniture I've seen in your house!" But untrustworthy? No, I don't think so.

In the bookstore, I left Billy at the performing arts books and headed upstairs for the poetry section. I was thumbing through a book of Chinese poetry looking for a poem Gwyn had sent me in his last letter when I heard a familiar voice coming from somewhere else on the floor.

"Man, Arnie, that cat can blow! I'd love to jam with him."

"Yeah. I know what you mean!" came a second, unfamiliar voice.

Book in hand, I wandered to another aisle and saw Floyd talking to a short man, whose open jacket revealed a dashiki a lot like the one I own.

The guy saw me smiling and tapped Floyd. "Hey man, I think someone knows you."

Floyd turned his head, saw me and gave me a dazzling smile. "Hey girl, how you doing?"

"Fine. And you?"

"Good. Oh, this is my man Arnie—the finest flutist in New York. Next to me, of course. Arnie, this is Nina, fellow student and intellectual."

Arnie and I laughed and shook our heads. "This cat's too much," Arnie said and shook my hand.

"So, what you up to?" Floyd asked.

I showed him the book.

"This woman's always reading poetry," he said.

"What's wrong with that?" I bridled.

He didn't answer, just smiled.

"Yo, Floyd. I gotta split. See you later," Arnie said.

"Okay, man." They slapped five and Arnie left.

"We just jammed together," Floyd explained. "Nearby. So I decided to come here and buy some magazines and stuff."

"Find what you were looking for?"

"Not yet . . . Hey, listen. I thought I saw a notice outside for a reading by a couple of Black poets at N.Y.U. tonight. You interested? If you are, I guess I could be persuaded to attend," he said.

"It sounds good, but I've got work to do."

"Nina dearest, time to . . ." Billy stopped short. "Oh, I didn't see you."

"Billy, this is Floyd. He also goes to Queens."

"I think I've seen you around. You're involved in politics, right?" Billy said.

"Yeah," Floyd said curtly. Then to me, "This your work?"

I thought he was kidding, so I laughed.

"Well, I don't want to muscle in on your time. 'Specially

since you such a busy chick. All them *poems* to read." He practically spat out the word and then hurried down the stairs.

Billy's nostrils flared. "Whoo, what was all that about?"

"I honestly don't know," I said. "That man can be very difficult."

"Oh yeah? What's his problem?"

"I don't know. A lot of passion, I think."

"For you?" Billy asked quickly.

"Oh no. His is a political sort. He's very bright, charismatic even, I think."

Billy scowled at the staircase. "He seemed goddamn rude to me."

"Yeah. Well . . . Look, I better get home and work on my paper. You ready to leave?"

"Yeah," Billy answered.

So I paid for my book and we took the subway back to Queens, reading Chinese poetry and talking about ballet. But I kept wondering about Floyd and why he acts the way he does and thinking that Billy was definitely not the right person to talk to about him. I wonder if I'll ever figure him out.

But, as I said before, despite the ambiguities of Floyd and college, December's been pretty good. And I haven't even mentioned the most exciting news of all, which Avi sprang last week in her inimitable fashion.

Nancy and I were at Dorrie's, stringing cranberries and popcorn.

"I've never had a Christmas tree. My parents were dead against it," Dorrie had said wistfully.

So, even though Christmas was three weeks away, Nancy and I trotted down to Nelson's Nursery and found a fat little fir (which was about all we could afford) and dragged it back to Dorrie's. Unfortunately, Dorrie had left. So we waited in the cold for half an hour, blowing on our fingers and singing

"The First Noel" loudly and off key. By the time she returned, we were ready to chop the damn tree into firewood and burn it.

But Dorrie was delighted and quickly set about baking cookie ornaments and instructing us on how to string garlands.

The cranberries kept squishing and the popcorn kept breaking into bits and Nancy and I were getting really annoyed until we all got stoned and then it didn't seem to matter. Dorrie went out again to get some candy canes ("I can't have a tree without candy canes," she said) and came back with Billy. He looked somewhat askance at our holiday ministrations, but we plied him with pot and he began to grin and cover himself with cranberry chains.

"How are your dance classes?" I asked.

"Good. Really good." He smiled. "In this getup, I could do the hula." Then he began to gyrate his hips until Dorrie told him she couldn't stand the strain and went to make coffee.

I couldn't stand the strain either and insisted he work on making paper flower decorations. But he didn't get very far because the door flew open and Aviva flew in.

"Merry merry!" she sang.

"Have some popcorn." Nancy replied.

"No, no, that can wait. We're going caroling."

"Caroling! You've gotta be kidding," Dorrie said, coming in from her kitchen with three steaming mugs.

"Nope. Pour that stuff in a thermos and let's go. I need the practice."

"For what?" I said.

"For the l.p. we're cutting next week," she answered.

"The what!" Nancy shrieked.

"Oh Aviva!" I yelled.

"Wow!" Dorrie exclaimed.

And Billy did another hula.

"How did it happen?" I asked.

108

"Ah," said Aviva, "Remember that fancy-suited dude who swaggered into Wheels last month and swaggered out at the end of the second set? Well, he's been swaggering around for a while now and he finally swaggered over to Sam and introduced himself as Chip Bloch ('As in "off the old" . . .') and said he was a producer for Vishnu records. 'I'm interested in bright new bands with lots of brass and a hard-edged but not-quite-acid rock sound. How about coming to my office and we can have a talk?' he said. The upshot is, we start cutting next Wednesday!"

"Holy shit!" Dorrie said.

"You can say that again."

"Holy shit!"

"Shut up. Let's go caroling."

"An l.p.! Wow!" I said. "The Rabbit's Foot lucks out."

"That's a good album title," Avi said.

Then she bustled us into our coats and scarves and out into the streets of Queens, where we assaulted the neighbors with versions of "God Rest Ye Merry, Gentlemen," "Joy to the World," and "O Hanukkah, O Hanukkah, Come Light the Menorah." And Billy kept dancing a hula.

Afterward, I went home and wrote to Gwyn, promising him an immediate copy of the record in Colorado. And then I made a list of everyone else I want to give a copy to.

Tomorrow's the recording session. I'm cutting class and I can't wait.

Chapter 10

So many dials. Hundreds of them. Don't know how that guy can figure out which to turn. We're sitting in the soundproof engineer's booth. Behind the heavy glass window, the band is rehearsing a raunchy old blues called "I Need a Little Sugar in My Bowl." Nancy keeps cracking up over the vulgarity. This session has been kind of repetitious and not as exciting as I thought it would be, with the band playing the same song over and over, so I'm doodling on a pad, trying to write a blues song—something I've never tried before. I keep watching Sam alternately blowing his sax and making suggestive remarks. It's like studying some robot. Nothing seems real on the other side of the glass. Sam's wearing a bandana around his neck. I remember Amelia Theresa saying something about him looking like a pirate.

"I'm a pirate blowing 'round the horn," I scribble.

Nah, not a pirate. A sailor? No.

"I need a little sugar in my bowl/I need a little hot dog in my roll," Aviva sings.

Sex always cuts the mustard. Ugh, what a pun!

Sex. Pun. Sailor. Seaman. Semen. Ha! Horny horn.

I'm a seaman
blowin' 'round the horn.
I'm a seaman, baby
blowin' 'round the horn.
Been blowin' down southward
Since the day I was born.

Got it! Got it! I laugh out loud.

"Shhhh," says an engineer.

"Shhhhh," says Chip Bloch.

"What are you laughing at?" asks Dorrie.

I show her.

She giggles and smacks a hand over her mouth.

"Okay," says the engineer. "That sounds good. I've got the levels set. Let's try a take."

Silence. Then. Ba Bom. Ba Bom. Heavy opening blues riff.

Aviva starts to sing.

And on the other side of the glass the heavy padded door with the red light over it swings open.

"Cut. Cut!" screams the engineer. What the hell is happening here?"

"I don't know," says a techie.

What's happening turns out to be Amelia Theresa, with Pat and Lolly hanging on to her arms and trying to drag her back. We can't hear what she's saying because the engineer has shut off the mike, but we see her sweep over to Sam, wrap her arms and the feather boa she's wearing around him and plant a huge kiss on his chops.

"What the hell is this? Where's Mike? He's supposed to be watching the door!" the engineer is still yelling.

Dorrie, Nancy and I are poking each other and laughing.

Pat says something and takes Terry's arm once again.

Lolly, her belly grown enormous since the last time I saw her, waddles toward the booth.

111

"Look, there's no room in here for all these broads!" the engineer complains to Chip.

"Take it easy, Ed. There's room. I'll make sure they don't interfere with your work."

Pat has managed to tug Amelia Theresa into the booth.

Chip has managed to calm Ed. Dorrie, Nancy and I have managed to stop laughing.

And "I Need a Little Sugar in My Bowl" begins once again.

Murray hits a blooper on the 'bone.

Cut.

Begin again.

Nice. Rough-smooth. Then Chester breaks a guitar string.

Whoops.

Cut.

Take it again.

Aviva's headphones fall off.

Ha ha.

Cut.

Time out.

"Man, this is bo-ring," Nancy says. "I'm gonna get something to eat. Anyone want to come?"

"Yeah," says Lolly, "I'll come."

"Me too," says Dorrie.

And the booth door opens, disclosing Billy.

"On second thought . . ." says Dorrie.

I suddenly think of another verse:

Well, I steer my ship
By the light of the moon.
Well, I steer my ship, baby,
By the light of the moon.
Like to take it nice and easy
So I don't come home too soon.

"But I'm not really hungry," Billy is saying.

"Well, just sit with us, then."

"Are you coming, Nina?"

"Me?" I ask, fuzzy-brained from my creative effort. "No. I want to do some writing."

"I'd like to talk with you. . . ." Billy looks right at me.

Slowly, I begin to see the pain in his face.

"What's wrong with talking to me?" Dorrie, suddenly strident, demands.

Billy winces. "Nothing. There's nothing wrong with talking to you."

"Are we going or not?" Lolly asks.

"Why don't you come, too, Nina?" asks Nancy.

I look from Dorrie to Billy and back. I'm stuck. I don't really want to go out for food. But I want to find out what Billy wants. But Dorrie looks like she doesn't quite fancy my company.

"I need a little steam on my clothes/Maybe I can fix things up so they go," Aviva's voice belts out.

"Sing it, sing it, sing it!" yells Amelia Theresa.

"Okay, let's go," says Billy, with a sigh. "I'll catch you later, Nina."

"Okay," I say.

Mike the techie, having returned and been bawled out by Ed, opens the door for them all.

I exhale a big breath. What now? I wonder.

The blues is winding to its big finish.

Terry is wiggling her shoulders and humming in a throaty alto. Pat has her eyes closed, listening intently to the music.

Bom. A good take.

But Chip wants another couple.

I exhale again. And stare blankly at my half-written blues.

Feh; I'll finish it later. I set aside the sheet with my words and begin a letter to Gwyn.

Dearest Gwyn,

In happy anticipation of January I've promised to lose five pounds. Isn't that an alluring thought? All the lighter to ride on your charger into the sunset.

Breeched by the white shine
   atop the tower,
Caught in the mixed glitter
   of the stones and the sun,
The courtier
   awaits the sea.

This recording studio is another world. There's this gray room—looks like felt on the walls. And a big piano over in a corner. And these big silver microphones like cheese graters hanging all over the place. Then, there's the sound booth and all this equipment. Oh yeah, that's where I'm sitting right now. Sitting and thinking. As in the immortal words of what's-his-name, "Sometimes I sets and thinks. Sometimes I jest sets." A just jest, eh what?

Man, you sure talk much of needing a wife to let you get some work done. Sounds more like you need a maid.

Have you found out the exact day of your arrival yet? I wish we could be together on New Year's Eve. Then my cornucopia would overflow. And is Margaret coming to the U.S. too? I'm looking forward to meeting her.

I pause, read over what I've written and scratch out the entire last paragraph. Why am I lying about Margaret? I don't really care whether or not I meet her. And that cornucopia bit, ugh! My cornucopia, indeed. My horn of plenty.

Suddenly, a bolt of lightning (or maybe a shower of cornucopias) blazes in my brain.

Well, horn of plenty
I gave it that name.
Well, horn of plenty
I gave it that name.
Don't mess with no seaman,
Or you'll never be the same.

I hoot with pleasure, scribble it down, ditto the opening verse and, holy shit, I've written a blues. I smirk to myself for a while and then pick up my letter again. Should I enclose my song? I decide against it.

Instead of a Christmas tree, I should have a bush of broom in remembrance of . . . But there's no broom in New York City. Maybe we can find a new broom, which they say sweeps clean.

Have you found out the exact day of your arrival yet? I'll meet you at the airport. I'll be wearing a red carnation . . . or a sprig of broom.

By the way, is Margaret coming to Colorado? I hope she gets the post she deserves. . . .

"Hey, this is good!"
I jump about two feet and fall off my chair.
"Floyd, what are you doing here? You scared me."
He grins. "That's my forte, baby!" He helps me up. "I'm playing on one of the tracks," he explains.
"Stop your fooling, and stuff something in my bowl!" sings Aviva.
"Good take." Chip gives the high sign. "We'll play it back in a minute."
"Man, what a funky song," Floyd says.

"Yeah, it sure is."

"I mean yours."

"Mine?" Then I notice he's holding my blues in one hand, his flute in the other. I feel my cheeks getting hot.

"Hold on." He starts playing his flute, a real bluesy sound. Then he stops, and begins to sing.

"I'm a seaman,
blowing 'round the horn."

My mind gets blown immediately. His voice is amazing. A whine. A growl. A caress. All together. Even Ed the engineer doesn't tell him to shut up. And Chip is listening real closely. And in that instant, I also realize that Aviva's voice, good as it is, shouldn't be singing the blues.

"Been blowing down southward/Since the day I was born."

Then his flute ripples, pouts, beckons, screams.

I close my eyes, letting it wrap silvery strings of notes around me. He stops abruptly. I blink.

"Can I use your lyrics?" he asks.

"Use them?"

"Yeah. In my gigs."

"You want to use my lyrics?"

"You struck deaf, mama? Yes, mademoiselle, I should like to sing your lyrics to this here tune I just wrote."

"Oh yes. Please. Take them."

He shakes his head. "Nina, girl. You sure some dumb chick. Listen. Never just give away your stuff. Make a copy. Sign your name. Write me a note that I have permission to set to music and copyright these lyrics. If the song is published, you will get a percentage. If recorded—another percentage. We'll write a contract between ourselves."

"Why bother with all this? I don't need to get paid."

"Listen, I know white folks be rich, but you ain't that rich."

"I ain't rich at all."

"Fine. We'll write a contract. Contracts can also save friendships."

I ponder that one a moment.

"Listen. I'd like to use this tune in my New Year's Eve gig. Maybe you'd like to come along?"

"I don't know. It depends on what Aviva, Dorrie and Nancy want to do."

"What have they got to do with it? I'm asking you, not them."

"You mean, like a date?" I blurt out.

"Shee-it," Floyd swears. "If you want to call it that, go ahead. I'd like you to hear me play, is all."

"Oh. That would be okay, I guess. If you don't mind the Crew coming along. I already made plans with them. You see, I don't date," I say, feeling increasingly foolish. "You know—that boyfriend I told you about."

"The one in England?"

"Yes."

"Shee-it."

There's an awkward silence, broken by "I Need a Little Sugar" blasting out over the speakers.

Bom-ba-bom. It sounds pretty good. The band is smiling.

"Great!" says Chip into the microphone. "Take a break."

I watch the band lay down instruments and go into a huddle—probably over the next song. Amelia Theresa runs into the studio and smothers Sam with kisses.

Floyd picks something off the floor. "What's this? Another song? " 'Dearest Gwyn,' " he starts to read.

"Let me have that. It's a letter."

"To your boyfriend?" he asks, still reading.

"Yes." I grab for the letter and miss.

He shakes his head and reads my poem out loud. Then he says in a tight, strained voice, "You really are a strange chick.

117

You live in a fairy-tale world, don't you? Prince Charming and all."

"What are you talking about?" My voice comes out harsh. Ed shushes me.

"Aw, damn, Nina," he bursts out. "Can't you see where you're at? You can write something like this tough blues and you send stuff like this courtier crap to this dude of yours. Why do you want to pretend you're all air and no earth?"

"Shut up."

"Yeah. Go ahead. Don't listen. Go play croquet and sip tea with your pinky sticking out. Do the fucking minuet for all I care. Just don't do it around me." He puts the letter into my hand and walks into the studio, where I watch Aviva and company give him five.

I turn and see that Pat is still sitting there, quietly looking at me.

Embarrassed, I try to slough the whole thing off. "I don't know why, but I seem to rub him the wrong way. Every time we see each other, we have an argument."

"You think that's why he freaked out?"

"I guess."

"Maybe he digs you."

"Digs me? Nah. He asked me to hear his music and all, but . . ."

"What is your English boyfriend like?"

"Gwyn's incredible. Thin. Medium height. Straight brown hair. Piercing blue eyes."

"Not what he looks like. What's he act like?"

"Like . . . like . . . a poet!" I say proudly.

"What does a poet act like?"

"What do you mean?"

"Well, does he go around reciting verse all the time?"

"No. He does quote things and he writes poetry, but he doesn't walk around orating or something."

118

"Then how does he act like a poet?"

I'm starting to get annoyed. "He . . . looks at things . . . differently . . . and talks about them differently."

"How does he see them differently?"

"Look, I can't explain what he's like. You'll have to meet him." I turn back to my letter.

But the door pushes open and Dorrie, Nancy, Billy and Lolly come pouring into the booth. Everybody looks jolly and sated with food except Lolly, who seems oblivious to everything except for that new life moving around inside her. Billy is laughing a lot. I look more closely at him. His smile is tight. And there's still that pain in his eyes. "What is it?" I want to ask. "What's wrong?" But he doesn't seem to want to talk in front of everybody.

"I've got to go now," he says.

"Awww, do you have to?" Dorrie asks.

"Yeah. See you." He looks at me.

"I'll call you later," I say.

He nods and leaves.

"Why are you going to call him?" Dorrie asks.

I'm tired of her jealousy. "He's my friend, too, Dorrie," I say sharply. Then I relent. "Did he tell you what's bugging him?"

She waves away my question. "Oh yeah. His dance classes aren't going so well."

I don't reply. I know he didn't tell her the truth.

"They doing anything different yet?" Nancy asks.

"I think they're starting 'On an Island,' " I answer.

"Oh good."

The band begins playing again and we all listen quietly (or hummingly, in the case of Amelia Theresa). But I keep thinking about Billy. Something is really bothering him. No, not bothering. Frightening. That was the look in his eyes. I must call him later.

"Hey, we need some clapping on this track. Everybody into the studio!" Sam yells.

So, giggling and prickling (what if I make a mistake, like I sneeze or something, on this cut and they have to redo the whole record), we file into the studio. I avoid looking at Floyd, who plays flute on this song.

"Okay, now, on the first verse, it goes clap-clap. Clap-clap. Clap-clap, clap-clap-clap-clap-clap-clap-clap-clap. Everybody got it?"

"No," we all said.

It took us half an hour to learn how to clap.

I tried reaching Billy tonight, but he wasn't home. But Floyd called.

"Nina, I guess I got to apologize to you again."

"I guess you do," I said coolly.

. "I don't know what else to say," he said.

There was a silence and then I lost my cool and said angrily, "Trying to correct my politics is one thing, but trying to correct my love life is something else."

"You're right," he said quietly. "Your love life is none of my business."

After another silence, he said, "But you mean, you don't mind my trying to correct your politics?"

I couldn't help it—I laughed. "I guess I'm getting used to that."

"Don't get too used to it—then you'll stop asking questions and thinking for yourself. Hey listen, why I called besides to apologize, that blues we wrote—I've worked out an agreement between us and I'd like you to read it. Can I bring it over?"

"To my house?"

"Yeah, something wrong with that? Your parents gonna call me 'boy' and whup your behind or something?"

"No," I said curtly. "But I think it would be better if we met somewhere . . . uh . . . neutral. At a restaurant for lunch or something. I mean, we're talking about signing a contract, so I think we should be, uh, businesslike about it."

"Oh yeah. Businesslike," Floyd answered sardonically.

Here we go again, I thought. "Oh, forget it," I said, disgusted.

"No. You want to be businesslike, so let's be businesslike. Lunch tomorrow, one o'clock. I'll write it in my appointment book."

"Floyd . . ."

"You pick the place."

"Oh, I don't know. Gino's," I said, lighting in exasperation on a familiar hangout from my pre-England days.

"Gino's. Right. See you then." He hung up.

"Ooooh!" I howled at the phone. "He makes me so mad!"

"Maybe he digs you," Pat had said.

Digs me, my ass! He's out to drive me crazy! Yelling and apologizing and mocking and apologizing. Telling me what to do, how to think. Accusing my parents . . . Then I stopped myself. No, Nina, he didn't accuse your parents. He accused you. No, he didn't even do that. He got your number. And got it right. It was true. I didn't want Floyd to come over because I didn't want to deal with my parents' questions about him. Why ask for trouble? as Dad always says. But Floyd's just a friend, I could have told them—just like Cassie, another black friend I once brought home. A friend is a friend. An easy, neat explanation. But the fact is I'm really confused about my feelings for Floyd—and each time I see him I get more confused. He's so bright, sharp, sarcastic. Sometimes he makes me so nervous. Because he's sarcastic? Because he's black? Because he's a man? Or because he's attractive. Because he attracts me. Hell, attracts me? Admit it, Nina, big, black, handsome Floyd turns you on. And I realize if I invited him here I'm afraid my parents would read it in huge letters on my chest: FLOYD TURNS NINA ON.

I wonder if Floyd can see it too and that's why he picks on me. After all, he doesn't pick on Aviva and she always sasses him like crazy. Ah shit, bad enough to have the hots for another man, but a black militant man yet. Oh Nina, are you ever asking for trouble! Maybe I ought to stay away from him completely.

But the thing is even though it—my attraction—and he, Floyd, make me nervous, I really like him, too, as a friend and, well, as a teacher. I can learn a lot from him. I already have. I guess what I'm worried about are some other things I might learn.

Oh Gwyn, you better get here quick. You just better.

Chapter 11

I am going to be straightforward and businesslike today.

"It's cold, isn't it," I say politely, sliding into the booth across from Floyd.

"Yeah, it's cold," he answers.

"Did you order?"

"Not yet. I was waiting for you."

"Shall I look at the agreement first?"

He looks amused. "By all means," he says wryly and hands it to me.

It's clear and simple, a fifty-fifty split of our percentage if and when the song is published, if and when recorded, etc. "It's fine," I say.

"Good. I'm going to copyright the song, then."

"Is that complicated?"

"No." And he shows me another form and explains the procedure.

"Fine. Where do I sign?"

"Right here, ma'am," he drawls.

I stifle a laugh and scrawl my name.

A waitress appears. "You want to order now?" she says crossly.

"Yes, sugar," Floyd says wickedly.

The waitress cracks a smile. "Save the sugar for your coffee. What'll you have?"

So we order Gino's famous meatball heros and coffee and then Floyd says, "Well, business is finished. Now what do we do?"

I shrug.

"I know, let's talk about the weath-ah some more," he says in an English accent. "Do you think we'll have snow? I do love sleigh riding, don't you?"

I giggle. "Oh yes. But not as much as ice skating. Ice skating is truly divine," I reply, also in an English accent.

"Ah, yours sounds authentic," he says. "Did your boyfriend teach you to talk pro-pah?" he asks lightly.

"No, actually he's Welsh and never talks pro-pah, according to the English."

"Oh, they are bourgeois," He sighs.

I change the topic. "Floyd, where do you live?"

"In Jamaica. I have a place I share with my sister."

"Your sister? That's kind of nice."

"Yeah. She's nice. A little overbearing like my mama, but nice. Anyway, that was the only way we could both afford a place."

"Was it difficult leaving home? I mean, did your parents mind?"

"Sure. Parents usually mind. Then they get used to it. I go home every couple of weeks for a good meal and that keeps them happy. Keeps me happy too. I can't cook worth shit. And Aggie—my sister—who can cook, is hardly around."

Appropriately, the waitress arrives with our food.

"Thanks, sugar, I'm starving," Floyd says.

The waitress gives him a wink.

124

"I guess you haven't visited your parents in a while then."
Floyd laughs. "That's right."

While we eat, he regales me with stories about crazy gigs
he's played.

". . . he was so high he left his pants in the john and tottered
out to play piano in his underpants."

I laugh and laugh.

"Yeah, it is funny, but pathetic, too. Dope's really a killer.
A way of keeping black folks under control."

"You don't even get stoned, do you?"

"Not anymore. I like to keep control of myself." Then he
tells me another funny story.

Later I ask him, "Floyd, do you think Aviva's talented?"
He looks surprised. "Sure. Don't you?"

"Yes, I do."

"Then why do you ask?"

"I guess what I really want to know is will she make it?"

"That's a different question entirely. In the rock world, talent
don't equal success. It's a rough, sometimes ugly, business,
rock 'n' roll."

"Ugly?" I am startled. Some of the places the band has
played haven't been too great and Avi's sex life has struck
me as a bit sordid, but the rock world itself has seemed a
glittering circle—a golden ring, even. So I say, "But it seems
so . . . exciting, glamorous. Once you start making it, that
is."

"Shit, Nina, that's 'cause you ain't inside it. You oughta
tell Aviva to watch her behind. 'Specially with the guys in
the band."

"I think it's a little late for that," I say.

"Oh. Like that, is it? Too bad." He finishes his coffee and
wipes his mouth. "Ooh, that was good. You finished? You
want to take a walk? It's cold all right, but kinda pretty outside."

"Okay," I say.

We split the bill and leave. I think about how relaxed we are together for a change. Maybe he does like me, as a friend or something, after all. Or maybe he really doesn't know he turns me on.

We end up at Flushing Meadow Park, site of the New York World's Fair. We stare up at the big, stainless steel Unisphere—symbol of world harmony.

"You ever go to the Fair?" he asks.

"Yes. Four times. Twice with my parents, once with my best girl friend, Janie, and once with the boy I was snowing into taking me to the Senior Prom."

He laughs. "Snowing?"

"Yeah. His name was Kenny Green. I didn't really like him but I wanted to go to the Prom so bad. Everyone was going—even Janie, and she was in eleventh grade! So I went on all these terrible dates with him so he'd ask me to the Prom, which he finally did, and I had a really boring time. Pretty awful, huh?"

He shrugs. "Listen, I went to the Fair practically every other week with a bunch of guys to try and pick up girls. We used to sneak ahead on all the lines and get dirty looks from everybody, but especially the Fair Guides who didn't like a scruffy batch of Ne-gro kids hanging around no-how. But we sure had fun." He chuckles at the memory.

"Oh, I thought I recognized you—you slipped in front of me on line at the Coca Cola exhibition, right?"

He snorts. "You bet, mama."

"I liked the Coca Cola exhibition best," I say. "Do you remember it—the sights, sounds and smells of five different countries? With a Coke machine in each tableau—like one in the middle of a jungle."

"Rampant imperialist capitalism!"

"True. So what was your favorite?"

"IBM," he says.

And we both laugh.

"Talk about imperialist capitalism," I say.

"Well, what did I know at seventeen? And IBM had all these fancy multimedia things. Just knocked me out." He pulls up the collar of his leather jacket. "Whew, it is cold. Look at that squirrel. His coat's thick and almost white. Sure is gonna be a rough winter."

"You can tell from a squirrel's fur?"

"Oh sure. And from other things, too. Like the thickness of a nut's shell. Or when certain birds migrate. My granddaddy taught me. He has a farm in Georgia I used to visit when I was a kid. I remember most sitting under a tree and eating big, juicy peaches, letting the juice trickle down my chin. Man, I'd sure like to go down there again."

" 'Do I dare to eat a peach?' " I mutter and immediately get embarrassed.

"What was that?"

"Nothing. Just a line from a poem by T. S. Eliot that came into my head." I repeat it.

"What does it mean?"

"Oh, this man, J. Alfred Prufrock, is really uptight about a lot of things. He's prematurely old; he measures out his life 'with coffee spoons' and asks things like 'Do I dare disturb the universe?' He's afraid to do, to plunge into anything—even something as simple as eating a peach, which is also a symbol of sorts. It's ripe and sensual. In China . . ." I break off.

"In China . . ." he urges me to continue.

My cheeks are flaming now, but I have to answer. "In China, the peach was a symbol for the female genitalia."

"Oh, I like that," he says softly. "It's very beautiful."

His face is so near to mine, I can feel his breath on my lips. My stomach is churning madly. "Nina . . ." he whispers and runs his fingers under my collar and up and down my neck. His lips brush against mine.

I jump back. "Floyd, I think we better go. It's cold and I've got to write a letter."

He squinches up his face. "A letter. To your boyfriend?"

I feel like kicking myself, but I just say, "Yes."

He kicks at a stone. "Yeah, let's go home and not disturb the universe," he says coldly.

Oh Floyd, I don't know what's happening here, I want to yell, but instead, I just turn, and we walk silently out of the park.

Chapter 12

The last strains of "Let the Sunshine In" are dying away. Dorrie is wiping her eyes. Nancy is humming to herself. Aviva is toking away. Billy is drumming his fingers on the arm of his seat (I still haven't had a chance to talk with him alone. He had left town and just returned today.) And Floyd is cursing.

"Shit," he mutters. "Damn stupid bourgeois minstrel show!"

Nancy stops humming. "What's eating him?" she asks.

"I'll tell you what's eating him," Floyd snaps. "Pretty little white folk and pretty little black folk all dancing together in natural rhythm. No cares, no woes. No hunger, no unemployment, no reality! Shit!"

"It's a musical, Floyd," Aviva says. "Not a treatise."

"What's that supposed to mean? That because it's some half-witted entertainment for the masses, it doesn't have to have any decent values?"

"But it's trying to break out of the old-style musical molds," I say. "And it's trying not to be racist. I mean that song 'Colored Spade' . . ."

"Yeah, right. 'Colored Spade.' Great example, Nina. Lists

129

a bunch of stereotypes and everyone laughs. And *agrees.* Where's the positive image?" He looks pointedly at me. "That dude up there balling white chicks? Great image!"

"You think he shouldn't be balling white chicks?" Aviva asks.

"No baby, I don't."

"Awww, and I thought you cared," she says.

For a moment no one speaks. Then the tension breaks. Floyd laughs. We all join in.

An usher appears, urging us to vacate his theater.

"Easy, man, we're the oppressed masses," Billy says.

The usher stiffens. "You'll have to leave anyway. We have another show to perform in less than four hours."

"Oh, you acting in it?" Avi asks.

"Please leave now or I'll have to summon the manager."

"Summon away."

The usher stalks off.

"Uh-oh," says Nancy. "He's lost his cool."

"Tsk-tsk," Avi answers.

But I'm still upset that Floyd is upset. "I still don't understand your objections, Floyd," I say. "I mean, everyone in this show was equal—nobody was better than anyone else, nobody was putting down blacks."

"Right, everything was just hunky-dory and we all love each other so much and nobody's uptight, right?"

"You don't think it can be that way?"

"I don't think it can be that way. Unless Blacks have as much power in this country as whites—power over our own schools, communities and government. If we can get that power peacefully, fine. If not, we will use whatever means are necessary."

"Floyd, you don't mean you advocate violent overthrow of the government? Things take time; they have to evolve . . ."

"Damn, Nina, you talk like *Time* magazine, you know that? All white and mealy-mouthed."

The shock waves reverberate. I stand up, shaking. "I'm going," I quaver.

Then the usher arrives with the manager in tow. The manager is fat and balding and very managerial.

"Now, what seems to be the trouble here?" he asks condescendingly.

"Nothing, sir," Billy says.

"Nothing at all. We're waiting for the dawning of the Age of Aquarius," Aviva says with great innocence.

"Are you waiting for someone in the cast? The stage door is out that door to your . . ."

"Excuse me," I say, pushing past him and the usher and out the door to which the former is gesturing.

When I get outside, I feel the tears starting to flood. "Aw, crap," I mutter and head for an alley where I can be alone. It's not just the play or even the government he's attacking this time. It's me personally. And I don't know why. I've been so confused about him since the other day. "Oh, crap," I say again.

This must be the stage-door alley because the guy who played Berger is just coming out with one of the actresses. I don't want to talk to him, tell him how good he was. Don't want to talk to anybody. Better split.

"Nina."

I jump.

Floyd grabs my arm before I can get past him.

"Let me alone!" I growl.

"Nina, I'm sorry."

"Listen, you put me down almost every time we see each other. And then you apologize and then you do it again. I've had enough. I don't understand why. Last time . . ." You

131

tried to kiss me, I almost say. But I don't want to bring up something that was probably a momentary aberration.

"Nina, let me say something. Please."

"Why? So you can insult me again?"

"Just listen. I said some stupid things before. I shouldn't let my personal feelings get in the way of my politics. I don't want to hurt you, to attack you. But I'm angry. I'm angry all the time. And I've got good reasons to be angry. And you, well, you're smarter than all the rest of the Crew—smarter and tougher. And when you start talking like some candy-ass liberal, I can't stomach it. I want to shake you."

I am stunned. What is this man talking about? Smarter? Tougher? Than Aviva? No way.

"You could help a lot; you could do something. But then you start spouting *Time* or getting stoned. Shit, Nina, you don't value me and you don't value yourself. It makes me sick."

"Then why bother with me at all?" I hurl. There, now, lay it on the table.

He touches my cheek and searches my eyes. "If you don't know that, you don't know nothing."

Oh God. What is he telling me? Confused, I push him away. "You're right. I don't know nothing. Nothing at all."

We glare at each other. Two cats. Spines arched. Backing away from each other, from the stream of actors brushing their way past.

Finally, Floyd eases down his shoulders. "Nina, come with me now. You go with Aviva and company, you're just gonna get wiped. I'll introduce you to some other people—people who are doing something."

"Hey, Nina!" Aviva's voice cuts through the cold air. "Hey, where are you? Is Floyd molesting you?"

Floyd's whole face contracts. "Nina, come with me. Come on."

132

I feel fixed to the pavement. Unable to move toward Floyd. Unable to move away.

"Where are you?"

An actress bundles past, singing a snatch of "Easy to Be Hard."

Floyd balls his fist and hits the wall. "Ah shit, Nina. You just gonna stand there, ain't you? Just stand and wait for that Prince Charming you write to to come over from England and take you away from All This. To where it's clean, green and obscene. Then you won't have to see my Black face or anybody else's ever again."

Furious, I strike at his face. He just stands there and lets me hit him. "You . . . you . . . creep!" I yell and try to punch him again.

But he grabs my wrist. "No. Once is all you get."

Then, in a blur of skin and denim, Billy is there. Yelling, "What are you doing to her, man?" And twisting Floyd's arm behind his back.

"No!" I cry.

Like a scene from a comic book, eyes wide, hands up, frozen, Aviva, Dorrie and Nancy stand at the mouth of the alley.

Floyd and Billy are grappling on the ground, arms interlocked.

Somebody steps out of the stage door, gasps, runs back inside.

"Stop it!" I yell. "Stop it!"

Aviva snaps awake. She and Dorrie run over and reach for Billy and try to pull him off. But he's too strong. Nancy and I tug at Floyd.

Then we hear a siren.

Instantly, we all stop.

"Get out. Quick," Floyd pants.

I help him up.

We all run out of the alley as the cop car pulls up.

A fat white cop is throwing open the door. I see his hand on his gun.

"In here," I breathe frantically, and Nancy and I pull Floyd into the nearest doorway.

Two seconds later and Aviva and Dorrie and Billy are inside with us. Avi is cramming something into her mouth. "Grass," Dorrie whispers.

"Shit," I say.

"Shhhhh," Floyd hisses.

"You want something?"

"Ahhhhh," I yell. It sounds as though my voice multiplied five times over. Then I realize that everybody else has gasped too.

A buxom woman with dyed black hair is giving us a mean stare.

Then, for the first time, we notice the pictures on the walls. Erotic line drawings with MASSAGE PARLOR written under them in red letters. We all seem dumbstruck. Except Floyd who says, "Cops after us."

The woman's face softens. "Back here. Come on." She leads us through some black velvet curtains into a little cubbyhole of a room. More curtains and a table/bed of sorts. A young black woman in a flimsy pink negligee thing peeks in.

"Out, Hattie. And tell Josie to go out front."

"Cops again?"

"Yeah." She turns to us. "Just stay here. I'll tell you when you can go."

Somehow, no one wants to sit on the table/bed. So we stand. Billy and Floyd, who has a cut on his cheek, avoid each other's eyes. A thick sullenness blankets the room.

After a while, Hattie looks in. She motions to Floyd. "Hey, mister!"

He looks up.

"You want me to do you while you're waiting?"

He smiles gently. "That's a kind offer, sister. But not today."

She smiles back. "Okay," she says and saunters back out with a little wiggle of her hips.

And suddenly, I feel very tired and sad. Gwyn's face bobbles up before me. But somehow, even it's not comforting.

I turn to Floyd. I want to say something. But it's hard with the Crew there.

Then the buxom woman comes back. "Okay. You can go."

The Crew scrambles out of the room. Floyd reaches in his pocket and pulls out a five. "Sorry I don't have more," he says, handing it to the woman.

"Wait. I have some," I say, pull out another five and put it into her hand.

"Thanks," she says and ambles away.

"Floyd . . ." I begin.

"Don't. It won't work," he says.

"Can't I say anything?"

"No. Not now."

"I'm sorry."

"So am I." He shakes his head and goes out into the street. When I get there, he's gone.

I'm trying to sort out my feelings about what happened this afternoon. I didn't realize. I thought I was the only one who felt . . . attracted. Even the other day in the park. I thought that was just . . . a passing fancy or something. If Floyd likes me . . . But why should he like me? A middle-class white girl. A political dimwit. Maybe he's not mad at me for liking him. Maybe he's mad at himself for liking me. *If* he likes me. I don't know. I'm more mixed up than ever. There's Gwyn. But then I ask myself, just suppose there weren't Gwyn. What would happen then between me and Floyd? I get so anxious thinking about it, my chest hurts. Would I feel so anxious if he were white? I don't know. Maybe

135

I am racist without even knowing it. Maybe it is something I've been taught from infancy. But then, how do I change it? Maybe being aware of it is the first step. I just don't know.

And Billy starting a fight like that. What was he doing? Defending me? Why? From what motives? Maybe that's for him to figure out. I know that I hated it—and at the same time I was flattered. God, what an embarrassing thing to realize.

The phone's ringing. What now?

"Hello?"

"Nina. Billy."

A pause.

"I'm sorry. About the scene today."

"I don't know whose fault it was."

He pauses again. Then he says, "You know that guy in *Hair*? The one who went to Vietnam and got killed?"

"Claude. Yeah, what about him?"

"You think he really had another choice?"

"What are you getting at?"

"I'm going for my army physical on Tuesday."

"No. You can't be!" The pain. The fear. Now I know what he's been carrying inside him.

"Yeah, I can be. I'm being reclassified. That's what I've wanted to tell you about. . . ."

"You can't go. Billy, you can't!"

"Have I got a choice? I can't face jail—I'm not brave enough for that. And Canada. Man, uprooting myself? Never being able to see my family or friends in New York again? I can't do it."

"But you can't go to Vietnam. You'll be killed."

Silence.

Finally, he tries to be jaunty. "Maybe. Maybe not."

"Listen. You've got to flunk the physical. We'll tell Aviva. And Nancy and Dorrie. Christ, why didn't you tell us all the other day at the recording studio? That's when you found

136

out, right? Why did you skip town when you knew I was trying to reach you?"

"I wanted to tell just you. I didn't want a big scene. But when I couldn't tell you then, I got depressed and decided I wanted to be alone for a while."

"We're all your friends. Look, we'll get together tomorrow and think up a plan."

"I don't know . . ."

"We have to try."

"Okay. We'll try. But you tell everyone else, all right? I just don't feel like it."

Dorrie, I think. You don't feel like telling Dorrie. "I'll call them," I say.

"Oh God, Nina, I love you. I mean, you're a good friend."

"Tomorrow. Seven o'clock. Probably Dorrie's. I'll call her and get back to you. Stay by the phone."

"Roger. Over and out."

"Billy!"

"Sorry. Just a little gallows humor. A little dance of death."

"Stop it!"

"Call me back."

"I will."

I couldn't face telling Dorrie either. I told Aviva and asked her to call Dorrie and Nancy and get back to me. She did. The meeting was set. Dorrie was freaking out. Aviva would spend the night with her.

Oh God, what a day! What a time. My little world. Falling apart. Floyd. Billy. We've got to stick together. We've got to. Pot and tapioca forever. It's too cold out there. Too hard. Gwyn can make it soft and warm. Oh Gwyn, thank God you're coming. Thank God! You will make it better. Floyd's wrong about you. You're not some remote, white, fairy-tale prince. But I know you will make it better.

137

Chapter 13

"Are you sure there's nothing wrong with you? No fallen arches? Ulcers? High blood pressure? Nothing?"

"Nothing. I'm disgustingly healthy."

"Too bad," Aviva says.

"We'll have to come up with a disease," Dorrie says.

"I heard that if you keep a penny under your tongue you'll get a fever," Nancy muses.

"If you put a clove of garlic up your ass, you'll also run a fever," I say.

"Yeah. And when you fart everybody else will run, too," Aviva says. "But a fever isn't going to get Billy deferred."

"You could raise your blood pressure. Lots of coffee would do it," Dorrie says.

"It might. But we wouldn't know for sure," Aviva says. "Hey Nancy, your father's a doctor. Couldn't he write a note saying Billy has some rare disease?"

Nancy looks embarrassed. "He wouldn't. He doesn't believe in lying."

"Does he believe in this war?"

"No. But he still wouldn't lie to get someone out of the army."

"Billy, you don't believe in this war either. Why don't you apply for a CO deferment?"

"It's too late. And too hard to prove. I've got no history of conscientious objection."

"If you bind your knees real tight, they'll swell," Nancy says.

"So?" Aviva asks.

"You could get out by claiming arthritis or joint disease."

"That might be worth a try," I say.

"I know someone who got out by shooting off his big toe," Billy says.

"Oh, stop it!" Dorrie yells.

"Black lace panties," Aviva says. "You could wear black lace panties and claim homosexual tendencies. After all, you are a dancer."

Billy smiles. "Very appealing! Lace is so soft. But I can't do it."

"Sure you can," Aviva says. "You might even enjoy it."

Billy laughs. "No. I mean, I don't think I could pull it off. No pun intended." Aviva and I crack up.

"I'll lend you my panties," Dorrie says.

"Whoo Whoo! I didn't know you were so kinky," Nancy shrieks.

"Why don't you lend him your banana knife instead," Avi says.

"Huh?" Billy asks.

"Didn't you ever see the famous picture of Dorrie and her banana knife?"

"Avi, please," Dorrie says, turning red.

But Aviva walks over to Dorrie's dresser. "Where's the picture?" she asks.

"In the top drawer," Dorrie mutters.

Aviva takes it out and hands it to Billy.

"Hey, nice muscles," he says.

Dorrie turns redder. "I'm softer now," she mumbles.

I look at her curiously. The whole scene is strange. Dorrie's always been proud of her muscles, always kept the photo right on her dresser. But it isn't the time to ask what's going on. So I decide to get back to the topic at hand. "The guys in the Rabbit's Foot haven't been drafted. How'd they get out?" I ask.

"Sam and Murray are too old to be drafted. Pete's married and has kids . . ." Aviva pauses.

"Yeah, that's right," I say slowly. "You can get out if you're married and have kids."

"I'm not married," Billy says.

"You could get married and then divorced when the war ends. It can't last much longer," Nancy says.

Billy is silent.

Nancy slowly realizes she has said the wrong thing.

Heavy silence. I look up at the ceiling.

Finally, Dorrie says, "I'd be willing to marry you. We don't have to live together or anything. Unless you dig my muscles." She tries to laugh, but there is a desperation in her voice. I feel acutely embarrassed.

"But you'd have to have kids," Nancy says.

"No," Billy says gently. "I don't want to marry to get out of the army. It wouldn't be fair."

"To the army or to you?" Avi asks.

"To the person I'd marry. I have to marry for love, not war."

Dorrie's eyes begin to water. "Excuse me," she says and heads for the bathroom.

"Oh shit, I didn't want to do that," Billy says.

"Never mind. We shouldn't have suggested it," I say. "Anyway, what about Chester and David. And John?" I ask Aviva.

"Chester was already in the Navy."

"You're kidding!"

"Nah. He signed up when he was eighteen. He bragged about it once."

"Jesus!"

"Yeah. David, I don't know. His parents are rich. I think maybe they paid somebody off."

"Can you do that?" Nancy asks.

"Why not? You can always pay someone off. And John. I think he's got a 4F. Something wrong with his plumbing."

"Like a ruptured spleen?" I ask.

Avi and I look at each other, grin and simultaneously sing:

"Sarge, I'm only eighteen, I've got a ruptured spleen
And I always carry a purse,"

Nancy chimes in.

"I've got eyes like a bat
And my feet are flat,
And my asthma's getting worse.
Oh, think of my career,
My sweetheart dear,
My poor old invalid aunt.
Besides I ain't no fool.
I'm a-going to school.
And I'm working in a defense plant."

We laugh.

"How does the rest go?" Nancy asks.

"I've got a dislocated disc and a racked up back,
I'm allergic to flowers and bugs . . ."

"Uh, how does the rest of it go?" I ask.

Dorrie sings from the bathroom,

"And when the bombshell hits
I get epileptic fits . . ."

"And I'm addicted to a thousand drugs," Billy adds.

Dorrie comes out of the john and the two of them finish:

"I've got the weakness woes
I can't touch my toes,
I can hardly reach my knees
And if the enemy ever came close to me
I'd probably start to sneeze."

"All together now. Double time," Avi shouts.

"Sarge, I'm only eighteen, I've got a ruptured spleen
And I always carry a purse,
I've got eyes like a bat
And my feet are flat,
And my asthma's getting worse.
Oh, think of my career,
My sweetheart dear,
My poor old invalid aunt.
Besides I ain't no fool.
I'm a-going to school.
And I'm working in a defense plant."

We collapse onto the floor, puffing and giggling.

"Let's audition for *Hair*," Nancy says. "We can sing 'Draft Dodger Rag.' "

"Okay. If we can successfully get Billy to dodge the draft, we can try out for *Hair*," Avi says.

"With Floyd; he'll have to try out with us," Nancy adds.

"I don't think Floyd will want to," I say quietly.

We grow somber again.

"Craziness. This war is sheer craziness," Dorrie says.

"That's it!" Avi shouts. "You have to get out on sheer craziness. A mental case. You have to be a mental case."

"I'm crazy, but I'm not that kind of crazy," Billy says.

"You will be when we finish with you. Now, shhh, let me think."

"He could recite Ophelia's mad scene from *Hamlet*," Nancy says.

"Nance, they don't defer people on account of bad acting," Avi retorts.

"Couldn't he just act crazy?" Dorrie asks.

"And what, pray tell, does 'just acting crazy' mean? Drooling? Attacking the army shrink? Being catatonic like some character in *Marat/Sade*?

"My cousin is crazy. She thinks she's Queen Esther," Nancy says.

"Queen Esther from *the Bible*?" Dorrie asks.

"Yep."

"That's interesting. How does she act?"

"Queenly."

"This is getting us no place." Avi sniffs.

"I don't think that if you act like you think you're Napoleon it will work," I say. "That's too much everybody's stereotyped loony—delusions of grandeur and all that rubbish. Maybe we shouldn't be thinking about the psychotic. Maybe something more sociopathic."

"Meaning?" Billy asks.

"Antisocial."

"That's a good idea," Avi nods approvingly. "What would be a really antisocial nutso thing to do?"

"Pulling your pants down and taking a crap on the floor," Dorrie answers so quickly we all stare at her and burst into giggles.

"I know because that's what one of the kids once did on my bus. Kids don't know from propriety."

"That's terrific! Could you do it?" Avi asks Billy.

"Take a crap on cue? I doubt it."

"Crap. Crap. Crap. Crap is definitely the bowels of the matter," Avi muses.

"How moving," I respond.

"Oh, stop being an ass," Avi answers.

We laugh. Then silence falls once again. But soon Avi's face lights up. "Look, Billy. How far are you willing to go to get out of the Army?"

"Pretty far. If I can do it, that is. I mean, I'm no good at acting a part—like Napoleon or someone. Why?"

"Okay. I've got a stupendous idea. Truly gross. But it won't require much acting. You just have to keep a straight face. And it's painless too—unlike bandaged knees—although it will be a bit uncomfortable, I imagine." She's getting more and more animated. "Oh, what a peach—nay, not a peach—a legume of an idea!"

"Well, for crying out loud, tell us what it is already," Dorrie huffs.

"Well, all this excremental talk gave me the idea. Okay. Billy. You take a jar of peanut butter. Skippy or Peter Pan. Any brand will do. But it must be smooth—not crunchy." She holds up an imaginary jar of peanut butter. "You dip into the jar." An imaginary dip. "And . . ." She pauses tantalizingly.

"And . . ." Nancy urges.

"And you schmeer it lavishly all over your posterior."

"Your ass?" Nancy squeaks.

"You got it."

"Ugh," Billy and I say simultaneously.

"Yes. Then. Then, you put your clothes on." Avi mimes putting on her clothes.

"Double ugh."

"Then, you trot down to your friendly draft board where you strip for the physical. Here, Dorrie, you be the doctor."

"What do I do?"

"Ask me what this schmehehe is that's all over my derriere, dope!"

"Oh. Eh—hem. Well, Mr. Klein. What is that schmehehe all over your butt?"

Slowly, Avi turns her head, lifts up her rear and stares at it. "Gee, I don't know."

"Oh good grief!" I yell.

"Shhh. Don't interrupt." Then Avi carefully mimes dipping her index finger in the goo and brings it to her lips. "Hmmm," she says, "tastes like peanut butter to me."

"Echhh! Retch! Blaaaaa! Barf!" we say.

All but Billy. He bursts out laughing. "I love it!" he gasps. "I love it! It's elegant. Simple and elegant. I'll do it!"

"You're kidding!" Dorrie shrieks. "You can't wear black lace panties, but you can do this and keep a straight face?"

"I'll practice."

"Here?"

"No, at home in front of a mirror. If I can watch myself and not crack up, I'll be able to do it at the draftboard. Also, I'll get stoned."

"Good idea," I say. "Let's all get stoned. Now."

"Wow," Nancy says. "Far out!"

"Far out is right," I agree. "The Peanut Butter Solution."

"Wow," Nancy reiterates.

For all of us.

Dorrie insisted on driving Billy to the draft board and hanging around, even though the physical and stuff is an all-day affair. Aviva had to rehearse, so Nancy and I have been hanging out together; neither of us has classes today. We're waiting for the news.

Billy said he really was going to go through with it. This morning he arrived at Dorrie's fidgeting and complaining about how sticky his ass was.

"I'll never be able to eat peanut butter again," he moaned.

We were falling over ourselves laughing.

But I knew we all felt weird. And worried. This is no joke. This is the Army, Mr. Klein. Grab your bayonet and Kill, Kill, KILL! Damn. I don't want to think about it.

"Hey, Dorrie's back!" Nancy shouts. We run out to the car.

Dorrie looks exhilarated. "He did it," she says. "He actually did it!"

"And . . ." Nancy and I demand.

"And he'll find out whether or not he gets deferred by December thirty-first."

"God, that long?" I say.

"Yeah. Cross your fingers."

"Where is he?"

"Home. Taking a long bath."

"Ha!" I chortle.

"How did it go?" Nancy asks.

"He said he did it as rehearsed and the doctor freaked and called in the shrink."

"And . . ."

"And the shrink said it smelled like peanut butter to him."

"No!"

"Yes."

"That's no good," I say. "The shrink thinks he's faking."

"Billy thinks the shrink was humoring him to see what he'd do next."

"And what did he do?" Nancy asks.

"He offered the shrink a taste."

"Oh no!" We crack up.

"The shrink declined and told him to go home and take a bath."

"Which advice Billy is following," I say.

"God, cross your fingers," Dorrie says again.

"By December thirty-first." Nancy sighs.

I hope it's going to be a Happy New Year.

146

Chapter 14

Happy New Year. The old year is dying. The new may also be a dying year. That is a good year for dying.

Billy is going into the army.

The letter came yesterday. Status 1A. Eligible anytime for call-up.

Funny how a letter can bring life or death, grief or solace. Gwyn sent me a Christmas card which promises a big New Year's surprise. I was—and am—excited. But Billy's letter took the edge off my excitement. And I don't want to be licking the cream off my whiskers around Billy and Dorrie. In fact, I feel kind of guilty being excited at all.

Dorrie is still trying to convince Billy to get married. Billy is playing stoic—telling her just because he's 1A doesn't mean he'll definitely be drafted. And even if he is, he may not go to Vietnam, he says. But we look at the statistics and know he hasn't a snowball's chance in hell—unless he goes to Canada or maybe hell itself.

What a New Year's Eve this is going to be.

And then there's the Rabbit's Foot's opening tonight at the

Cheetah—a classier discotheque than Wheels. So we all promised to be there to cheer them on.

Rah. Rah.

In the midst of all this, I have two papers due—"Teaching Shakespeare in New York City's Public Schools" for Ed. 39, my last education course before student teaching, and "The New Contraceptives" for Hygiene. Yes, I know: Hygiene is for freshmen. But at Queens College, it doesn't matter when you take it, so long as you take it. And believe me, you can have it! I'm the only senior in the class and I feel like I'm from another planet. I don't think the kids know what the *word* contraceptives means. Nah, they know what it means, but not how to use them. Except condoms. Would you believe, condom jokes still abound? Anyway, since we've got to read our papers ALOUD, I'm trying to educate these kids a little. But it's frustrating—the more I write about pills and diaphragms and IUD's, the hornier I get.

So I'm working on Shakespeare instead—a loftier subject. Except, how the hell do you teach Shakespeare to kids who think *Mad* magazine is great reading (which, in fact, it is— but keep it under your hat). How can a kid who watches Captain Kirk zap someone with a laser gun or whatever it is every five minutes relate to Hamlet, who takes five acts to kill the man who murdered his father? Better yet, as Floyd would say, how can a kid who doesn't get enough to eat give a damn about Julius Caesar? An emperor. A greedy bastard. Like so many other greedy bastards who sap your money and strength. Who promise golden roads and give you no heat. Who conscript you, telling you to die for the glory of the corrupt state. What the hell do I want to teach for anyway?

I give up. Time for a tea break.

"Something wrong, Nina?" My mother comes into the kitchen.

"The paper I'm working on is giving me a pain."

"Oh. . . . Are you going out this evening?"

"Yes. I told you I am."

"You did?"

"Yes. The Rabbit's Foot is playing at the Cheetah."

"Oh that." She waves her hand. "You know, Miriam called me this afternoon. Her boy is home . . ."

I stand up. Not again. Doesn't she ever learn? Charlotte's boy was enough. "Mom, I have to finish my paper."

"Well, all right," she huffs.

"Tell Miriam thanks, but no thanks."

Her lips tighten. "I don't like those discotheques. They look like Sodom and Gomorrah."

"Sodom and Gomorrah didn't have electricity as far as I can tell." I scurry back to my room and my paper.

Damn the public school system, I think. A white bourgeois establishment if I ever saw one. God, I really am beginning to sound like Floyd. Floyd. How is he? I wonder. Where is he? He said he had a gig tonight—he invited me to it. I ought to call him. But why the hell should he want to talk to me after the way we parted? Never mind. I'll call him anyway. I feel possessed with the desire, the need to call him, to set things right. Shit, I don't have his number. Phone book. He lives in Jamaica, he said. Last name—Cooke. Call the operator. Not listed. Call Aviva. She's on her way to rehearsal. Shit. Who would know?

Got it. Call Sam's loft—they must be there. I've got the number somewhere.

"Hello. This is Nina. Who's this? Can't hear you. Chester. Hi. Listen. Do you have Floyd's number? No? Does Sam. You'll check? Thanks."

Long wait.

I tap my pencil.

Finally, he returns, reads a number and tells me to shake it once for him.

I hang up and blow a raspberry at the phone.

I start to dial Floyd's number. Then I stop. What am I going to say to him? Apologize again? Ask him what's happening? Nuts. I can't call.

Oh yes I can. I will wish him a Happy New Year and then let *him* talk.

Ring. Ring. Ring. Ring.

I'm about to hang up when someone picks up the receiver.

"Hello," a woman's voice answers.

"Hello. Is Floyd there?"

The voice turns sharp and suspicious. "Who is this?"

"Nina Ritter. Is this 526-9780?"

"Yes. This is Aggie, Floyd's sister. He mentioned you."

"He's not home?"

"Honey, don't you know? He's in jail."

"What!"

"I say he's in jail. Got picked up two days ago on his way to a Black Panther rally. They busted him 'cause he didn't have no draft card on him."

"You're kidding!"

"I wouldn't kid about a thing like that."

"When's he coming out?"

"Soon as we raise bail. Maybe by tonight."

"Can I do anything?"

"You got two thousand dollars?"

"No."

"Then you can't do nothing."

"What about his gig?"

"He asked Arnie—you know Arnie?—to fill in."

"Look, can I reach him in jail?"

"Girl, you must be stoned."

"No. I'll call later."

"No. I'll tell him to call you."

"Okay. But after ten I'll be at the Cheetah."

"It ain't life or death, is it?"

"No. I'm sorry. I just . . . wanted to wish him Happy New Year." My voice trails off.

"It'll be a lot happier if he ain't in the joint. But I'll give him your message."

"Yes. Thanks."

"You're welcome. 'Bye."

"Good-bye."

After I hang up the phone I realize that my fists are clenched. That damn draft, that damn war keeps surfacing like a bloated corpse. The stench of it, the pestilence of it seems everywhere. I don't want to think about it. But I can't not think about it—it's there constantly, a nightmare peeking through the cracks in my fingers held against my eyes. And my own impotence enrages me. I start beating my pillow. Billy. Floyd. Who next?

The goddamn phone is ringing.

Death on the line.

No. I'm getting morbid.

"Hello."

"Hello. This is George Gross. Is this Nina Ritter?"

George Gross. Death is named George Gross? "Yes, this is she."

"Oh hi. You don't know me. I'm Miriam Gross' son."

Miriam's boy. Jesus! Damn my mother! "You're right, I don't know you."

"Well, I could give you a chance to."

What the hell do I say to that? Nothing. I will not say one word.

"I hear you're not doing anything tonight."

"You've been misinformed."

"Oh?"

"Yes. I have an appointment in Gomorrah."

"Huh?"

151

"Or was it Sodom? Happy New Year."

I hang up.

Amazing. Death sweeps its black veil over the land, but the Charlotte's boys, the Miriam's boys keep twitching out of the shadows, stuttering "Wanna have fun? Wanna have a few laughs? Gimme some. Gimme some. Gimme some."

And there's nothing I can do but return to my paper on "The New Contraceptives," and instruct the freshmen in hygiene on how not to bring more babies into this lousy world. But I doubt they'll listen.

Gomorrah (alias the Cheetah) is all aglitter. All black and gold. No neon here. But there is tawny animal-skin wallpaper festooned with little twinkling Christmas lights, making the walls appear to have some strange skin disease. There's a sizable dance floor with several tables ringing it and then a sort of balcony or terrace with black velvet booths. Only it's not real velvet and it itches. But at least the booths are secluded. I'm sitting in one sipping white wine. Just this one Happy New Year drink—I don't want to repeat my birthday fiasco.

The kids who are crowding the floor certainly don't look drinking age. I wonder how many forged driver's licenses/birth certificates/school I.D.'s are being flashed tonight.

Once again, everybody's here—this time decked out in especial splendor. Aviva's wearing the baby-pink, tight satin gown Nancy, Dorrie and I gave her for Christmas. David is wearing a white suit! Sam's cowboy hat has a band of tinsel strung around it. John is in his usual jeans and sleeveless T-shirt. But even he is bedecked—a circlet of gold leaves in his hair. I wonder why he and Aviva haven't yet gotten together. I'd like to pride myself, thinking she's taken my advice about sex partners, but I doubt that's the reason. To be honest, I'm glad she and he haven't made it. I don't know why. After all, he's not my bloke.

152

Anyway . . . Prize for best outfit has got to go to Amelia Theresa, who is entirely gold and silver. I mean entirely. Not only is her leather suit half gold and half silver, and not only is she wearing one gold boot and one silver boot, one gold glove and one silver glove, but her hair has been dyed gold and her face painted silver. As Nancy would say, Far out! Lolly, in her billowing green dress, looks like an enormous Christmas tree. Next to them, Pat is conservative—in a black top hat and tails. The kids on the floor are having a hell of a time trying to figure out whom to look at first.

The band is hot tonight, playing funky versions of Christmas carols and "Auld Lang Syne," loving the crowd, loving the holiday spirit. Too bad the rest of the Crew isn't so up. Billy, gray-faced, is sitting near me getting bombed out of his skull. Dorrie is joining him in his cups. Nancy, stoned as usual, is listening to the band and playing an imaginary fiddle. "Ooooh, great riff, great riff," she croons.

Chip Bloch is buying all of us free drinks. I tell him thanks, but no thanks. But Dorrie and Billy gladly take him up on his offer. Aviva is singing Grace Slick's "Don't You Want Somebody to Love?" Yeah, I think, I want him right now. Then, someone taps my shoulder.

"Floyd! You're out! You're okay!" I fling my arms around him. Then I get embarrassed and break away.

"I'm out. I'm okay," he says.

"What are you doing here? You had a gig."

"Too late to catch it. Arnie'll do fine."

"I called . . ."

"I know. Aggie told me."

"Oh Floyd. Why the hell did the cops pick on you?"

"The cops pick on any likely party who's heading for a Panther rally. It was dumb of me not to be carrying my card."

"Oh, you didn't burn it?"

"Girl, do I look like a fool? I'm not going into the army, but I don't believe in advertising that fact."

"But why were you going to a rally with those people?"

"Those people. Ah shit, Nina. I thought maybe you learned something . . ."

"Floyd, please. It's New Year's Eve. Let's not argue. Whatever I said, I'm sorry I said it."

"Shhh," Nancy shushes. "I can't hear anything."

I turn to apologize to her and notice Dorrie and Billy engaged in a heavy breathing session in the next booth. "Whoops," I say and turn back to Floyd.

"Look Nina, I don't want to argue tonight either. I shouldn't have just run out on you after that fight. I've been wanting to call. I'm glad you did. But you got to know we argue for a reason. Listen, if I give you some books and stuff on the Panthers, will you read them?"

I think about it for a minute. "Okay. I'll read them. But please don't expect me to agree with—or even understand— everything immediately."

"That's fair," he says.

We smile at each other.

"Hey, you're not stoned," he says.

"No," I answer.

"That's good."

A guy with a funny hat and bow tie comes up to our booth and asks Nancy to dance. "Sure," she says and, giggling, descends to the floor.

Billy and Dorrie get up. "We're leaving," Billy says. "Happy New Year."

"Happy New Year." I smile broadly. Looks as though Dorrie's Number One resolution will be fulfilled.

Then I say, "Floyd, I don't think the only reason we argue is our political differences."

For the first time, he looks abashed. "You're right," he

154

says, pauses, then blurts out, "Oh hell, Nina! I gave myself a whole lot of reasons why I shouldn't feel the way I do about you. But those reasons aren't worth a damn!"

Then someone yells, "It's midnight!"

With a clank, the ceiling seems to open. Golden balloons and colored streamers float down. The Rabbit's Foot throws huge handfuls of confetti from the stage. "Happy New Year! Happy New Year!" the crowd shouts.

Floyd turns my face to his. "Happy New Year, Nina," he says softly.

Then we kiss.

It is not a mere New Year's kiss. It is burning, roaring. The force of his feeling overwhelms me, grabs me in the pit of my stomach. And I have to pull away.

"Nina, come home with me."

"Floyd, I . . . Why?" I say stupidly.

"Oh Nina. Because I want to make love with you." He is looking at me intensely, his brown eyes moist and warm. His wide lips are parted slightly, asking for another kiss. I feel a thrill shoot through me. No one has ever been so direct before. No one. Not even Gwyn.

Gwyn. Oh God. I can't. "Floyd. I can't. You know I . . ."

"Please, don't tell me about your English lover. He's three thousand miles away. I'm here. And, goddamn it, woman, I want you."

He kisses me again.

I whimper.

"Lady, lady, lady, please," he whispers into my hair.

I feel ready to faint. Instead, I stand up. My knees buckle. Floyd grasps my arm. "Easy," he says.

I let him steer me to the door. What am I doing? Where are we going? I can't. I can't. I can't. The words ring in my ears. But Floyd's hand is stroking the small of my back and I'm shivering all over.

"Let me get your coat," he says.

Blindly, I fish for my ticket in my purse. I can't find it. I stoop and begin to empty the purse on the floor.

"Nina. Happy New Year."

No. That voice. Can't be. I look up. There, in the doorway is—oh my God—Gwyn. My eyes. Blank. Blind. No. Can't be.

"Gwyn!" I cry.

"Nina!" he says.

I rush into his arms, rain kisses on his face, neck.

"Nina, Nina." He laughs.

I stop, realizing he—and I—aren't alone.

"What? How? Oh Lord, I don't believe it," I stammer.

"I did promise you a New Year's surprise," he says.

I don't know how to act. I turn to Floyd. He looks as though someone hit him between the eyes.

"Floyd. This is Gwyn. Gwyn. Floyd."

Gwyn sticks out his hand.

Floyd extends his tentatively, staring at it as if it belonged to someone else.

They shake.

"And this is Margaret," Gwyn says.

I see her for the first time.

A tall, slim, blond woman with an English-rosebud complexion. "Hello Nina," she says. "I've heard so much about you."

"Well, shall we sit down?" I say.

"Sure," Margaret says.

Back into the noisy room. The band is taking a break. Floyd excuses himself and goes to talk to David.

"Avi. Avi," I call.

She comes over.

"This is Gwyn. And Margaret."

Avi looks him up and down and gives me a smile.

156

I'm beginning to float—but something keeps trying to tug me underwater. I kick it away.

"Good grief," says Avi. "What are you doing here on New Year's Eve?"

"Well, actually . . ." Margaret begins. "Gwyn, you'd better tell."

"Well. We're both going to be fellows at the University of Colorado next—er, this—month. So we thought we'd come in a bit early and celebrate."

"Your fellowships?"

"No, actually. Our honeymoon."

"Your what?" It's my voice, sharp and loud. But it's not coming from me.

"Our honeymoon. We were married last week," Gwyn says.

"Excuse me. I must use the loo," Margaret says.

"I'll show you where it is," Avi says, quickly leading Margaret away.

The salt is in my mouth. My lungs are bursting. I can't speak.

"Oh Nina," Gwyn is saying. Far away. Above the water. "I've missed you. I've wanted you."

Can't breathe. Drowning.

"I know you must be confused. 'He's married,' you're saying. But it doesn't change anything between us."

Something in my hair. Lips. Pushing me further under the water.

"I will have to come to New York. And we can be together. God, I've missed your breasts."

Flailing. Must swim. Must get air. Push through the water. So many people in the water. In my way. Swim faster. Stroke, Kick.

Up. Air.

I gulp huge breaths, look at the cold stars. Shivering. It's

157

so dark. Something coming. Big gray thing. A whale? Very like a whale. Look. Look. Nearer. Nearer. Roaring. Puffing like a grampus. Squealing. Whales don't squeal.

"Watch out," the whale yells.

"Look out for the bus," a porpoise screams.

A black arm shoots out and drags my head out of the water. A smooth arm. A warm skin. A panther skin. Not a porpoise at all. "Oh God, Nina," it cries. "Are you okay? Were you hit?"

Hit. By a whale? Bad whale. The panther leads me away. "Taxi!" he calls.

We get into it and ride out of the ocean.

PART TWO

Chapter 15

Dear Nina,

I was happy to get a letter from you and saddened by its contents. Gwyn. The worst four-letter word in the English language. Well, flippancy won't help, so let me try to be straightforward.

Gwyn and I were lovers for almost two years, and during that time, he had at least a dozen affairs. I never minded his having sex with other women. The affairs were not *affaires du cœur*, but *affaires du corps*. What I did come to mind—and mind dreadfully—was the way in which he manipulated women, myself included. Brilliance and the urge to control everything are a deadly combination. And I believe that Gwyn is indeed brilliant. And ruthless. Like Iago. Like Steerpike in the *Gormenghast* trilogy. Gwyn had—and I'm sure still has—an incredible knack for producing the right line for each woman. If you were the timid sort, Gwyn would come on manly and protective. If you were romantic, out would come the poetry and flowers. If you enjoyed the bawdy, Gwyn would choreograph a scene straight out of *Tom Jones*. If you were a feminist, he would, chameleonlike, become one too, speaking with ease of sex objectification and the like. I fear that Gwyn's definition of feminism is letting the woman screw on top, if you get my meaning.

At any rate, he fooled me for a long time as much as he fooled you. That's why I told you to be careful. But warnings and advice are useless anyway. It would have been far better if I had kicked him in the balls. I am sorry you did not do the same. God pity poor Margaret!

I hope you will exorcise that Welsh wretch from your heart and mind. I know it will be hard. But women have rarely had it easy.

Please write me again.

With affection,
Elspeth

EXCERPT FROM A JOURNAL, JANUARY 1969
To His Cold Mistress

The amount of pain does not
    matter;
It's your aptitude for pain
    that counts.
Why, I once knew a girl
    who could make herself cry
    twenty times a day
    and still beg for more.
But, of course, her aptitude was
    exceptional.

162

Now, you interest me
    because your aptitude is enormous.
I've seen you—
    the way you make people raise their lances
    the way you walk on hot coals
    the way you choose snowdrift fellows for lovers.
It's amazing.
You would make an excellent subject
    for study.
But
    there's just one thing . . .
I don't like you.

Snow pattering light on frozen ground. A perfect time
to be suicidal. But I won't. Commit suicide, that is. After
New Year's Eve when I almost let myself get hit by that
bus, everyone is being very solicitous—and watching me
closely. Avi gave me this journal. "Write. It'll do you
good," she said. It'll keep her from stabbing herself, is
probably what she thought. Well, I'm lucky I have good
friends I can trust. And really, I don't want to die. I
want to live. But it's so damn hard.

The worst is that I can't cry. Or yell. I've worn grooves
in the wall, but I can't cry. Lost ten pounds, though.
Look chic.

Yesterday, I got a letter from Rhys. Gwyn had asked
him to be best man. Rhys had refused. Good Rhys. I
wonder if Gwyn wore tux. He's so skinny. Skin just hanging off his ass. Let me have men about me who are fat.

There are no men about me at all, fat or otherwise.
Billy's like a ghost when he's around, which isn't often.

163

Floyd? I'm too embarrassed to talk to him. I could have a fling with Chester. He's always trying to grab my boobs anyway. Or what about if I called Stan Wasserman and said, casually, "Hey, how about it, Stanley, boy. Want to exercise your organ?" Wouldn't that get him? Or maybe I should finally meet the famous Mark the marksman who's so good with his sticks. Aw, hell!

No more letters. Maybe that's the hardest. But I'm never going to write to him again. Oh Elspeth, I wish you'd told me everything you knew before I let myself fall. I wonder if it would have made any difference anyway.

If one more person tells me Time Heals All Wounds, I'm going to scream. And if my mother gives me one more "Shape up, Nina" pep talk, I'm going to commit matricide.

Ah shit, what a world.

Chapter 16

"I'm really glad you decided to come," Aviva says. She is very earnest. The freckles stand out on her face, scrubbed shiny before the makeup ritual begins. Aviva, as predicted, has dropped out of school. And she has also gotten her own studio apartment in Manhattan, on 28th Street. She wanted Nancy to move in with her, but Nancy said her parents wouldn't like it. Mine wouldn't either, but that wouldn't matter if I could afford it, which I can't. "You'll stay over tonight, too?"

"Aviva, don't worry. I'm not about to . . ." Kill myself, I was going to say, but I change it to "desert you." It is her big evening. Third billing at the Fillmore, Canned Heat topping the bill. God, any other time I'd be leaping out of my skin, so excited for her. But I feel numb.

Actually, I'm better than I was in January, the month of disaster and bad poetry. You'd think misery would improve one's writing, but it doesn't.

The worst thing was Floyd. His hearing came up quickly, and because he had his draft card and was a 2S (student deferment), the judge let him off with a warning. Then, just one week later, at course registration, we ran into each other and started joking around—Floyd trying to make me laugh, me trying to forget my embarrassment around him. I've been avoiding him since New Year's Eve.

"Hey, mambo!" Floyd called. "You gonna take more social dancing?"

"No, I decided to be more militant this time."

Floyd's eyebrows shot up. "Oh?"

"Yes. I'm going to take fencing."

"Oh. Well, it might come in handy if we reenter the Middle Ages, which, given this government, we may very well do."

"I'm also student teaching this term at Long Island City High School."

"Yeah? That's cool. Are you looking forward to it?"

"Yes and no. I'm kind of nervous. And critical of the public school system. I learned that from you."

"Ah, but if there were more teachers like you, maybe I wouldn't be so critical."

"How do you know whether I'm any good?"

"I know you will be."

Touched and embarrassed by his compliment, I blush and ask, "How about you? What are you taking?"

"Still fighting for Afro-American Studies and taking calculus."

"Calculus?" My eyebrows shot up.

"Yeah. I've always dug math."

"Math! And you said Russian literature was useless!"

He grins. "Yeah, well. Sometimes I fly off the handle a bit."

We waited on line after line until we finally got the courses we wanted. Then we went outside to get something hot to drink at the Union and to talk.

But just as we got outside, two guys in gray overcoats walked up to us.

"Mr. Cooke? Could we talk with you, please?" one said.

"No, you may not. I'm otherwise engaged," Floyd said.

166

"I'm afraid that will have to wait." He pulled out a flat black wallet and flashed it at Floyd.

"Hey, what is this? You want to see my draft card again?"

"No. We want to talk to you about another matter."

"What's happening, man?" Floyd's friend Jerry had drifted up.

"Nothing, man," Floyd said. "Catch you later. Take Nina to the Union and buy her some cocoa, okay? Go on, Nina. I'll call you tonight."

I knew something was terribly wrong, but I went with Jerry.

That night he didn't call. Aggie did. "They busted him on a phony narcotics charge," she told me.

"No! Why?"

"Why? Honey, you got to know why by now."

"They're really after him, aren't they?"

"He's a revolutionary. Cops and colleges don't like revolutionaries."

"Aggie, how much is the bail?"

"You ready? Fifty thousand dollars."

"No! That's impossible to raise."

"Right. So they can keep him in jail for a long time."

"Aggie, I've got to see him."

"You can't. Look, I gotta go. I'll call you if anything happens."

Two weeks later and Floyd is still in prison. I feel bad, but so numb I can't really touch the pain.

"Nina, you haven't heard a word I said," Avi says.

"Sorry. I'm thinking about Floyd."

"Oh Christ, that mess is awful."

I nod. Awful. Terrible. Damn! Words are so inadequate.

"What happened between you and him on New Year's Eve?" she asks, and sits at the vanity she dragged all the way from Queens in my old Chevy. I watch her carefully blending silver and green shadow on her eyelids to match her billowy pants.

What happened? It's sort of fuzzy—like your eyes get when you've been underwater too long. We took a taxi to Jamaica. I remember staring at the lights in the tunnel. We didn't speak during the ride. We got out somewhere—a quiet street with lots of big, dark, looming trees.

We sat in a tiny kitchen. Floyd made me a cup of some kind of herb tea. "Drink it. My grandmother's recipe," he said.

I obeyed and scalded my tongue.

"No, no. Let it cool first."

"Your parents aren't expecting you home tonight?" he asked after a pause.

I stared blankly. Parents? Who were they? Oh yes. I remembered. No, I shook my head, they weren't expecting me home.

"Okay. I'd better get you something to sleep in." He went out and came back with a large yellow nightgown. "Sorry, this is all I could find. Aggie's a lot bigger than you, I'm afraid. She won't be back tonight, though."

I took the nightgown and fingered the buttons. I felt like a child, pliant, obedient. But something furiously adult-size was welling up inside me. I followed him into a bedroom.

"You can change here." He went out.

Slowly, I took off my dress, my slip, my shoes, pantyhose, underwear, and left everything in a heap on the floor. When I was naked, I just stood there looking at myself in a big mirror on the wall.

A knock.

I didn't answer.

Another.

Finally, the door opened. "Nina, are you . . ." Then he saw me and stopped dead.

I said nothing, just watched him.

He exhaled, then came over warily. "Nina, you're shivering," he said and touched my arm.

And then I threw back my head and screamed. "Oh my God! How could he? How could he? No! No! No!"

Floyd gripped me tight while I just screamed and screamed and beat against his chest. Eventually, I collapsed and somehow Floyd got me into Aggie's nightgown and his bed. He crawled in next to me and cradled me against him, pushing my damp hair from my eyes and stroking my forehead. And he sang to me, a tender, crooning song. Finally, I fell asleep in his arms.

The next morning, I didn't know where I was. My head and throat ached. I felt stiff all over and hollow inside. Then Floyd came in and I remembered.

"You want to stay or go home?" he asked.

"I'd better go home," I said.

He nodded and brought me my clothes, which he'd folded neatly. Then, he made me breakfast and took me to Dorrie's place to pick up my car.

I couldn't thank him. How do you thank someone who saved your life? And I was ashamed of revealing my nakedness, emotional and physical, to him. So I just squeezed his hand and said good-bye and drove back to Long Island. And now he's in some goddamn cell and I can't do a fucking thing about it.

"Nothing," I tell Aviva. "Nothing happened."

"I thought you dug him." She looks at me.

I don't know what to answer. Finally, I say, "He's my friend."

"Oh." Then she goes back to her makeup and begins to talk of Grace Slick's grittiness and John's great bass playing and how she still doesn't know how to move when she's up there on stage. I want to be kind to her, the way Floyd was kind to me.

"You move very well," I say.

She turns. "You really think so?" The question is serious.

Aviva is more critical of her performance than anyone else could ever be.

"Yes, I think so," I answer, with proper gravity.

"That's good. Because Neen, I really want to make it. Big. I know I'm good. At last. But that don't mean shit in the rock world. Believe me."

"I do."

"My parents think I'm ruining my voice."

"I know."

"Ah crap, who needs their approval anyway?" She shrugs and then takes off her flannel shirt and puts Band-Aids on her nipples.

I am stupefied.

"When I sing, they get erect," she says. Then she pulls a maroon mesh top over her head and drapes it strategically over the rest of her. "Well?" she asks, standing up.

I am kind of taken aback. No bra is one thing; no clothes is another. Also, it looks strange. The Band-Aids make it seem as if she's one expanse of pink, nipple-less flesh wrapped in a net. She's still waiting for an answer, so I finally say, "You look like a Walt Disney mermaid."

She looks into the mirror and begins to laugh.

I laugh, too. It feels good to laugh.

When we stop laughing, Aviva says, "He's really an all-time jerk."

"Who?"

"Gwyn, that's who. You know, I wrote to him."

I instantly freeze. "You what?"

"I wrote to him. I told him what a bastard he is."

I gasp slightly, involuntarily. "He's not a bastard . . . He's . . . Look, three thousand miles is a long . . ." I don't know why I'm defending him, but I can't seem to help it.

"He's a goddamn bastard, and the sooner you accept that, the sooner you'll stop wanting to kill yourself."

"I don't want to kill myself!" I yell.

"Then what was that little episode with the bus about?"

"You didn't write him about that, did you?"

"I certainly did."

"Oh Jesus, Aviva. Goddamnit!" I start to cry, thick tears that hurt my eyes, run down into my throat. "God . . . God . . . God . . . He . . . is . . . a . . . rat . . . bastard." I say it over and over—all the things buried deep that I couldn't say out loud.

Aviva holds my head against her Band-Aided breasts and says softly, "You're worth a hundred of him."

I cry harder.

Just then I hear Dorrie and Nancy burst in in a rustle of bags and a clink of bottles.

"It's gonna snow!" Nancy yells. "The weather report says maybe a big one!"

"I've got even better proof—the scar under my knee says snow," Dorrie says.

They see us and stop dead.

"She okay?" Nancy finally asks.

"*She* is perfectly fine," I say hoarsely, but with great dignity.

"She had just admitted out loud what we have been aware of all along," says Aviva. "That Gwyn the Great Welcher is a rat bastard."

"Hear, hear," applauds Dorrie, and Nancy seconds her.

"Good. Now that that's over, maybe we can get down to something serious—like food, dope and rock 'n' roll."

We all laugh, but I am forcing myself. For Aviva, it *is* all over—I made my statement and now I've washed that man right out of my hair. But it isn't so fast or so easy. I cried in her arms and in Floyd's arms, but I still ache from loving Gwyn. I believe what Elspeth wrote me, too. But still I wish I were with Gwyn. How can a person love a rat bastard even when she knows he's a rat bastard? And how does she stop

171

loving the rat bastard? Does she find another rat bastard to take his place? I start to laugh. "That isn't what I had in mind."

"What?" Nancy asks.

"Did I say something?"

"Yeah. You said, 'That isn't what I had in mind.' "

"Oh. Well, it isn't."

"What?"

"He's on second," Aviva says, mouth full of corned beef.

"Who?"

"He's on first," I say.

"You two. I don't know," sighs Nancy.

Dorrie snickers. She knows what's coming next.

"He's on third," Aviva and I chorus. Then we look at each other and grin approvingly.

And I decide I'm going to try—at least for tonight—not to think anymore about Gwyn. Or Floyd. Or even Billy.

A jangling mass of beads and nerves, we make our way downtown to the Fillmore East. Instead of calming us down, the grass seems to be making us whiz. And the cold air is helping it along.

"You sure this isn't mixed with speed?" Aviva chatters. "I'm not gonna mess with that stuff again."

"When did you try speed?" I ask.

"When you were high on Gwyn."

I wince. "Meaning?"

Aviva just shrugs. "November or so. Took it with Pete. . . . Man, you know that guy has the longest tongue in the world?"

"Like a snake?" Nancy giggles.

"Like an anteater!"

I turn and look out the car window.

The Fillmore line is already in sight. Even in this freeze,

172

it's wrapped itself around 6th Street—a millipede in a pea coat.

"You can practically smell the good stuff already," Dorrie says.

"No, you can't," Nancy says. "All our windows are closed."

"I was not being literal," Dorrie retorts.

"Neither was I," Nancy answers.

"Huh?"

"Calling all potheads. Calling all potheads," Aviva intones nasally.

We snort and sputter and stumble out of the car onto Avenue A, two long blocks away from the Fillmore, but the only parking place we can find.

"Rock World, here comes your newest A-Number-One Star!" Nancy yells, holding up Aviva's arm. Then she shivers. "Oooh, I gotta go to the bathroom."

"How come the damn management doesn't reserve parking for its rising stars?" Dorrie grumbles, as we all pull collars higher and bunch hands into pockets.

"Listen, at least we'll have a nice, warm dressing room to sit in," Avi answers.

"Do we have time for a nice, warm plate of blintzes at Ratner's beforehand?" I ask.

"No, but you can have a nice warm swig of cognac when we get inside."

"If you all don't hurry up, I'm going to take a nice warm pee in my pants," Nancy growls.

As we sprint to the stage door, several curious heads crane in our direction. And assorted comments drift our way. "Who's that?" "They performing?" "There an all-girl group on the bill?" etc.

Up several flights, Nancy leading, searching for a toilet. Faded walls. Identical doors painted turd brown. My life is starting to look like a chronicle of seedy settings, I think.

"Where is it?" I ask.

"Fourth floor, Sam said on the phone."

We hit the fourth floor. Nancy has her legs squeezed together.

"You look like one of the kids I pick up doing the 'I Gotta Go' dance."

"Please, don't make me laugh." Nancy grits her teeth.

"Hey, is anybody around?" Avi yells.

A door opens. A guy with an enormous Afro looks out. "Hel-lo, mama. Need a hand? And I do mean a hand."

"Where's the Rabbit's Foot's dressing room?"

"Oh, you one of their old ladies?"

"No, I sing with the group."

"If you sing as good as you look, you'll do okay."

Suddenly, I start giggling. How many times have I heard that one before?

"What's with you?" Dorrie nudges me.

"Nothing," I say, giggling harder.

"What's with her?" the guy asks.

"She's just stoned," Aviva says.

I sit down, gasping and giggling.

"Come on, find the dressing room," Nancy groans, sitting next to me. "There's got to be a toilet there."

Another head pops out over the Afro. It's David.

"Jesus, can't you be on time," he says.

Aviva draws herself up and says, coldly, "Can't you display any decent manners?" She brushes past him into the room.

Nancy immediately jumps up and heads for the door. David blocks the entrance. "Your entourage has to stay outside," he says.

"Balls!" Nancy yells, pushing him aside.

"Like the lady says, 'Balls!' " Dorrie says and we walk inside together, me still giggling.

David is right. The room is too small, cluttered with instruments, ancient makeup tables, boxes and beer cans, and filled with not only the Rabbit's Foot but the group that has second billing, Santana or something, of which the guy with the Afro is a part. I thought that at least in the Fillmore there'd be a fancy dressing room. A big-time, glamorous dressing room for hitting the big time. But no such luck. Anyway, Dorrie and I wedge ourselves into corners and survey the scene. Aviva has squeezed herself next to Sam and is inspecting her makeup. Sam, in purple pants and floppy shirt hiding his flab, is swigging the brew and tootling on his sax. Pete is adjusting his black leather vest over his bare chest. Murray, in what looks like white tux, is stretched out on a cot having a snooze. John, his long hair looking more unkempt than ever, is tuning his bass. Chester is missing. And David is glaring at us.

"I don't think Avi's going to make it with him," Dorrie whispers to me, nodding at David.

"Not unless he tells her that if she sings as good as she looks they've got it made," I answer, and then crack up.

Dorrie gives me a mystified look and pulls out a joint.

"Good idea," Pete says, and Dorrie passes him the joint. Nancy comes out of the toilet with a contented smile and takes the joint from him.

I finish laughing and look up to see John looking at me. I look back for a good minute. He doesn't turn away.

"How come you're always staring at me?" I finally say. Which isn't exactly true. I mean he's not always staring at me.

"I like your face," he says simply.

And suddenly, I feel confused. This is not the answer I am expecting.

"Would you like some beer?" he asks.

"Yeah." I smile. "I would."

Dorrie grins at me and scrunches over so John can sit next to me.

I sip the lukewarm beer. John slides an arm across my shoulders. I smile slightly, settle back against it and close my eyes.

There is a sudden silence in the room. Then Sam's voice cuts through. "Whoo, that's some outfit!"

I open my eyes. There's a burst of whistles and stamps. Aviva, her coat draped over the back of her chair, poses with her hands behind her like a centerfold model.

I glance at John. His right eyebrow is raised and he's studying Aviva intently. I sit up and reach for a joint.

Then, the door swings open and Chester bursts in. One look at Aviva is all he needs. "Yowza!" he bellows and reaches for her breasts.

"I'm going outside," I say to no one in particular, and I push out the door, welcoming the blast of cool air that greets me.

Leaning against the wall, I try to think. What am I doing here? What is all this? Oh Gwyn, damn you! I hit my fist on the wall. It hurts. "Owww," I shout, and clench and unclench my fingers. A noise makes me spin around.

"Hi," John says. "You okay?"

"Oh yeah. Fine. Thanks."

He doesn't press me, and we just stand there in the cold hallway. A red-haired woman in a black dress slit up the side to her thigh appears from nowhere. She pounds on the dressing room door and announces, "Rabbit's Foot on stage!"

"Okay," Sam calls out.

John turns to me. "Wish me luck?" he asks.

I smile. "Good luck."

He leans forward and kisses me.

I am startled, but in a nice way. His lips are full and soft and I haven't been kissed since New Year's Eve.

We smile at each other. "Good luck." I say again.

He goes into the dressing room to get his bass, and I head downstairs, murmuring to myself, "Fuck you, Gwyn. Fuck you."

176

The house is humming with that unmistakable pre-performance noise, even though the Light Show is on. We slide into our seats next to the Group Ladies, Lolly, Pat and Terry.

"Isn't it won-der-ful?" Terry says to me in her spaced-out voice.

"Yeah. Look at those lights!"

"Ummmmm," Terry answers.

Electric pink and green swirls surround the stage, which seems ready to float out of the building. Pete's drums, already set up, glow orange.

"Ahhhh," the audience breathes.

Sweet smells waft through the air.

I inhale deeply and rub the palms of my hands along the red plush of the armrests.

Black shadowy figures appear doing something to the bulky amps, themselves shadows on the floating stage. It takes me a while to realize these new shadows are people. They move silently in and out of the luminous perpetually changing zones, motioning here a blue arm, there a purple head.

Then they seem at once to disappear. And the lights all go first red, then blue. A spotlight hits the stage, and into it steps disc jockey Jumping Joe Samuels, guest M.C.

"Hey, all you cats and chicks. Toke that weed, and pay me heed!"

Scattered cheers.

"We got for your aural pleasure one hell of a show to-night."

More cheers.

"Starring Santana . . ."

Still more cheers.

"Canned Heat . . ."

Big cheers.

"And lights by the Joshua Light Show. And now to start the grass growing is . . . the Rabbit's Foot!"

Polite, stoned-out cheers.

The spotlight blinks out.

Then, in a blaze of golden light, the Rabbit's Foot flash on stage and immediately crash into "Super Chick."

Aviva begins to sing, swaying and dipping, sliding her fingers up and down the microphone, ripping the air with little growls. Sam digs it and blows his sax like nobody's business.

"That's right, Sam baby, you sell it!" Terry calls out.

The audience around us titters.

Sam and Murray do a brass duet.

"Whoo," Terry whoops, and then stands up and begins to dance.

"Terry, sit down," Pat says, but Terry goes right on gyrating.

I glance around. No one else is dancing. Some people are listening, but a lot of them are talking or toking, waiting for the "real" acts to start. I look at John on stage—he's so focused, so concentrated on that bass.

The band finishes "Super Chick" and goes on to "Tree of Life," a pretty ballad Avi wrote the words to.

The talking gets louder.

"They sound good tonight," Dorrie says to me.

"Yeah," I answer. "Too bad nobody's buying."

Dorrie looks around. "I see what you mean."

Two more numbers, the latter I never heard before. Chorus of "Baby, baby, baby" from Aviva. She presses her mouth close to the mike, breathes the words over and over, faster and faster, rising in pitch and trembling all over. She's not trying to be Joplin anymore. She's got her own style now, and it's dynamite. The audience begins to applaud. I shiver and close my eyes. Nancy leans over Dorrie and nudges me, "Here comes the bass solo," she says.

"So?" I answer, but I look at John just as the colors change

178

and he's struck by brilliant white light. I stare at his intent face, his fine fingers plucking the bass. And suddenly, he is an angel, playing an earthy white bass instead of a delicate golden harp, but an angel nevertheless. Yeah, I know I'm stoned, but it doesn't matter. Nothing matters except John touching the strings.

When the group finally finishes, I sigh deeply and lean back heavily in my seat.

"You wanna stay for Canned Heat?" Dorrie asks.

"Hmmmm," I answer.

"What?"

I am sweating. And my fingers ache from clutching the armrests. But I don't tell her. Finally, I say, "I think I'll go backstage. You?"

"Yeah. Let's go."

We all get up. My legs feel a little shaky, but I make it up the stairs.

John is leaning against the wall outside the room.

We just look at each other.

I hear Aviva's voice from inside cry, "High-toned sex is what does it!"

The Group Ladies enter amid squeals and shouts.

"Coming in?" Dorrie asks.

"Later," I say, still looking at John.

She and Nancy go inside the room.

"I watched you," I say.

"Yeah?" John asks.

"Yeah."

"How'd you like it?"

"I liked it. I liked you."

"Good."

I nod. My breathing is shallow. I wonder if my eyes look "hungry," as they say in true confessions magazines.

"Come over here," he says. "You're too far away."

179

I slowly move nearer until I can touch him. I pick up his hand, look down at the fingers. "Terrific," I whisper.

He picks up my face, bends down and kisses my ear.

I shudder.

"Cold?" he asks.

"No," I say. Hot, I think.

And then we kiss, pressed tight against a faded wall in the Fillmore East. I close my eyes and the wall disappears. I am leaning against a tree. There's grass and violets and a man who smells like clover. . . .

"Gwyn," I murmur into his shoulder.

"What?" he asks.

I open my eyes quickly. "John," I say. "John," I repeat, loudly this time.

"Yes," he answers.

I smile at him.

"I have to go, Nina. I'll come and see you tomorrow night, okay?"

"Tomorrow night . . . okay."

We kiss again.

"I have to go," he repeats. "See you tomorrow."

He starts down the stairs, then turns around. "Where?" he asks.

"At Aviva's. You know where she lives?" I find myself holding my breath.

"No," he answers, and I exhale deeply.

I give him the address. We kiss once more. He is gone.

I enter the dressing room. Everyone is waving cups of something and cheering. Aviva pauses and looks pointedly at me.

"John coming back?" she asks.

"No."

"Well, is he any good?"

Cries of "Whoa!" "Hot stuff!" "Yip yip yip!" "Sexy!" etc. Then, a pause. Everyone turns to me.

I smile. "The best," I say as nonchalantly as possible.

Aviva's eyes flare just once, and then she says, "Have some champagne."

I take a cup.

"You like the new number, 'Baby, Baby, Baby'?" she asks.

"Very sexy," I say.

"Should be. I wrote it after you told me how you and Gwyn made whoopee in an English meadow."

More cries of "Wowie!" "Tell us about that one." "Sex-y!"

Dorrie and Nancy say nothing.

"Bitch," I mutter.

"What?" Aviva asks.

I look up and smile icily. "It's a very good song," I say. "I don't think Gwyn would like it, though."

"Yeah, he'd probably find it too blatant. But John likes it."

"I hope so. He plays solo in it."

"That's not the only reason," Aviva says with a leer.

"You're drunk, Avi," Dorrie says calmly.

"Yeah, it's true. I am."

"Let's go," Dorrie insists.

Suddenly, Avi is docile. "Help me up," she begs.

Dorrie hoists her out of the seat.

"Good night, Band," Avi calls.

"Mañana, Aviva," Sam calls.

"Don't keep your legs closed!" Chester bellows.

"Don't worry, I won't." Avi laughs.

Nancy propels her out the door.

"Thanks," I whisper to Dorrie.

"Don't mention it," Dorrie says. And then, "He's nice."

"Yeah."

"Keep him nice."

"Yeah. I'll try."

We head out into a flurry of snow.

Chapter 17

"I don't think you're going to make it home today."

I open my eyes. A fuzzy Aviva is sitting at the edge of the bed holding out a cup of tea.

"Huh?" I ask.

"Time to wake up and greet the Winter Wonderland." She presses the saucer into my hand.

"Thanks," I croak, and take a sip. "You seem unusually chipper today. What gives?"

"Come look out."

Balancing the cup and saucer in one hand, I stumble out of bed to the window. "Good grief!" I exclaim.

The whole world is white. Huge drifts of snow covering fire hydrants, melding sidewalks into gutters, stopping buses dead in their tracks.

"Wow!" I exclaim again.

"Terrific, isn't it?"

"Maybe it'll last forever and I won't have to teach!"

"Jeez, I thought only students felt that way."

"What's all the shouting about?" Dorrie's muzzy head peeks out from her blankets.

"Snow!" I say. "The biggest goddamn snowstorm New York's had in years."

Dorrie's out of bed in a bound, nearly tripping over Nancy's inert form on the floor. Like a little kid, she stares wide-eyed out the window.

I can see her mind float back to Ashtabula, Ohio, where she grew up and the snow piles high *every* winter.

"Hurry up. Let's go out. Come on, Nancy. Wake up! Everybody out!" she yells, jumping into her clothes so fast she might've never taken them off in the first place.

"Huh? What's going on?" Nancy rasps sleepily.

"Snow. Snow. Snow!" Dorrie sings. "We're all going out."

"Yeah. Why not?" Aviva says.

And before you know it, four giggling ex-teenagers are pitching snowballs and falling face down into the wet white with the best of 'em.

Everywhere people are giggling and going whump into the snow.

"Hi." A perfect stranger waves at me and then throws a snowball smack into my ear.

"Same to you," I say, and pitch a snowball that knocks off his hat.

A shopkeeper peeks out of her door. "Psst, come here." She motions at Aviva.

Aviva wades over.

"No, all of you."

Dorrie, Nancy, the perfect stranger, a couple of other snowballers and I slog forward.

"I gotta pot of hot chocolate onna burner. Anybody want some?"

"Wheeee! Hot chocolate! Wheee!" cheers the perfect stranger.

"Yippee!" Nancy shouts.

And we all slide into the store.

"If I hadn'ta slept in the backa the store last night, I never woulda been here today," the shopkeeper says.

"Well, at least you won't go hungry," Avi says, looking at the stacked shelves.

"Oh no, that I won't."

We all cluster around a tiny space heater and drink our chocolate. It's a nice cozy feeling.

When we finish drinking and warming up, we decide to build a snowman in a small nearby park and promise to come back later for more hot chocolate.

"This is just great," Nancy says. "I won't have to go home tonight and my parents can't say a word."

"Yeah. Me either," I say. "Hey Avi, are you going to be able to stand all of us in your place?"

"Sure. It'll be fun. We can buy some stuff and have a big feast."

"I wonder where Billy is," Dorrie says. "I know he hasn't been around much, but I thought he'd show up last night."

That makes me remember John and last night. He said he'd see me tonight. But in this snow, I doubt he'll make it. Too bad.

Then Nancy says, "Oh, don't think about him now. We can be just the four of us—just The Crew, like we used to be."

"Yeah. Okay," Dorrie says, brightening. "One for all, and all for . . . Mmmf."

Aviva has smacked a snowball right into her mouth.

We all giggle and start pelting each other again.

Then we get to work on our snowman.

"This snowman's going to be different," Avi says.

"How?" Nancy asks.

"He's going to be anatomically correct." She cackles.

"Oh brother."

"Can you be arrested for erecting penile snowmen?" I ask.

184

"No, just snowmen with erections."

"No. No penises, erect or otherwise," Dorrie says. "We're going to have a nice, clean, old-fashioned, suitable-for-family-viewing snowman. And if you say one word against it, I'm not going to let you play with my dolly anymore."

"I wouldn't play with your dolly for anything. But okay, we'll let you have an old-fashioned snowman," Avi says.

"Good." Dorrie nods. And she starts rolling a humongous snowball.

It was a lovely day. After we built our snowman and had more hot chocolate at Mrs. McCleary's store, we decided to go to a movie. We went to the Bay Theatre and saw *Monterey Pop*, a documentary about the rock festival in California. It was great—especially since we were the only ones in the audience and we were stoned and singing along with half the movie. When Janis Joplin came on singing "Ball and Chain," Avi, like Mama Cass in the festival audience, just about swooned. "Goddamn, can that woman sing!" she exclaimed. "Goddamn!"

After the movie, and replete with three boxes of popcorn, we went back to Avi's apartment and made this huge meal and polished it and two bottles of wine off.

We were so goofy by then, we decided to dress up in leotards and other stuff that Avi has and act out characters in dance. After Avi did Minnie Mouse as seen in a Martha Graham ballet ("If Billy saw us now, he'd die," I said), and we all fell on the floor laughing, we figured we'd better go to bed. Nancy and Avi are sharing her double bed this time. Dorrie gets the "guest bed." And I get the floor. But I don't care. I feel too good. And too sleepy.

Wish Billy had seen us. I miss him. Never there when I call. Miss Floyd, too. I hope he's okay. So cold in a cell. Can't think about it. Very bad. Gwyn seems far away. Very

185

good. He probably never built a snowman. He is a snow-man.

The phone. Someone's ringing the phone. Why does the phone always ring in the middle of the night? No, not the phone. The door. Someone's buzzing.

"Shit!" Avi yells. "Who the hell could that be at this time?" She stomps out of bed, flicks on the light and presses the intercom.

"A Mist Mud . . . see . . . Mis Ter."

"What?" shouts Aviva. "I can't understand you."

"Shut up," Nancy growls. "I want to sleep."

"Mr. Marden to see Miss Ritter," the crackly voice says. "John Marden?"

"I'll ask . . . Yes. John Marden."

"Send him up." She nudges me with her foot. "Hey, Miss Ritter, you better wake up. You have a new admirer."

"I am up," I say.

"Hey Nina, you can have the bed. I'll sleep on the floor," Dorrie calls from the alcove.

"How suggestive!" Aviva says acidly.

It's a tense moment, but I decide I'm not going to talk (or neck) with John in the middle of the floor, so I gratefully accept.

Dorrie comes over and stretches out on the cushions.

"I wish I had a bathrobe," I say, looking down at my baggy flannel p.j.'s—all I had packed for what was to be an overnight stay.

"John won't mind that you don't," Aviva says. "But you can borrow mine, if you want."

"What will you wear?"

"Nothing. That is, my nightgown, of course."

"Thanks, but never mind."

"Will you let me sleep?" Nancy groans.

"Oh wake up, you twirp, we're having an exalted visitor," Aviva says.

Knock. Knock.

Aviva throws open the door. "Well, this *is* a surprise. But you're just in time for early morning tea. *Very early* morning tea. Do come in."

John puddles into the room. And I mean puddles. His boots, pants legs are soaked. Ice is melting off his hair. His nose is dripping. "Hi, Nina," he says.

"Hi," I answer.

"God, what happened to you?" Avi exclaims.

"I visited a friend in the Bronx. Then, I was riding the subways for a couple of hours. I got lost. Finally, I got off and walked."

"Don't you know your way around?" I ask.

"Not really. I'm from New Hampshire."

"Well, for God's sake, take off your things. I'll make some tea," Avi says.

"I better do it in the bathroom. I'll get everything wet."

"Better take off those pants," Aviva says.

John hesitates, turns back to look at her.

"You can wrap your lower half in the bathsheet that's hanging there."

"Okay," he says, and slops off to the loo.

"John is now in the john," Aviva says and goes into the kitchen alcove. (Everything in this apartment is an alcove. Instead of two and a half rooms, it's more like two alcoves and half a room.)

"God, Nina, he must really dig you," Nancy, finally awake, says.

"I guess," I say shyly.

No one speaks for a while until Aviva comes out of her kitchen with the tea. "So you want to be a Group Lady," she says to me.

"I don't want to be anything."

"Nothing? That's sad."

"You know what I mean."

"I always look at people's hands. John has beautiful, long ones," Nancy interjects.

"All the better to fondle you with, my dear," Avi says.

Then John comes out of the bathroom. His long hair is pulled back into a ponytail. His shirt sleeves are rolled up. And from the waist down, he is duly wrapped in a towel.

"Oh John, we were just talking about your hands," Aviva says. "Do you think men with long hands make better lovers?"

Whether it's from the cold or the steam heat or embarrassment, John is red in the face. "Gee, I don't know," he says.

"I don't either," she says, pointedly, and hands him a mug.

We all drink silently.

"If you're from New Hampshire, you must be used to this snow," Dorrie says.

"Yeah. I am."

"We get a lot of it in Ohio, too."

He nods.

Silence.

"Well, I'd like to go back to sleep," Nancy says, "so could you move to the other side of the room?"

"Spoilsport," says Aviva.

Nancy gives her a look.

"Oh sure," I say. "Come on, John." I turn off the light and walk to the alcove. John follows. So does Aviva.

"You look great in that towel. A male Dorothy Lamour," Aviva says.

"Huh?" John looks puzzled.

"She wore a sarong in all those old Bob Hope/Bing Crosby movies."

"What's a sarong?"

188

"Oh, never mind," Aviva responds crossly. She sits down on the bed.

So does John.

There's no room for me between John and Aviva, so I sit at his other side.

"Last night was really something," he says.

"It really was," Aviva agrees. "But someday, I'd like them to be cheering as loudly for us as they did for Canned Heat."

"I don't think about the audience too much. I'm too busy concentrating on my playing."

"You play very well," I say.

He smiles and slips his arm around my shoulders.

"Tell me, John, what do you think about that organ riff David plays in 'Blaze'? You don't think it's too static?"

"I like it, that riff," I say before John can answer.

Avi flashes me a "what-do-you-know" look and turns to John. "Well, what do you think?"

"Static? You mean, is it boring? No, I don't think so. But Sam comes in too soon sometimes. And the rhythm . . ."

And off they go into a musical discussion I can't follow at all, punctuated by phrases like "modulating to E flat" and "sweetening the bridge." When there's a lull, I ask, "Hey John, are you going to sing lead on any of the songs?"

"Me? No, I can't sing."

"Yeah, you sound like a camel," Avi says.

"What does a camel sound like?" John asks.

"Like you. But actually, I've got a good idea for a song that requires a camel's voice . . ." And she starts talking about a duet for the two of them she's writing.

I find myself getting sleepy.

I'm dressed all in silver and black sequins. Got a top hat and a cane. No, not a cane—it's a microphone. John's in white with gold camels all over his shirt. We're both singing. Then I take the lead, belting out some bluesy song:

Well, I'm leaving tomorrow
And you know I will.
Well, I'm leaving tomorrow
Bet you know I will
Don't give me any stiff-assed jive
I'm going where the people are still alive
And you know I will. . . .

The crowd below me is screaming, hollering for more. My voice grows louder until it fills the whole theater. Sweat's pouring off me, but I give it my all. Then, Aviva runs out on stage in a frilly maid's outfit—short, black dress, white apron and cap. She wipes my brow and runs back off.

The Crew cheers me on. I throw the mike away. Don't need it anymore—my voice is so loud. The band is playing louder too, but they can't drown me out.

Finally, exhausted, I finish the song and collapse. Aviva and John carry me off stage. Avi fans my forehead. "She's always like this after a performance. But she'll be fine. What a talent!" She gazes at me in admiration, as John kneels at my feet, kissing my toes. "Are you asleep?" he asks between kisses. "Are you asleep?"

"Hmmm."
"Are you asleep, too?"
I sit up with a start.
"You were asleep," John is saying. "Sorry I woke you."
"Oh, that's okay. I was . . . just . . . having a strange dream . . . you and Aviva . . ." I stop, remembering the dream and not caring to repeat it. I seem to recall there was a good song in it, but I can't remember the words. "Where is Aviva?" I ask.

190

"Here," he says, and I notice that she's sleeping with her head in John's lap.

"Help me get her to bed, will you?" he asks.

"Okay."

I stumble to my feet and hoist Aviva off John. Then he picks her up.

"Ummm, is it time yet?" she mutters.

"No," I say.

John lowers her onto her bed. I tuck her in.

"Go away," mumbles Nancy.

"Shhh. Go back to sleep," I say.

John and I walk back to "my" bed. "I didn't think you'd make it here tonight," I say.

"But I did."

"Why?"

"Because I wanted to see you." He kisses me gently.

"Ummmm."

He kisses me again.

I wrap my arms around his neck and nuzzle his cheek.

We kiss more ardently. I'm fully awake now and I'm getting aroused. I push my breasts against his chest.

"You're nice," he says. "You remind me of a girl I knew in New Hampshire."

"Oh," I say, curling up on my side, cheek on hand, hip jutting out.

"Yeah." He strokes my hip.

I sigh and move it slowly under his hand.

"I wonder if my jeans are dry," he says. "This towel's ridiculous."

"Then take it off," I say.

"I will if my pants are dry," he says and goes to the bathroom.

Maybe he's shy. But he doesn't seem that kind of shy. I undo the top button of my pajama top.

He comes back with his pants on, leans over and kisses me, then stretches out next to me.

We embrace, neck.

He kisses very well. Not slobbery or dry-mouthed, but just right.

I take his hand and put it on my thigh.

"Do you want to smoke a joint?" he asks.

"Right now?"

"Yeah."

"Not really."

"Oh." He turns on his back. "I'm tired."

"Do you want to go to sleep?"

"Yeah. I think so."

"Okay."

In a minute, he's breathing slowly and rhythmically.

Good grief, I think, I feel like a restored virgin. Maybe I could catch me a unicorn.

Chapter 18

My class of sophomores sat before me trying to decide whether to be sympathetic or a pain in the ass.

Mr. Knoedler, my supervisor, insisted that I teach a class on "apostrophe s" because the students don't know it at all. "You mean they don't know their 's' from their elbow?" I cracked. Mr. Knoedler looked shocked. I decided this is not going to be a great working relationship.

Anyway, he said when we were introduced last week, "You come right in and teach a lesson. Then you observe me for a week and teach another lesson and you'll see how much better your second lesson is after a week of observation."

In other words, I am to make a fool of myself, let him come in, show me up and then make a fool of myself again.

Well, the Great Snow of 1969 gave me a brief respite—too brief, for here I finally am looking at thirty-four pairs of sophomoric eyes.

"Good morning, class. I'm Miss Ritter, your student teacher."

In the back of the room Mr. Knoedler nodded encouragement.

"I'm sure you'd all rather be out playing in the remaining snow and so would I . . ."

The class smiles. Mr. Knoedler frowns.

"But all good things come to an etcetera, and here we are for the rest of the term."

Good things. Actually, the snow was beginning to pall on me. A pall of snow. Appalling snow. Four days and four people in a studio apartment. By the end of Day 2, we were beginning to get on each other's nerves. Nancy was pining for her violin. Dorrie kept trying to reach Billy on the phone. And me. Well, me brings up John.

"Miss Ritter, can I be excused?" A little blond girl raises her hand.

Mr. Knoedler shakes his head "no."

"Er . . ." I consult my seating plan. "Monica . . . Could you wait a bit, please?"

"No, I can't. It's an emergency."

Mr. Knoedler is still shaking his head.

"Oh . . . ummm . . . Well, let me give the opening exercise first."

Monica pouts and scrunches down into her seat.

"I've handed out a sheet with ten sentences on it. Please put in an apostrophe where it's appropriate."

"Hey, Miss. What's an apostrophe?" A handsome boy with corn rowed hair asks.

"Oh, didn't I explain? It's . . ."

"Terence," Mr. Knoedler scolds, "you know perfectly well what an apostrophe is. You were told last week you were going to have a lesson on the apostrophe by Miss Ritter. Why are you trying to annoy her?"

"I'm not trying to annoy her, Mr. Knoedler. I forgot what it is."

"Then you have a very short memory, my lad."

I wince along with Terence.

"The apostrophe," I say too loudly, "is a mark like this."
I scribble on the board. The chalk squeaks.

"Aieeee," the class squeals.

"I'm sorry," I say. "Anyway, this mark is used to indicate—
to show—possession. Here's an example: 'Give me George's
ball.' " I write it down.

The class titters.

I'm puzzled. "This apostrophe means the ball belongs to
George and no one else."

"That's good. You can't have Fred owning George's balls,"
a voice pipes up.

The class bursts into hysterical laughter.

I turn red.

"Quiet! Stop it at once," Mr. Knoedler shouts.

His shouting makes me regain my composure. I hold up a
hand. "I agree with you . . . er . . . Hank," I say, after stealing
another quick look at my seating plan. "It would be terrible
to have balls just passed indiscriminately back and forth."

The class laughs again.

Mr. Knoedler turns red.

"But that is exactly why we need the little apostrophe.
This charming punctuation mark resembling a tripped-out
comma . . ."

The class giggles again.

"Can insure that George's ball doesn't end up in the wrong
hands."

The class totally cracks up.

Mr. Knoedler begins to rise.

I hold up my hand again. "Now, please do the exercises I
gave you and we'll go over the answers in five minutes."

Giggling, murmuring, the class picks up their papers and
begins to read.

Mr. Knoedler crooks a finger at me and motions me over.
I obey.

"Ah, Miss Ritter," he says. "You . . . er . . . handled that . . . er . . . well. But, you must be . . . er . . . careful . . . of being too . . . er . . . intimate . . . that is, familiar with the students. You want to stay . . . er . . . above them, not sink to their level."

"I understand, Mr. Knoedler," I say.

"Good." He looks relieved. "Now, circulate and make sure all of them are doing the exercises and not reading Captain Marvel comics. Oh, and help them if need be."

I nod and begin to walk around the room. The students smile up at me as I pass their desks.

"Is this right, Miss Ritter?" a girl wearing bright red lipstick asks.

"That's good . . . er . . ."

"Luz."

"Luz."

I pass on. A boy with long hair like John's grins cockily at me.

"Keep it up," he says. "We haven't had so much fun this whole term."

I grin back. I feel good. I go back to my desk and think about John.

We awoke curled back to back like twin fetuses. He gave me a sweet kiss, got up and rolled a joint.

"Did you sleep well?" I asked for want of anything better to say.

"Yeah. Fine. And you?"

"Fine."

A silence.

"Have you played the bass for a long time?" I asked.

"Six years."

"That's pretty long. . . . What would you be if you weren't a rock musician?"

"Be? Dunno. Maybe a pilot. I've always liked the idea of

flying. Or maybe some kind of carpenter. I like to make things with my hands."

"Did you make a lot of things in New Hampshire?"

"Yeah. All kinds of stuff."

"That's nice."

"Yeah."

He handed me the joint. I took a long drag.

"Hey, you want to see where I live now?"

"Is it far?"

"No. Down on East Sixth Street."

"Okay. If you think any buses are running."

They weren't. We decided to go back to Aviva's.

John wasn't very talkative. He started to make a house out of toothpicks and string. Aviva was fascinated. She wouldn't leave him alone.

"Show me how," she insisted.

Dorrie and I decided to watch television. Nancy moaned about missing practice and got stoned.

By evening we were all kind of tired.

The next day, things were moving again, so John and I went down to East Sixth Street. Avi wanted to go too, but Dorrie insisted they check on the snowman and rebuild him if necessary.

"Ahem, Miss Ritter. I believe the five minutes are up." Mr. Knoedler's voice snaps me out of my daydreaming.

"Oh yes. Thank you, Mr. Knoedler. Let's go over these sentences."

The lesson proceeds sedately.

"So, old Knoedler is your supervisor." A teacher named Ruth Torres has come up to me in the cafeteria. She is a striking dark-haired woman with big, limpid eyes.

"Yes. He is."

"Difficult, isn't he?"

197

"Well, he's a bit of a tartar."

"Bit of a jerk, you mean. Back to 1869 time."

"I guess so."

"I hear you did quite well, though."

"How do you know?"

"Larry told me."

"Larry?"

"A kid with long brown hair. One of my favorite students."

"Oh yes, I know the one. He reminds me of my boy . . ."
I stop.

"Reminds you of someone?"

"Yes. Sort of." Of my boyfriend. Is John my boyfriend?
As opposed to my boy friend. A peculiar semantic distinction.

Sam was asleep at John's apartment, a small, sloppy place
with a bathtub in the kitchen, dirty dishes in the sink and
John's clothing flung all over the place.

"Oh, hi," John said nonchalantly.

"Hey, hi." Sam pinched my cheek. "Hi ya, lady." I was
rather surprised. Then he said, "Did ya hear the news? Lolly
had a baby yesterday."

"Oh, that's nice. A boy or girl?"

"A boy."

"Where is she?" I asked.

"At home."

"At home?"

"Yeah. That's where she had the baby."

"Can we see her?" I asked.

"Sure," Sam answered. "They live only a couple of blocks
away."

So we went over to Pete and Lolly's.

Pat and Amelia Theresa were there. Lolly, looking oddly
deflated, was holding a tiny little wrinkled infant to her
swollen breast and saying, "Come on, suck it, you
little bugger."

I felt strange, sort of shocked, I guess. I never saw a woman nurse a baby before.

"Isn't he adorable!" Amelia Theresa cried. "He looks just like you."

"No, he doesn't," Lolly said. "He's funny-looking like his father."

"Shut up," Pete said. But he was smiling.

"Hi, Nina. How are you?" Pat asked.

"I'm okay."

"Of course she is. She's John's Old Lady," Amelia Theresa said. "I told you—Aquarius and Libra."

"Are you?" Pat asked.

I got embarrassed and didn't know what to say.

"She's one of us," Amelia Theresa cooed again at the baby. "Right, little Sasha?"

"There he goes," Lolly exclaimed as the baby began to suck on her brown nipple. She smiled at me.

I smiled back. Suddenly, I liked watching her and that tiny new life.

"You and John going to have a baby?" Amelia Theresa asked.

"Terry, behave yourself," Pat said.

John put his arm around me. "You don't plan things like that," he said.

I jerked and coughed.

"Something wrong?" he asked.

I shook my head and resolved to visit my gynecologist as soon as I could get back to Long Island.

We hung around a while longer and then John had to practice, so I went back to Aviva's.

"Are you falling asleep?" Ruth Torres asks.

"I'm sorry. I've done that twice today. I have a worse attention span than the kids."

"Your boyfriend must be hot stuff."

199

I laugh. Then I say, "Actually, he's kind of shy—especially for a rock musician."

"Now, that is a rarity. My brother's in a band and I can't say any of the jokers he plays with are shy. They'd be grabbing my ass fast enough if Carlos weren't my brother."

I laugh and yawn.

"Oh muchacha, you are exhausted. Here, have some more tea."

"Thanks, I will. Whew, I am pooped. If I were a man, I'd have a nice bluish stubble on my face to scratch."

She laughs.

"Tell me, what do you teach?" I ask.

"History."

"That's interesting."

"It can be. If you chuck out most of the white male supremacist texts we've got here."

"You sound like a friend of mine."

"The one who looks like Larry?"

"No. This one's in jail."

"Uh-oh. Is that where I'm headed?"

"Well, I don't think you're a Black Panther."

"Hmm. No. But I've gone to a few Young Lords meetings."

"The Hispanic revolutionary group?"

"Uh-huh."

"I'd like to know something about them."

"I can't invite you to a meeting, but there's a newspaper. . . ."

"Oh, I'd like to read that."

"Okay. I'll get you one. What about your friend? How long will he be in prison?"

"I don't know. He hasn't been tried yet."

"Uh-oh. Bad news."

"Yeah, I know. Oh hell, there's the bell. Knoedler gave me study-hall duty."

"He would. Look, I'll see you tomorrow."

"Yeah."

"And Nina—I'm glad you're here."

"Thanks, Ruth. I feel the same about you."

So, I ask myself on the way to study hall, can an English teacher find true happiness with a rock musician boyfriend? Tune in to the next exciting installment and maybe she'll find out.

Chapter 19

I saw Billy yesterday. He called me in the afternoon just when I got home, tired and cranky from having taught a lesson on an exceedingly boring poem Knoedler dug up somewhere, and then having fenced for an hour at Q.C.

"Hello stranger," I said. "I've been calling you for weeks . . ."

"Nina, could you come over? I know you're busy and stuff, but I've got to see you." Then his voice broke.

"Are you okay?" I asked.

"Not really."

"All right," I said, hung up and, with a groan, got back into my car.

Billy's house is a splintery old frame house badly in need of a paint job. He lives there with his father, a strange man who practices and teaches yoga and meditation. His mother split when he was a baby. No one has ever heard from her again.

He answered the door in his tights.

"You still have great legs," I said as I walked in. "Been practicing?"

"Yeah. I've got a performance tonight."

"Tonight? How come you didn't tell anybody? In fact, how come nobody's heard from you in a while?"

He shrugged. "I don't know . . . I sort of . . . haven't wanted to be around anybody since . . ."

"Since?"

"Since New Year's Eve."

"*Oooooooommmmmmm.*" A buzzing echo reverberated from somewhere in the house.

"Let's go into my room. I don't want to disturb my father."

Billy's room, which I'd never been in before, was as surprisingly spare as John's had been sloppy. He has a desk, a chair, a bed, neatly made, and an old sandalwood trunk, beautifully carved and sweet-smelling. On a mantlepiece I noticed three small, many-armed stone Hindu deities.

"Who are they?" I asked.

"Brahma, Vishnu and Siva, gods of creation, preservation and destruction. But they're actually all manifestations of the same god—Brahma."

"You mean creation, preservation and destruction come from the same source?"

"Yeah, something like that." He picks up Siva and fingers the god's swords.

"Are you into Hinduism?"

"No. My father brought these back from a trip to India. He's not a Hindu either, even though he is a yogi."

"Do you do yoga?"

"Sometimes. It's very soothing. You would like it." He put the statue down and rubbed his forehead.

"Billy, how come you don't see any of us anymore? Especially Dorrie. She told me you made love on New Year's Eve and . . ."

"Is that how she described it? We didn't make love; we fucked. That was what it was. Plain old unadulterated fucking." He hit one balled-up fist into his other palm.

"But Billy, why are you so upset? It's what Dorrie wanted."

"It's not what I wanted. And it's not even what she wanted. It was an illusion of what she wanted. The whole time she murmured. 'Do you love me, Billy? Do you love me?' I said, 'Yes. Sure. I do.' But it was a lie. I was drunk and aroused and . . ."

"So you've been avoiding her. And all the rest of us because we remind you about her."

He nodded. Then he shook his head. "No, I've been avoiding Nancy and Aviva for that reason . . . but you, I thought you'd disapprove of me."

"Why? Why would I feel that way?"

"I don't know. Maybe *I'd* feel that way if you just . . . fucked someone."

"Why?"

"Because you . . . Oh, I don't know."

"I'm not a saint, Billy. I get horny, too."

"Yeah? Well, if you wanted to, we could . . ." he said, with his old twinkle returning.

"You be careful, William Klein. One day, I may take you up on that offer," I teased.

"I wish you would," he said.

I couldn't tell if he was joking or not. He looked so serious.

"Look," I said, "why don't you tell Dorrie you feel bad about what happened?"

"What, say I feel bad we fucked?"

"Oh, Billy, I don't know. I can't give you advice. Is that what you want from me?"

"No . . . there's something else." He took a deep breath and turned his sad brown eyes to mine. "I got my call-up notice."

"You couldn't have. It's supposed to take five or six months before they actually call you up."

"I'm just a prize specimen, then, because they got me in less than two."

"When are you supposed to go?"

"Next week. Oh Christ, Nina!" Sobbing, he threw himself at my feet and buried his head in my lap. "I'm scared, Nina. I'm so scared."

I stroked his hair and cried with him. "Please . . . go to Canada . . . Billy, please . . . go to Sweden. Somewhere . . . anywhere."

"I . . . can't . . . I can't run away and go into hiding. I've got to go . . . face the whole thing . . ."

I picked up his face and looked at him. "What are you talking about? Face what?"

He didn't answer, just kissed my palm and lay still in my lap.

Finally, he said, "Nina, will you come see me dance tonight? We'll be performing at good old Q.C. I'm going to dance gloriously. It will be my best performance."

"Yes, of course I'll come. But will you let me tell Dorrie and the Crew?"

He wiped his eyes. "Yes. All right."

I called them all, told them to come to the Colden Auditorium at eight o'clock.

"But why hasn't he called me?" Dorrie asked.

"I think he felt guilty."

"About what?"

"Well . . . er . . . deflowering you."

"He didn't deflower me. I was already deflowered. Besides, if he loved me, it wouldn't matter."

"Dorrie, give him time. Maybe he will come to love you."

She sighed and hung up.

That night as I watched Billy dance, I thought he was a god. Brahma, Vishnu and Siva as one. He moved like a knife through the air, like a dragonfly in the wind. He was life. He was death. He was grace; he was pain. He danced for us all. He danced for the stars.

Today we went to the bus station to say good-bye. Billy's hair was all shorn—his mustache too.

"You look like a Hare Krishna freak," Aviva said.

"Yeah. I guess I do. Except I don't have the topknot."

Dorrie stood like a zombie. She had taken too many Valiums and she couldn't even cry. Nancy was very subdued. I trembled all over with a chill that came from inside.

"Why don't you add a pirouette to your left-rights?" Aviva said.

"Avi, shut up," Nancy said. "You're making it worse."

"Am I?" she asked Billy.

"No," he said. "It's already as bad as it can get."

Puffing and grinding, the bus engine roared awake. All over the terminal, mothers, wives and sweethearts kissed their men good-bye. If it hadn't been for the outfits, it would've looked like a scene from a lousy 1940's movie.

"I've got to go," Billy said.

We all kissed him quickly. He picked up his duffel bag and mounted the steps. Then he turned. "Wish me luck," he called.

"Good luck," we murmured.

Then the bus pulled out of the station, slowly, inevitably on its way.

The last thing we saw was Billy's white face pressed against the green windowglass. Dorrie screamed his name once and then fell abruptly silent, as though she were wondering where the scream came from.

When I got home, there were two letters. One was from Gwyn.

Dear Nina, [it read]

My ability to give pain, to be creator and destroyer, seems boundless. I am sorry. But how to live my own life in the midst I must learn.

I wish to hurt neither you nor Margaret. But to pour streams of love from hand to hands.

Ah me.

"Each man kills the thing he loves." Wild Wilde was write.

Nina, please accept my love. Come to Colorado. Let me see you, show you my heart.

Peace be.

Love,
Gwyn

I crumpled it and threw it into the garbage. "Pompous ass. Rat bastard!" I screamed. All those letters designed to bring my heart into my mouth. To make me quiver with desire. Even that goddamn journal he left "casually" lying around in his room for me to discover. Everything staged for my benefit. No, for his benefit.

The other letter was from Floyd:

February 28, 1969

Dear Nina,

I guess there won't be any calculus for me this term. If they decide to put you away, they do it for real.

When I listen to my cellmate—and the other prisoners—and their miserable stories: couldn't get no job; couldn't find no place to live; have five kids, one on the way and don't even have enough food for myself and my old lady—damn, it makes me finally and fully understand what Brother Huey and Brother Bobby wrote in the Black Panther Party Manifesto: that all Black prisoners should be freed because there was and is no "fair" trial for us until we are tried by our peers. The same goes for Hispanic prisoners, Native American prisoners, Chinese prisoners, poor whites and all oppressed peoples.

But, for me, I hope my trial, fair or not, comes soon. It's hard being here. Can't have any of my books or friends to visit. And the prison library is rather lacking. I did find a poetry anthology which had in it "The Love Song of J. Alfred Prufrock." I actually liked it.

Tell me, Nina, have you gotten rid of your devils? Are you all right? Please, no more stepping in front of buses. No more white knights, either. And keep away from the ganja man.

I hear there was quite a snowstorm. There are no windows to look out of anywhere in my cell block. Did you enjoy it or hate it? Did you build a snowman or sit and grumble? Write me what you did.

Floyd

I read the letter twice and then cried for a long time. That a shit like Gwyn could be walking around free to destroy more women, while Floyd—and Billy too—were caged was proof of a savage, amoral universe. It didn't matter how good you were—in fact, it seemed the better you were, the quicker you were punished for it. So the hell with it. "Let's be hedonists," I once told Nancy. Well, goddamnit, I'll follow my own advice. I reached for the phone and called John.

"Are you free tonight?" I asked.

"Yes. Do you want to come over?"

"No. I want to go to a bar."

"A bar?"

"Yes. You know. Bar. Booze. Glug. Glug."

"Oh. Okay. How about Ricky's Place."

Ricky's Place. The sleazbo joint the Rabbit's Foot, to a man, adored.

"Yeah. Fine. See you then."

I'll be too tired tomorrow to teach, but I don't give a damn. To hell with responsibility! Up with decadence!

ON THE RUN
Poems of the Rabbit's Foot by Nina Ritter

Sax-on Blues
(For Sam)
Well, I'm a seaman
   Blowin' round the horn.
Well, I'm a seaman, baby,
   Blowin' round the horn.
Been blowin' down southward
Since the day I was born.

Well, I steer my ship
   By the light of the moon.
Well, I steer my ship, baby,
   By the light of the moon.
Like to take it nice and easy
So I don't come home too soon.

Well, horn of plenty
   I gave it that name.
Well, horn of plenty
   I gave it that name.
Don't mess with no seaman,
Or you'll never be the same.

Well, I'm a seaman
  Blowin' round the horn.
Well, I'm a seaman, baby,
  Blowin' round the horn.
Been blowin' down southward
Since the day I was born.

Wacks and Waves
(For Murray)
Everybody's always squawkin';
I'll let my 'bone do most my talkin'.
There's always somethin' that they're knockin';
I'll just keep on with my rockin'.

Razzamatazz
Playin' my jazz
Wearin' a crazy hat.
Thinkin' where I might be
Ain't the thing for me
'Cause I know just where I'm at.

If I don't, I have no face
And I must be in some other place.
But if I'm there,
I still don't care
'Cause this place
  Becomes
    That.

Mr. Dylan and Me
(For Chester)
They call me the Jester
  'Cause I am.
I ain't had schoolin'
And the news don't scare me.
All I care about is:

210

My women
My guitar
My next meal
My women
And they're the same thing.
I figure
   Life is just trying
   to forget
   about dying
So I'm doing the best I can.

   Cheetah
   (For Pete)
   He sees no pastels
   He beats out flames
      Blue beat
   s
      Orange
         beats
      Red beats
         flame
   in his eyes
   He sees no pastels.

   Ivory
   (For David)
   He erects
   Ghost towers
   Where ivy broods
      on the walls.
   Implanted there,
      His organ
       Music
      Swells

Fills
    The hollows
      With its climax
But no notes stir
    the ivy,
For they too are ghosts.

Pentacles
(For John)
Imagine
  a cloud
Shaped
  like a bus
Making stops
  in the sky
And all the people get on
  silent
  and seeing
Ask me why
  I don't talk
    much?
Why,
  I'd miss
  the bus.

Poem for Aviva
?

EXCERPT FROM A JOURNAL, MARCH 1969
Knoedler was out sick today, and his substitute decided
she didn't need to stick around when I was teaching (if

212

the principal had found out, she would've been killed). So there I was, alone for the first time in *my* classroom. I was supposed to teach a lesson on punctuation. "Well, let's take the colon," I began. "There's the colon, the semicolon and the spastic colon, which is what Mr. Knoedler has today." Some of the kids giggled. Then Terence raised his hand and asked if, instead of grammar, we could listen to a record of poetry he had with him. I asked to see it and he handed me an album called *The New Afrikkan Poets*—three Black poets I'd vaguely heard of. "Okay," I said, "if someone can rustle up a record player." Larry said Ruth Torres had one, so he went and borrowed it.

The record was heavy—angry, staccato poems full of the words "motherfucker" and "honky" set to a conga beat. Some of it was hard to take, and the class reacted strongly, first with dead silence, then with pleasure, delight, fear, disgust, fury. "Right on!" "This is racist." "They hate white people." "This stinks!" "Did you hear— he said 'motherfucker'!" and other comments filled the air. I let the comments flow. Finally, her voice ringing out over the others, little blond Monica said, "I want to know why is it all right for them to call me 'honky,' but not for me to call them 'nigger.'" She looked right at Terence. And instead of getting angry, Terence began to explain how white people had been saying "nigger" for years, in one way or another, and that for years, Blacks have been angry at this abuse and oppression, but have only recently begun to express that anger, and how it was better to get the anger out in words than to slug someone. He reminded me of Floyd, and I found myself

213

wishing he could be here, knowing he'd have liked to hear this. Monica nodded and said that she thought she understood, but didn't think that name-calling was going to further better race relations. Then, Larry said that rhetoric was essential to creating a new image with which a person could identify. The angry—and dynamic—Black man who used certain catch phrases and words to identify himself as such was an important new image. Terence agreed with him. I gently led the discussion on to how the poems we had heard were not only controversial in content, but stylistically controversial too, and quiet Rita, who's hardly said a word before, raised her hand and surprised us all by explaining that in Africa poems were mostly sung to music, but that the widespread and accepted use of Black English in these poems was indeed uncommon. The discussion went on even after the bell rang and I had to throw everyone out. It was amazing. Larry and Terence and Monica and Rita said I was the best teacher they'd ever had. "But I didn't do anything," I said. "You let us talk," Terence responded, "which is something no one else lets us do." "Except Ms. Torres," Larry interjected. "Well, you're lucky then, man, 'cause you got *two* good teachers!" Terence said.

I felt really good. Went out for coffee with Ruth, my head still humming from the class.

"You got a lot of guts," she told me. "And you made sure it was a serious discussion and not a circus."

"I guess so," I said.

"Nina, you really *are* something. You'll probably last two minutes in the school system, but what a glorious two minutes!"

I wish every day could be like this one was, instead of the draggy grind Knoedler imposes, but, at least, when I have my own class in the fall, maybe I can instigate more discussions like today's. I guess I really do want to teach. That's what I wrote Floyd in the letter I just sent him. But my teaching seems to be in the way of my night/love life and my night/love life seems to be in the way of my teaching. It's like I'm two different people living in two different worlds. I'm not turning out to be a good decadent, and I'm not a good responsible citizen either. Is this what they mean by an identity crisis?

March 10, 1969

Dear Nina,

Jeez, I'm tired. I thought dancing was exhausting, but it's nothing like jumping, crawling, running up and down through mudholes, over sandbags, into trenches, shoving your rifle butt into some dummy's guts and shouting "Kill!" until you're blue in the face. The food stinks too.

I'm getting friendly with a guy named—would you believe—Corky. His bunk is next to mine. He's a real kid—only 18. Actually signed up. Hates college. Hates his parents even more. He's never tired. Don't know where he gets his energy.

I miss our good times, Nina. When I get leave, let's go dancing somewhere together and rub against each other's sweaty bodies a lot.

Been practicing meditation. It helps when things get to be too much.

Say "hello" to the Crew for me and tell Dorrie I will write.

Love,
Billy

March 21, 1969

Dear Nina,

Got up and realized it was the first day of spring and thought I ought to write.

Glad you are reading the books I suggested. I hope you are thinking about them. And feeling. I would be glad to read books you send too. My knowledge of poetry is kind of deficient. And I find perhaps I can learn things from poems after all.

I liked hearing about your teaching career and about Ruth. But when you wrote about the Rabbit's Foot, your letter sounded . . . careful. As though you were watching what you were saying, Is something happening you think I shouldn't know about?

What do I do here all day, you ask? I rap and listen—you can talk to other guys on the cellblock if you beat on and shout through the walls. I read whatever I can get my hands on. I write. I play cards and handball off the walls in the dayroom. I watch the news on TV. I exercise as well as I can—the cell's tiny, but I found out I can do push-ups on my bunk. I sing—because they won't let me have my flute. Twice a week for a short time, I'm allowed one visitor—my mother usually comes, and when she doesn't, my dad or Aggie or my brother Paul does—but we have to talk through a partition. I've seen my lawyer just once—he seems more and more useless. But mostly what I do here is try to keep myself

216

alert and away from despair. It's not always easy. We're locked in over sixteen hours a day. We eat in the cell with the toilet a few feet away. The stench gets pretty bad sometimes. There's a table in here, but my cellmate has been here longer than me, so he has what you might call seniority and gets to use it at meals. I use my bed. Sometimes when the plate is too hot, I have to use my pillow as a "place mat," which is a drag because the food spills over on it and I have to wash it out in a slop bucket and dry it on the bars, which is "illegal." Shit, and folks wonder why prisoners won't "rehabilitate." Treat a person like an animal and he'll live down to that classification.

Nina, my friend, I wish I could have a picture of you, but we're not allowed to put up any photos. But they'll let me read your letters, even if they won't let me see your pretty face. So keep writing.

Floyd

Chapter 20

"You know, I don't want to be a nuisance, but you really look beat these days."

I rub the bags under my eyes. "Yeah, I guess I do."

"Knoedler isn't driving you bonkers, is he?"

"No. That is, yes, but no. The kids are getting restless. Restless and angry. Not at me. They want more discussions like the one we had when Knoedler was out. But he hasn't been absent since. Damn, this is not the time for *The Scarlet Letter*!"

"Yes, I know. I completely chucked out the syllabus. We've been studying the history of U.S. imperialism instead."

"Ruth! You'll be fired!"

"No. Number One, I'm this school's only Puerto Rican teacher. In fact, I'm one of the only Puerto Rican teachers in the whole New York City public school system."

"I thought you said your mother is Jewish."

"She is. But if you're half Puerto Rican, you're all Puerto Rican. It's like you can't be half Black."

"Yes. I understand."

"Good. That means you're learning."

"Don't tease."

"Okay. Sorry. Anyway, Bryant would be seriously embarrassed if he fired me. And seriously in trouble—unless I fomented an insurrection in the school."

"You might."

"I might. But not overtly. Furthermore, Number Two, I have tenure. So unless, brandishing a machete, I lead the insurrection myself, I cannot be booted out."

"You're excited about the kids' restlessness, aren't you?"

"Yes, I am. I think it's vital and healthy and about time. Don't you?"

"Yes and no. It's a little scary, a little overwhelming. And I'm surrounded by it everywhere. Here—and at Q.C. when I have my fencing class. Sometimes I feel like Queens College is a time bomb about to explode."

"It probably is. The question is are you going to help ignite the fuse?"

"Oh Christ, I don't know, Ruth. Fuses-schmuses. What I really need is a good night's sleep."

"So, as my Yiddishe mama would say, 'Vy don't you take a nap?' "

"Now *that* sounds like a good idea."

"How come you're so tired? That boyfriend of yours acting less shy?"

I smile, but the truth is he hasn't been. Oh, we neck, all right, but that's as far as we've ever gone. I can't bring myself to ask him why. Maybe he really is an angel. "It's not that . . . " I say to Ruth, "but he's been performing a lot."

"You follow him and the band around every night and teach early the next day?"

"Not every night."

"Most nights, then."

It is true. I've been spending most of my evenings in club after club, listening to the Foot promoting their upcoming album (with a mystery cover Aviva says will surprise us all), hearing them argue about what's good and bad about this song or that, what should have been included on the album, what is or isn't commercial, getting stoned and necking with John. Had a big fight with my parents about all the time I spend out. "What kind of girl are you becoming?" my father roared. "Unfortunately, not that kind of girl," I said. And he slapped me. He hasn't done that in years. I was really upset. So was he. I dutifully came home every evening for the next week. But it was so boring. So I decided to move into Aviva's for a while, much to her delight.

"You must really dig this guy to be burning yourself out like this. I remember when I had a boyfriend who was into custom cars. Every night I hung around 'til three, four in the morning while he added a new fender or fitted in a new seat or polished the chrome, and then I had to get up and go to school. Wow, was I dead."

I look at her in surprise. "I can't see you with a car buff," I say.

"Why not? Lady, if you can go out with a rock musician, I could go out with a car nut."

"What happened to him?"

"I don't know. One day we were out driving in his car— that was a special day because he almost never drove the thing, just made love to it regularly. Anyway, we were driving along a quiet street in Brooklyn when from out of nowhere this car lurched around the corner and hit us. When I woke up, Eddie was crying over his smashed grillwork and I was lying there in a pool of blood. It took a level-headed resident to call an ambulance for me. Eddie didn't even bother to visit me in the hospital and I didn't bother to look him up when I got out."

"Jesus, what a story. And what a jerk!"

"Yeah, I've had some nicer boyfriends since. Listen, I'd

220

like to see this famous boyfriend of yours. And Aviva, whom you've told me about."

"Okay. You want to go to a concert?"

"Yeah. Saturday night?"

"Bueno," I said. "It's a date."

Aviva has been dropping little hints all through the asparagus soup, the chicken Kiev, the French apple tart about a surprise. Nobody seems to know what she's talking about—nobody being none of the Rabbit's Foot (minus Pete who had a previous engagement), the Whole Sick Crew, or Avi's family, all of whom she decided against what should have been her better judgment to invite to dinner at her house. The food, prepared entirely by Avi herself, has been spectacular. But the atmosphere has been weird. You might say there hasn't been much common ground for conversation. But Avi's been bustling about, playing hostess, being a strange combination of charming and puckish, as though she can't determine whether to make this dinner a success or to sabotage it.

"For how long have you been playing the organ?" Mr. Marcus, making another stab at politeness, asks David.

"Oh, I've only been playing organ for a couple of years. But I've played piano since I was a kid."

"Piano?" Mr. Marcus raises an eyebrow. I hear him think, What do you know; one of them is not a yahoo. "Who are your favorite composers for piano?"

David thinks a moment, then says, "Beethoven, Bartok and Fats Waller."

Mr. Marcus smiles. He's found, if not exactly a kindred spirit, then at least another gentleman of cultured taste.

"Snot nose," Chester, who drank most of the wine Avi provided, mutters.

Mr. Marcus gives him a chilly look.

"Is everyone finished eating?" "Does anyone want more

221

coffee?" Mrs. Marcus and Shoshanna ask simultaneously.

Avi frowns. "I think everyone is finished," she says. She doesn't want Mom and Sis playing hostess at her dinner party.

"I'd like some more coffee," John says.

"I'll get it for you," Shoshanna says, reaching for his cup.

"Why don't we take our cups with us into the living room where we can, perhaps, persuade David to play the piano. It's a Steinway," Mr. Marcus says.

"That's a good idea. A treat before the treat," Avi says mysteriously.

I turn to John. He's still holding out his cup, but now he's also halfway out of his seat. I think the Marcusian manner is confusing him. Surreptitiously, I stroke his leg.

He looks at me, smiles and stands up.

Shoshanna takes his cup and Mr. Marcus rises and ushers all of us into the living room.

"What's this surprise bit?" Dorrie whispers into my ear.

"Beats me," I whisper back.

Nancy lets out a giggle. I turn my head. Sam is whispering something to her and laughing. Like Chester, she's had a little too much wine.

We settle into the living room.

Looking at the piano, Murray says, "A Steinway, huh? I shoulda brought my trombone. It's a King."

Sam hears Murray's remark and cracks up. I gather it's an inside joke.

"Any requests?" David asks, sitting down at the piano.

" 'Fur Elise,' please," Shoshanna says.

David obliges, surprising everybody with a gorgeous rendition of the piece and following it with an equally gorgeous rendition of "Honeysuckle Rose." Everyone applauds.

I glance at Avi. She looks puzzled in some way. And suddenly I realize that Avi wants her parents to accept—and God help us—even like her band, but at the same time to

222

brand them a bunch of freaks. She wants to be both a rebel and a good little girl in the best Marcusian tradition. Bemused, I shake my head.

Then, Aviva is prevailed upon to sing. David starts to play "God Bless the Child," but Avi stops him. "I can't sing that stuff," she says.

"Of course you can," Mrs. Marcus says.

"You should try," David says. "It will teach you a lot about phrasing."

"Is this a conspiracy?" Avi cracks. "Play 'Nobody Knows You, When You're Down and Out.' " Then she gets a minxish grin on her face. "No, better yet, play 'Jelly Jelly Blues.' "

David looks at her in dismay.

"Play it!"

He shrugs and obeys.

"Whip it to them, baby!" Chester yells, as Avi launches into the raunchy tune, and he sits down next to me. "Hey, Aviva's sister has great tits."

"She does have a good figure."

"You do too, you know. Nice, big, full . . ."

"You're drunk, Chester. And everybody's staring at us."

"So what? Damn snobs. Been putting me down all night anyway."

"Chester, lay off," John says mildly.

"Chester, why don't you play your axe?" Aviva calls.

He stumbles to his feet and gets his guitar.

A couple more songs and then Aviva leads us all in a rousing rendition of "Hey, Jude." Even her parents join in. When we finish, David starts to play a new song of his, but Aviva stops him.

"Now it's time for the surprise," she says.

We sit up straighter.

"Uh-oh," Dorrie mutters.

"I just so happen to have the first, fresh-off-the-presses copy of the poster for our new album—*The Rabbit's Foot Lucks Out.*"

David starts. "I don't think this is an appropriate time . . ."

"Nonsense. It's terribly appropriate," Aviva interrupts.

Chester says, "How'd you get it so soon? We weren't supposed to get them until Friday."

"Chip gave it to me." She smirks.

Oh God, I think, not Chip this time.

Avi asks David to stand up and reaches inside the piano bench. She takes out a rolled-up poster. "A little unveiling music, maestro, please," she says.

David just sits there.

Chester strums some loud chords on the guitar.

I see a red flush creeping up on John's face. What's going on, I wonder. What is it with this album cover?

Slowly, Avi unrolls the poster revealing an extremely naked, garishly body-painted group of people who vaguely resemble the Rabbit's Foot, all posed in such a way as to conceal genitalia, but either reveal (or create) everybody's worst body flaws. Chester's potbelly hangs onto his knees. Avi's left breast dangles pendulously, while her right is covered by a plump arm. Sam's chest is wrinkled and flabby; so is Murray's bum. Only Pete, David and John look physically fit. But David wears a "God, is this embarrassing" expression, Pete looks as though he's cursing out the world and John looks stoned out of his mind.

"Gott im Himmel!" exclaims Mrs. Marcus.

"Oh my!" Shoshanna says.

Dorrie coughs.

Nancy bursts out laughing.

"That's what the album cover looks like?" I blurt out to John.

He nods unhappily.

"Aviva, this is hideous," Mr. Marcus says.

"Isn't it though?" She grins.

"I am a painter. I am not shocked by nudity," Mrs. Marcus says, "but your father is right."

"I just agreed with him. But there's nothing I can do about it."

"Surely you can force them to redo the cover."

"No, it costs too much," David says.

There's an embarrassed silence.

"How about painting black bars across all the good parts, the way they do on the posters on Forty-second Street," Shoshanna says.

Avi snorts. Then we all crack up. Even the Marcuses.

"That's not such a bad idea," Mrs. Marcus says. "I don't mean black bars, but why not more flowers and things to cover up the unfortunate flaws?"

"You can do that on your copy, Mother," Aviva says. She seems irked by her mother's reaction. "Nancy, will you stop laughing."

"I . . . can't . . . help . . . it. . . . Chester's . . . belly . . ." she gasps.

Chester looks miffed. "If you were sitting that way, you'd have a potbelly too, sister."

"Let's go," I whisper to John. "Avi's overdoing it."

"Okay," he says.

We get up.

"Going already?" Aviva demands.

"Yes. I have to teach tomorrow."

"Is John your pupil?"

Mr. Marcus raises his bushy eyebrows.

"Good night, Mr. and Mrs. Marcus," John says. "Thanks for dinner, Aviva."

Thank you, John, I think. "Good night. It was a great dinner," I say.

We exit quickly.

225

It's a beautiful spring night, warm and kind of tangy. We decide to walk for a bit.

"Why did she do that?" John asks.

"The poster bit?" I don't feel like going into a long explanation of my theories about Avi and her parents, so I just say, "I don't know exactly. She just does things sometimes."

"Yeah . . . I like her anyway."

"I do too." I do, don't I? "Hey, why did you agree to a nude photo?"

"Chip said it would help sell the album."

"Oh. Wasn't it embarrassing?"

"Yeah. Kind of."

We were quiet for a while. Then I say, "You have a nice body."

We kiss.

"John . . ." I begin. "Don't you like me?"

"Like you? Of course I do."

"No, I mean, wouldn't you like to . . ." Oh shit, I don't know how to say it.

"Get stoned? Yeah, I'd love to."

I sigh.

We share a joint, kiss some more.

Then I drive John back to Manhattan.

"You want to come in for a while? We can have another joint."

"No. Not tonight. I really have to get home. I have papers to grade."

"Oh okay. See you tomorrow."

"Yeah. Tomorrow," I say.

As I pass through the Midtown Tunnel and stare at the white lights I think that soon millions of girls will see John naked. But I'm luckier. I got to see the album cover before they did. Ain't that a kick?

Brought Ruth to the Academy of Music, where the Rabbit's Foot played second billing to the Young Rascals. It was a good gig and a lively audience. We ran into a couple of students we know—they grinned an oh-how-cute-it's-two-teachers-out-on-the-town grin at us. Afterward, I introduced Ruth to the Crew and the band and the Group Ladies.

"Oh, are you Spanish?" Amelia Theresa said.

"I'm Puerto Rican," Ruth answered politely.

Terry didn't seem to hear her. "My grandmother was Spanish. She wore a white lace mantilla at her wedding. I wish I owned one."

I threw a look of apology at Ruth, but she just smiled and listened to Terry ramble disjointedly on.

We went down to Ricky's Place and hung out awhile, listening to the band argue as usual. I thought Ruth might be grossed out by the bar, but she downed a couple of beers with great ease and left looking relaxed and stone cold sober.

In school on Monday, I asked her what she thought of the band. She said she thought they were good, especially Aviva. But I knew she was holding back something. "Okay," she said, when I prompted her. "My feeling is they don't seem to get along, and that kind of tension can break up a band faster than a keg of gunpowder. My brother will confirm that."

"Hmmm," I thought about it. "Well, what did you think of John?"

"He's handsome and quiet." And that was all she could

227

say about him.

I was disappointed, but she said, "Amigita, you can't expect me to know him after one hour."

"You think I'm wasting my time, don't you?"

"Nina," she said, "it's not for me to judge . . . but, forgive me, what I want to know is what do you need those people for?"

I just looked at her and said, "What kind of question is that? They're my friends."

She apologized again and said it wasn't her business. I said it was okay, but the truth is our conversation left me feeling kind of raw, exposing things I don't want to deal with. But somehow I feel sooner or later I'm going to have to and that makes me scared.

April 8, 1969

Dear Nina,

Feeling good today. Got me a new lawyer. She expects to get me a trial soon. She seems to feel confident we can win. Also found out my cellmate was just acquitted. Got a new one now who quotes the Bible all the time. Oh well.

Yesterday, we got to see a movie. It was some John Wayne turkey—all Great White Father and Manifest Destiny crap. Racist and violent, but oh Lordy, it was a break in the routine and it stimulated some interesting political conversation.

Nina, I think about you often. I know you and Aggie have been in touch. I wish I could see you. It's cold in this place and I don't believe in any comforting God.

He never helped any Black brother or sister I've ever heard about. I never had much freedom outside—only what a racist system allowed me. Like this poet Larry Neal wrote, ". . . America is the world's greatest/jailer,/ and we all in jails. Black spirits contained like magnifi/ cent/birds of wonder." But sometimes here—especially at night—when it's so dark and the men are moaning in troubled sleep—I swear I'd sell my soul to get out of here. If I believed in Satan. But the real devil is a many-headed monster—IBM, ITT, Con Ed, Con You, Con Me, Mr. President, Mr. Man. And I wouldn't sell my soul to that devil nohow.

Write to me, Nina. Tell me about April. Strange as it may seem, I used to like watching the magnolias bloom on my street. Tell me about the magnolias. And send me some of your fine lyrics and maybe I can set them to tunes.

Floyd

April 10, 1969

Dear Nina,

My platoon is going to be shipped out soon. We're not sure where yet. Could be Germany. Or could be Nam. But I get leave shortly and hope to know by then. And then we can dance up a storm.

I'm getting used to this place and it's not so bad here. Except at night. I never slept in a room full of men before. All the noises. There's one guy who cries every night. I still can't get used to that.

I wrote to Dorrie and she wrote me back. She sounds

okay. I'm a little afraid to see her though. Especially if I find out I'm going to Nam.

I dig your letters, so write me some more. Wish you could send some green stuff, but that would land us both in the stockade. So send me some leg warmers instead— I'll practice a chassé during a break in KP duty.

See you soon.

Love,
Billy

Chapter 21

The Electric Circus is even classier than the Cheetah—at least, that's what everyone says. No phony leopardskin wallpaper here—just phony black suede or velvet or whatever this stuff is. But a better quality phony than the Cheetah's. Here it doesn't itch. The rest of the place is silver. Mylar, they call it. Frankly, I think these places all use the same interior decorator.

Anyway, it's packed tonight. Recording executives, rock musicians, lucky fans and, of course, the formidable critics, d.j.'s, and theatre managers who are, after all, the real reason for this shebang, which is a party to celebrate the release of the Rabbit's Foot album. Those God-awful posters are hanging all over the place. Just before, I watched a gaggle of groupies, clutching their free albums, point to Murray's rear end and giggle. Besides the albums, we also got multicolored rabbit's feet and those really ugly "gold tone" necklaces with a hideous pendant of Vishnu—a reminder of the record company responsible for all of this. Funny how Vishnu keeps popping up all over the place. Oh Billy. Poor Billy.

"This is really something," Dorrie whispers in my ear.

"Yes. Something."

"When does the Foot appear?"

"Soon, I would guess. When Chip thinks the excitement has built up enough."

"Hey, look over there. It's Jorma Kaukonen. My God, Jorma Kaukonen! You think the rest of the Airplane are here?"

"I don't know. But this *is* exciting, isn't it?" I say, suddenly feeling very fizzly.

I begin to scan the crowd for other famous faces. Could Paul McCartney be here? Or John Lennon? My God, could they? Suddenly, I feel a twinge, remembering England, remembering Gwyn. He should see me now, with my handsome, soon-to-be-famous boyfriend, hobnobbing with Lennon and McCartney. Then I have to laugh at myself. Silly Nina. Lennon and McCartney would not show up for the Rabbit's Foot. They don't even show up for the Rolling Stones. Cor blimey, could *they* be here?

Nancy comes wallowing through the mob, her hands full of drinks. "Dorrie, Nina, I just talked to Jerry Garcia!"

"You're kidding!"

"No. I asked him something about his electric slide guitar. He was really nice."

"Did he and Kaukonen come into town just for this?"

"No. Kaukonen's visiting his old guitar teacher or something. And the Dead are giving a concert tomorrow."

"Wow, you really did talk with him!"

"Yeah, I did!"

"Look, there goes Chip," Dorrie says. He's got a gorgeous redhead on his arm.

"Hey Dorrie. About Chip. Is Aviva . . . ?" I ask.

"Yeah. I think so."

"Oh no."

"What does it matter, if she's having fun?"

232

"Is she?"

"Is she what?"

"Having fun?"

But then Chip ahems and announces that Vishnu Records is proud to introduce the most dazzling new group on the rock scene—a combination of California sun and New York brass, a group spanning the generations of jazz and hard rock, a startling union of rebels and flower children, heralding the Aquarian Age, the Sexual Revolution, the Rock Revolt!

"Blech," I say.

"Double blech," Nancy agrees.

"Hey, are they going to come out nude?" Dorrie asks.

"I hope not," I answer.

"Why not? That'd really shake up this crowd."

Then the Foot comes out on the silver stage, all beads and fringes, and the crowd cheers.

I feel my heart knocking my ribs and I'm sweating. Please, please, make it. Come on, John, thump 'em out of their skins! Come on, Aviva, blast 'em off their feet! Boom-Boom-Boom. The opening chords of—guess what—"Super Chick." Oh well. But they sure sound good and together. So together you'd never know they squabble all the time. I'm grinning like a fool when I notice the Group Ladies in a huddle right near the stage. Lolly's holding her tiny baby. Pat is wearing Murray's cowboy hat. And Amelia Theresa is waving a fan of ostrich feathers at me. I make my way over to her.

"Hello, Nina," she breathes. "You have to stay with us now. That's your man up there."

My man. I look up at John, his eyes shut in concentration, his hair a halo around his face.

"Ooh," a little groupie next to me squeals. "I really dig that bass player."

"Yeah," her friend agrees, "he's really groovy."

My really groovy man. Yeah. Okay. He's my man!

233

As if he heard my thoughts, John opens his eyes and looks at me. He smiles and winks.

The little groupies scream.

Amelia Theresa starts dancing all around, waving her fan in the air.

Then someone passes me a pipe. Hash. Finally. I take a deep drag. Then another. Wheee! I start dancing, too. Too bad Billy's not here to dance with.

"A big success, I tell you, a big success," Chip keeps saying over his blintzes at Ratner's.

"It's so late, Sam," Amelia Theresa says, snuggling into his beard. "Let's go home and make love."

"Yeah, yeah, baby, in a minute. So you think we got some nibbles, eh, Chip?"

"Not nibbles, man, bites. Bites!"

"Chip," Aviva says, running her fingers up his arm, "it is late. How about if we leave?"

"Oh Aviva. I'm sorry, doll—I forgot to tell you. I can't come over to your place tonight."

"Well, let's go to your place, then."

"I'm really sorry, you—that is—we can't. I'm having it redecorated. It's a real mess."

The gorgeous redhead from before looms over our table. "Oh there you are Chip. Ready to go?"

"Oh hi, Stella." Chip looks apologetically to Aviva, then back at Stella. "Sure. I'm looking forward to hearing you sing."

Stella smiles toothily. "Oh honey, you will," she says.

"I'm tired. I gotta split," John whispers to me. "Want to come?"

I'm stoned and sleepy and confused. I'd like to go home with John—maybe tonight will be the night—but somehow, I feel like I'd better stick with Aviva. Dorrie and Nancy have already split for Queens. "No, I'll go home with Avi," I say.

"Good," Avi snaps. "Let's go then."

"Hey, can I come too?" asks Chester with a leer.

Aviva looks him up and down. "Sure, Big Boy," she says in a Mae West voice. "Why not?"

"Hot dog!" Chester cheers.

"Wait a minute . . ." I begin. If Chester's going to be there, Aviva doesn't need me.

But Chester and Aviva are already halfway out the door.

I stumble to my feet and follow after them.

Aviva hails a cab.

"Hey wait . . ." I begin again.

"Come on," she says, pushing me into the taxi.

I sprawl across the seat.

Chester lands a hand on my rump.

"Hot dog!" he says again.

"Shut up," snarls Aviva. Then, to the cabbie, "Twenty-eighth between Second and Third and make it snappy!"

Ooh my head. Like lead. Head lead. Lead head. Hard bed. God, really hard. No mattress. Uh-oh. No bed. The floor. I'm lying on the floor.

Something in my hands. I crane my neck and bump something. Ooh. Lead head. A candle. There's a candle behind my head. And in my hands flowers. I'm holding a bunch of flowers. And there is another candle at my feet. Oh my God. I'm dead. Lead head dead. I start to cry.

A giggle. Two giggles.

Why am I crying? Because I'm dead. Stupid, you can't cry if you're dead. You're dreaming. That must be it.

More giggles.

I bring the flowers to my face and sniff. Real. This is no dream. "What the hell is this?" I sit up, knocking over the candle at my feet.

"I'll get it. Don't want to start a fire." Chester, his potbelly sliding over his naked thighs, bends down to pick up the candle.

I turn my head. Aviva, equally naked, is doubled up, laughing.

Oh my God, am I naked too? No, I'm still wearing my clothes.

And suddenly, my head clears. "You fuckers!" I yell.

Aviva laughs harder. Chester reaches for me. "Awww, Nina. It's just a joke. Come on and join us, sugar."

"Stay away from me," I yell. I scramble to my feet and grab my purse and coat from the floor.

"Come on, Nina. Don't be a nerd," Aviva says.

"Who's the nerd?" I shout and head for the door.

"You are. Where are you going to go at five o'clock in the morning?" Avi says.

I let the slamming door answer for me.

But once I hit the street I realize I don't know where to go. My car's at home. Damn! Dorrie was supposed to drive me home. But I guess she thought I'd be sleeping at John's. John's. Why not? That's where I'll go. He is my man, isn't he? Even Amelia Theresa said so. Oh my head. Christ, I'm a mess.

No goddamn cabs at this hour. The bus? I don't know. Oh, screw it. I'll start walking.

Ten blocks later and a bus finally chugs along. I dig out some change and give it to the driver.

"Another nickel, miss."

"Did the fare go up?" I ask.

"No, you only gave me fifteen cents."

I scrabble around in my purse. My money. Shit, what happened to my money? And then I have an image clear as day in my head of a ten-dollar bill lying on my dresser. Oh crap, I forgot to take it. "I'm sorry, I don't seem to have another nickel."

"Well, that's too bad. You'll have to get off at the next block."

"What? For a lousy nickel."

"That's the law, miss."

"Whose law?"

"Transit Authority, City of New York."

I look at the passengers on the bus. There's only four—a drunk, a half-necking, half-sleeping couple and a smart-suited business type. I have to appeal to one of them. I figure the business type is my best bet. "Just a minute," I tell the driver and lurch over to the business man.

"Please sir, do you have a nickel to lend me? I don't have any change."

"Drop dead! You dirty hippies make me sick," he spits out with such venom I back off and fall onto the drunk.

"Watcherself, honey," he says.

"Mister, do you have a nickel?" I ask desperately.

"Sure," he says and reaches into his pocket, pulling out a cache of change along with a snot-encrusted handkerchief, a broken comb and a book of matches. "Here, honey," he says, handing me a nickel.

"Thanks," I say. "Can I send it back to you?"

"Fugget it." He winks at me and coughs.

I lurch back to the impassive bus driver. I'd like to smash his face, but I give him the nickel instead. Five minutes later and we're at my stop.

I stumble off, swearing and praying. Please God, let me not be assaulted tonight.

But the streets are dead and I reach John's house in one piece. I walk right in—the front door is never locked—and bang on his apartment door.

Bang. Wait. Bang. Wait.

Finally, "Who is it?"

"Nina. It's Nina."

"Nina?"

"Nina."

Noises. Shuffling feet.

The door opens.

"Nina. Are you okay?"

"Fine. I'm fine." Then I burst into tears.

John puts his arms around me. "Did anyone hurt you?" he asks.

I shake my head. I know he means "physically."

"Must be the hash. Strong stuff," he says sagely. "You want anything?" he asks.

"Sleep," I say. "I want to sleep."

"Sure. Okay." He leads me to his room.

I don't even bother with my clothes. I just fall on his bed and turn out my brain.

EXCERPT FROM A JOURNAL, APRIL 1969

Something funny's going on with Aviva. She's played jokes before, but they've usually been good-natured. Hell, that one was not good-natured. It's lucky John was home. But you know, and this is probably an awful thing to say about your man, he was sort of useless. Didn't even try to find out what was wrong. I remember New Year's Eve, how Floyd held me and sang to me and fed me and took care of me. I guess I shouldn't compare, but I keep thinking Floyd's a man and John is, well, boyish. Then again, that's one of his endearing qualities. Johnny Angel. But I do sort of wish he'd be a bit more aggressive. I *think* I turn him on. Maybe he doesn't want to seem

238

pushy. But, Lord, I'm so horny, I don't think I can hold out much longer, so I guess I'll have to make myself more aggressive somehow. But how? God, what a lot of "buts" are in this paragraph!

Anyway, I don't know what is up with Aviva. She's been more irritable lately, too. In fact, the whole Crew is starting to act kind of strange. Dorrie hasn't worked on a sculpture in months. She won't talk about her feelings either. She just says she'll feel up to working again when she knows where Billy will be stationed. Oh poor Billy. And poor Dorrie. And then there's Nancy, who seems to think coming up with freaky escapades will make everything uptight and outtasite again. A couple of Sundays ago, she suggested we go to Grand Central Station, pick a train and get on it. But Avi said she was too wiped; I said I had to read *The Scarlet Letter*; and Dorrie just shrugged. Nancy looked so crushed, I said maybe we could take a brief ride in a car somewhere. Avi said she was too wiped even for that and Dorrie just shrugged again, so Nancy and I went off alone. We ended up at Calvary Cemetery.

I said I thought she didn't like cemeteries, but she said only at night; they were fine in the daytime. We came across a weird grave, a sleeping figure of a girl, her gown with its stone ripples cascading across a marker that read:

BENITA (1876–1896)
Asleep with God

"It's beautiful, isn't it?" Nancy said.
"In a bizarre way," I replied.
We sat on a cold bench and stared at Benita for a

while. Nancy was so quiet I felt I was with a different person. Then I realized that although I've known Nancy for a long time, I don't really know her at all. I've seen nice girl Nancy and crazy Nancy and serious musician Nancy, but who the hell is the real Nancy? So I asked her, "How come you're such a freak sometimes, but when you and I are alone together, you're much more straight?"

"Am I? I guess I am. I don't know why," she answered.

"Sometimes I get the feeling you do zany things like Miss Subways and jumping into the Bethesda Fountain to keep up with Aviva."

She said that was funny because sometimes she felt I was doing the same thing.

I thought about that one for a while, then I said, "Avi sort of goads you into doing crazy stuff, doesn't she?"

"Yeah. But it's fun, isn't it? I mean, that's why we're the Whole Sick Crew, right?"

"Yeah, I guess so," I said. "But don't you wonder if you do it so Avi'll approve of you?"

She dismissed my remark. "Why should I do that? Do you?"

"I don't know. But it's something I've been thinking about."

Nancy didn't reply and I decided not to push her. "Let's walk. My ass is cold," I said.

So we strolled on, reading out names and dates of birth, dates of decease. Then Nancy said, "Nina, sometimes I feel, well, sort of scared."

"Of death?"

"No. I mean . . . Sometimes . . . Well, it's great the Crew being together. I haven't really had friends before.

240

Close friends."

I asked her what she was afraid of, but I knew the answer before she said it: "That it won't last forever."

"Nothing lasts forever," I said.

"That's what I'm scared of," she answered.

And suddenly, I caught a glimpse of the real Nancy, soft and frail like the rest of us. So I patted her hand and said, "Yeah, me too." Then I suggested we get stoned and she thought that was a good idea, so she bade good-bye to Benita ("Be glad she doesn't answer back," I said) and got duly wrecked.

But our talk troubled me. Changes. I don't know how many of them I can take. There seem to be too many happening at once lately, and it's hard keeping afloat. I want the Crew to stick together too. What do I need these people for, Ruth asked. Well, they're all I've got right now. And John, of course. But if Aviva plays any more jokes like that last one, this crew member is gonna jump ship.

Chapter 22

On the way to fencing class, I thought about Robert Browning. That is to say, I thought about something Robert Browning wrote. Quote:

> Oh, to be in England,
> Now that April's there.

End quote.

It was a beautiful spring day—tiny maple leaves burgeoning and the grass coming up bright new green. And, oh God, how it made me think of England, long for England. For the tranquility of standing on Westminster Bridge looking at the Houses of Parliament or of sitting under a Stratford beech tree watching the ferryman pole travelers across the Avon.

"Hey, Nina!" someone called.

I had just reached the gym. I turned my head. It was Floyd's friend Jerry.

"Hi Jerry. What's happening?" I asked.

"Haven't you heard? Briggs and Levine are meeting with the president. A meet-our-demands-or-else meeting."

"What are the demands?" I asked.

He looked at me strangely. "You been away or something?"

"I only have one class here now." I didn't want to tell him I've also been otherwise engaged.

"Oh. Still you should . . . Well, never mind. Some of the demands are that we have open admissions to end a racist admissions system; that Afro-American studies be established as a department; that the police not be allowed on campus; that the college not surrender college records to selective service; that students have a say in the courses we take, and in the tenure awarded to professors; and that we have a right to appeal grades and treatment by professors."

"That's so broad," I said.

"Not broad—comprehensive. It's all interconnected, you know."

"That's what Floyd says."

"I got a letter from Floyd," Jerry said.

"Yeah. I did too."

"Makes me so angry. I love that brother. And now he's another casualty of the System."

"He can't be a casualty. He didn't do anything. He's got to get out of jail, doesn't he?"

"Does he? Even if they can't make this charge stick, they'll always be after Floyd. That's how the cops get promotions. That's how the cops survive. Picking off 'them niggers' like flies. So, no, Nina, Floyd does not have to get out of jail. Just pray he's got a damn smart lawyer and then he might."

"I'm scared for him, Jerry, really scared."

Jerry's dark face softened. "Yeah. I am too. But at least they haven't beaten him up like they do plenty."

"He wrote you that?"

"Yeah."

"God, it gets me crazy that there's nothing I can do for him."

243

"Yeah. Well, come on to the rally. That'll be doing something for him and all of us."

"I got a class."

"You can skip your class today."

"No. I can't. Look, I'll come over after class."

"Okay. Then I'll see you later."

I nodded and went to my locker.

"Stretch those thighs. Stretch those hamstrings," our teacher, Miss Burris, said to our class, now shrunk from its normal twenty people to six.

I stretched and grunted.

"All right, class. Today, we will learn *the beat*. It is an offensive move designed to psych out your opponent. It can be used in combination with the parries you've learned. Like so."

I watched her feint, beat, parry with such grace I started thinking about England again. England and all those courtiers and swordsmen.

"Miss Ritter, I'd like you to be my partner. Mr. Lewis, I'd like you to judge," Miss Burris said.

I gulped. "I can't . . . I'm not . . ." I stammered.

"You'll do fine," she said.

I bit my lip and went to the front of the class. Jim Lewis also came up to judge us. As I saluted her with my foil, I thanked heaven I wasn't stoned.

"*En garde!*" Jim Lewis commanded.

We obeyed.

Miss Burris thrust. I parried. Steel rang on steel. Another thrust. I parried again. She was being tough, aggressive. I had to keep on my toes. I lunged to touch her shoulder with my foil. She parried magnificently. I got excited. Annoyed and excited. And then something happened in my head. Suddenly, I wasn't Nina Ritter anymore. I was Hamlet, Robin

244

Hood, Romeo (weren't there any swords*women*?) And I was going to whip her ass. What's more, I knew how.

She lunged at me. I parried, but weakly, pretending to tire. She withdrew, then held her foil aloft, ready for the final thrust. And I was ready. Lunge. Thrust. Beat. I knocked her foil aside, lunged deep and bent the protected tip of my foil into her arm.

"*Touché!*" I yelled. "*Touché, Aviva!*"

"A hit. A palpable hit," called Jim Lewis. He's also an English major.

We took off our masks. Miss Burris was grinning. "Damn good!" she said. "You really surprised me!"

"Thanks," I answered.

"But you don't have to shout 'To Life!' when you score."

"What?"

"You said 'À Vie!' when you touched me."

"I did?" I replied. It was then I realized I had somehow said Aviva's name. Wow, I must be angrier at her than I thought.

"Anyway, that was an excellent use of the beat. Now, class, we'll learn parry . . ."

But Miss Burris was interrupted by one of the deans.

"I'm afraid we're going to have to cut this class short," the dean said. "There seems to be some trouble . . ."

But he never got to finish what he was saying either, because just then we heard a noise outside like the shattering of fifty windows.

Without thinking, we all ran downstairs in our fencing whites and looked toward the administration building.

Another crash of glass.

And then we realized that all the windows in the administration building were in fact systematically being broken.

"Holy shit!" exclaimed Jim Lewis.

I've got to get out of here, I thought. But when I turned

around, I was swept up by a swarm of students who bore down on me and carried me along to the building.

The crowd there was inflamed. "They're expelling Briggs and Levine," someone yelled.

"They expel them, they have to expel all of us!" someone else cried.

"That's right!"

"We'll give 'em a good reason to!" another voice shouted. It was Jerry.

I wanted to get away before he saw me, but I couldn't.

"Nina. Here!" He handed me a rock.

I just looked at it and then looked at the gaping holes in the administration building where the windows once were. I felt terrified.

"Let's go inside. Take over the building!" Jerry shouted.

"Yeah! Take it over. Sit-in!" came the response.

Students began to crawl through the gaping window frames, to tear open the doors.

"No, let me go!" I screamed as someone pushed me into the building. "Let me go!" I clawed at a guy and ended up with a striped scarf in my hands. But I couldn't get away.

The building was packed, and more and more people were squeezing inside.

"Head for the president's office," a girl I vaguely recognized commanded.

"Right on!"

The mass pushed toward his office.

And then the cops came. Not just cops. The T.P.F. The Tactical Police Force. With helmets and long hard truncheons.

"Oh God," I moaned, when I saw them through the window frame. "Please let me out!"

The crowd suddenly grew very quiet.

Truncheons aloft, the cops began to file through the door.

And then the president appeared.

"Who are the ringleaders?" the head cop asked.

"Pig!" someone shouted.

The cop whirled. "Who said that?" he demanded.

"Oink. Oink," came from another place in the crowd.

Then shouts began to come from everywhere. "Piggy. Piggy." "Oink. Oink." "Look at that snout. Look at that tail." "OFF THE PIG!"

The president disappeared back into his office with the head cop.

The taunts continued.

The cops began to turn red, to smack their truncheons into their palms. It was only a matter of time.

And then someone fell against me—it turned out later that it was Didi Hinkel, who had passed out; she was helping out one of the deans and had come out of his office to see what was going on. Anyway, Didi Hinkel fell against me. And I pitched forward right into a cop.

His blow landed smack on my head. It hurt like hell. But not for long. I had a quick flash of a long-haired girl saying, "They're busting heads!" in some other time and place. Then I passed out real fast.

I woke up in the hospital. That's where I am now. A concussion, the doctors said. But not a bad one. A week's rest and I'll be fine. However, I've got a lump the size of a peach. And man, did it bleed! My fencing whites are a total wreck.

My parents somehow managed to get my things out of my locker. But they wouldn't believe that I got involved in the demonstration by accident.

I didn't much feel like arguing with them so I let them believe whatever they wanted.

Another visitor I had today was Ruth Torres.

When I didn't show up for my high school class that afternoon, Mr. Knoedler called my home. My mother didn't know what was going on—no one had been able to identify me yet at the hospital. She panicked and called the college, which she was, of course, unable to reach. Knoedler went to the principal and Ruth happened to have been in his office at the time. The riot was all over the radio. Mr. Bryant, the principal, was freaking out, worrying about it stirring up "his" students. So Ruth guessed what happened to me.

She was the first one to track me down. And she was the one who identified me and notified my parents.

"So," she said when I was able to hear her, "you lit the fuse."

"No. No, Ruth. Someone just stuck a match in my hand and I couldn't blow it out."

"You're kidding."

"Unfortunately not."

"*Jesús!* But didn't you agree with the students?"

"Oh God, Ruth, please. Let's not even go into it. One thing I can say is that I didn't agree with the cops." I gingerly touched my bandaged scalp.

Ruth laughed, then apologized. "Sorry. I know it's not funny. So, how was that party you were going to the other night?"

"Let's skip that one too. . . . On second thought, no, I'll tell you all about it." So I did. Maybe it was the pain, or the fatigue, but I just poured it all out, all about Aviva and Chester and their cruel jest, and staying at John's and not making love again.

Ruth just listened quietly, then said, "Oy vay, these people are really messed up. The rock scene messes people up—if they're not messed up to begin with. Especially women. They get eaten alive. Maybe you ought to get away from that crew. All of them."

"You don't understand. Aviva's my friend, even if she is flipping out. And I love John. He's very gentle and sweet.

248

He's my man. I don't know why he won't make love with me, that's all."

"That's all? If sex is what you want, I can introduce you to lots of guys who are just salivating for the opportunity . . ."

"Ruth, now *you* sound like Aviva."

"I do?"

"Yeah. She used to offer me all sorts of weird guys. Mark somebody. Luckily, he and his group moved to California. And now Chester in a ménage à trois. I don't want just any guy. I've got a guy. It's just, well . . ."

"Maybe John is gay."

"Maybe. But I don't think so."

"Nina, there are other guys to fall in love with. And I'm not sure you're really in love with John anyway."

"Oh, but I am. He's so . . . angelic."

"Angels make rotten lovers."

"Anyway, how can you say you don't know if I'm in love with him? You don't know him—you said so yourself."

"But I know you some. And I know me. And you remind me of me in a lot of ways."

Then a nurse came in and said my parents were here and made Ruth leave.

"Well, I hope at least he comes and visits you," she said, and promised to call me tomorrow.

Later in the day, Jerry called me. He had been arrested, but was out on bail. "Hey, Nina. I saw those pigs bash you on the head. Found out you were in the hospital. You okay?"

"Yeah. I'll live."

"You're a real sister now. I'm starting a defense committee for all of us to expose police brutality. You're gonna be our star witness."

"Oh Jerry." I was exhausted by this time. Exhausted and fed up. "I didn't even want to *be* there," I said.

"But you were and you were tough."

"I was scared."

"You're going to be a big symbol for the whole movement. I wrote to Floyd."

"I don't want to be a symbol. And I wish you hadn't written him. He's got enough worries."

"He'll be proud."

"Jerry, I'm tired."

"You must be. I'll call you back tomorrow with details."

After I hung up I buzzed the operator and told her to tell any other callers to phone tomorrow. I wanted to think and sleep.

So now I'm lying here thinking. Everyone thinks I'm a heroine or a villain as the case may be. But what is my political stand? Hell, I don't even know. Is there really a connection between capitalism and racism and war and lack of students' rights? It seems there is, but I'm not sure. I feel so confused. I should read more. And talk to people. Ruth. Jerry. Floyd. Oh Lord, I wish I could talk to Floyd.

Thinking politics hurts my head (living politics hurt my head in the first place). Think about John instead. And what it will be like to have his naked body pressed against mine. Oh dear, that's making it worse. Look, John's wonderful and sex isn't everything, is it? No, but it sure is something. Oh Gwyn. Now, stop that, Nina. Man, things were so simple before I left for England, weren't they? Just me and Nancy, Dorrie and Avi, my first few friends. No men. No riots. Not even any drugs. Why the hell can't it be that way now? Instead of Nancy acting crazy and Dorrie strung out over Billy. And Aviva . . . Oh Aviva! I'm still furious at her for that joke. God, I thought I was skewering her in fencing, didn't I? What the hell is my relationship with Aviva all about? I told Ruth Aviva's my friend. But is she? I've been pondering that more and more. God, this thinking hurts my head too. I had better

250

stop. Maybe I'll watch TV. Isn't that what you're supposed to do when you're sick?

The Crew arrives en masse at visiting time bearing all sorts of presents, including a soft plastic billy club. They're trying to cheer me up, but I'm feeling worse and worse. Feeling angry and mixed up. Wishing so bad I could talk to Floyd and to Billy. Wanting to turn back the clock. I feel like any minute I could burst into tears and I don't want to in front of the Crew.

"We tried calling you last night, but the operator said you weren't taking any calls," Nancy says.

"Yeah. I really felt wretched."

"You look like the guy who plays the fife in that famous picture. You know the one . . ." Dorrie says.

"The *Spirit of '76.* Yeah. Well, revolution is the American Spirit, I guess."

"Oh, are you a revolutionary now?" Aviva asks.

I feel like shouting at her, but instead, I make a joke. "Sure. My head is definitely revolting."

She laughs.

I close my eyes.

Then Aviva says, "You're still pissed off at me, aren't you?"

I open my eyes and stare at her for a minute. Then I say, "Yes. As a matter of fact, I am."

"Why? It drove you into John's arms, didn't it?"

"That's far from the point."

"Well listen. Don't stay angry. I don't want to leave with you still angry."

"Leave where? The hospital?"

"No. New York."

"What?"

"The Rabbit's Foot is going on tour."

251

Dorrie and Nancy are as surprised as I am.

"For how long?" I ask.

"For two months starting this weekend. And I'm making you a present of my apartment while I'm gone."

"That's generous of you, but . . ."

"No buts. You know you can't stomach living at home. So say thanks and stop being mad at me."

I realize that she expects my anger will evaporate just the way she expected me to, poof, get over Gwyn. But she looks so innocent and full of goodwill. So "old Aviva-ish," her head cocked to one side and her eyes all bright, I just sigh and say, "Okay, I'll stop being angry."

"Good." She grins and tells me the itinerary of her tour.

But when John shows up later I'm more miserable than ever and all I want to do is hold him and have him hold me. "Two months. I won't see you for two months."

"I'll write," he says.

"Letters," I snort. "Goddamn! I hate letters."

He kisses me. "You're cute when you're angry."

Then he hands me a present—a heart-shaped box he made out of wood and velvet.

I start to cry. "You . . . love . . . me," I sob.

"Sure," he says. "Why not?"

Then the phone rings. I pick it up.

"Hi. I heard you got thumped."

"Billy!" I yell. My heart lurches. Oh God, so good to hear that voice. "You're on leave."

"Yeah. Two weeks."

"And then?"

"Vietnam."

I feel the bleakness coming right through the phone. "Oh no," my voice breaks; my mouth tastes like ashes.

"But let's not talk about it," he says quickly. "I want to know how *you* are."

I swallow hard. "All right," I finally say. "Will you come and see me?"

"Of course," he answers. "Today?"

"Yes."

When I hang up, I begin to cry again.

"What is it?" John asks.

But I can't answer him, and I'm not even sure whom I'm crying for.

POSTCARDS AND LETTERS

FRONT—PICTURE OF STEEL MILL

BACK—Dear Nina,

How lovely and clean is this city. It just steels your heart.

Love, Aviva

P.S. Played second billing to Country Joe and the Fish!

FRONT—THE CUYAHOGA

BACK—Dear Nina,

This has got to be the only river in the world that could catch on fire. I swear I'm telling the truth. Cleveland is unreal.

Love, Aviva

P.S. Pete's wife showed up in the audience. Seems she left Florida because it swamped her.

FRONT—A BREWERY

BACK—Dear Nina,

Milwaukee is good for what ales you. Except for
what ails Sam. Seems he picked up a case somewhere.
(Not of beer, my dear). I had myself checked, but
I'm clean as a newborn babe.

Love, Aviva

P.S. I'm taking good care of John, so don't worry.

May 1, 1969

My dear Nina,

Happy First of May and welcome to the revolution.
Jerry wrote me what happened. Yes, I am proud of you,
my friend, as he thought I would be. But I also know—
or think I know—your embarrassment and ambivalence.
You didn't mean to provoke, did you? Perhaps you didn't
even want to be there. But the fact is, Nina, whether
we like it or not, we are all caught up in the change
that's coming and the changes that continually happen,
and we're on one side or the other that makes those
changes happen. Better to seize the time and to know
where you stand than to let yourself be herded, fearful
and cowering, into a group.

Speech finished—and oh man, I didn't even ask how
you feel. Your head okay? Glad they didn't crack your
skull, but I always said you had a strong head line, didn't
I?

Take care of yourself.

Floyd

FRONT—THE BADLANDS

BACK—Dear Nina,

This is where I'd really like to visit. But Chip says we aren't going anywhere near there. Miniapolis was alright. We go to Denver next.

Love, John

FRONT—THE ROCKIES

BACK—Dear Nina,

The Hills Are Alive With The Sound Of Mucusssssssss!

Love, Aviva

P.S. Played second billing to Gary Puckett and the Union Gap.

FRONT—A GREEN TREE FROG AND BANNER OF SAN DIEGO ZOO

BACK—Dear Nina,

Saw this and thought of you. We go to San Francisco tomorrow. Play second billing to Swami Puttatherpal. If he can't make it, Guru Wattalottahooi will take his place. Looking forward to a week's rest in El Lay.

Love, Aviva

P.S. John has grown two inches. He's gotten taller too.

FRONT—ZUMA BEACH

BACK—Dear Nina,

This is the life. Wish you could come out here and stay awhile. The wether is beautiful. I am buying a new bass. Found a Fender. Been hoping to get one for a long time.

Love, John

Dear Nina,

Sometimes it's so green and quiet here I forget there's a war on. But then I hear the strafing and see the napalm falling, setting the trees on fire, and I remember. It's hard to dance here. Easy to get stoned, but hard to dance.

It's also hard to write. I've got to do mess duty now. I'll continue this tomorrow if I can.

Sgt. Climmer told a joke tonight about a gook who was made to eat a bowl of Ivory Snow and farted soap bubbles for a week. He claimed it was true. Corky laughed. I didn't think it was funny.

Someone said they censor our letters. Let me know if you were able to read the above.

Oh no. I've got to sign off again. I *will* finish this tomorrow.

I don't know how to write this. I feel so sick. More than sick. We were in a skirmish today. My friend Corky wouldn't stay under cover. He freaked or something. I saw him get shot but I couldn't do anything. We went to get him later. He was dead. They say he died instantly. I just don't know. There were some Viet Cong killed too. One of the guys wanted to castrate them. Somehow I stopped him. I can't write anymore now. Please tell everyone I'm okay.

Love,
Billy

May 27, 1969

Dear Nina,

It was a bad day yesterday. There was a shakedown—a cell search. That isn't strange—it happens practically every week. A guard comes up to your cell, makes you come out, strip and face away from the cell while other officers watch. Then he goes in and wrecks it, throwing your blankets and pillows on the floor, ripping apart your mail, stomping your clothes. When he's through, he calls you back in and tells you to clean everything up. But this time, the officer decided that wasn't enough and thought he'd better do a body search. I won't describe it—you can imagine what it is. Oh Jesus, Nina, I wanted to kick his balls up his gut so bad. The whole time it was happening, Wilfredo, my latest cellmate, cowered in a corner and muttered to himself. I don't know why they decided to do it to me—or what the hell they were looking for, so my guess is it was done to humiliate and degrade me. When the guards left, I got back into my dirty clothes and sat down on the bed and thought about how many people have it worse than me. But the whole time I was shaking with anger and it took everything in me to stop from screaming. A man could go crazy here, I thought. And that's when I decided I would not go crazy. That I'd work out mathematical equations in my head, re-write *Romeo and Juliet*, start studying law—anything to keep from going crazy. I'm sorry I have to write this to you, but I had to set it down on paper. You understand?

Floyd

FRONT—AN AUTO FACTORY

BACK—Dear Nina,

Sorry I haven't written in a while. Fact is this tour is exhausting (like Detroit—get it?) Will be glad to get home. See you in a week.

Love, Aviva

FRONT—AN AUTO FACTORY

BACK—Dear Nina,

Sorry I haven't written in awhile. I'm tired. We all are. I did buy my bass. It's great. See you soon.

Love, John

Chapter 23

It's very hot for June and the air conditioning in the terminal appears to be busted. It seems like a lot more than ten months ago that the Crew met me here, stepping off a plane onto my native soil. "Did you get laid?" Aviva asked then. I won't ask her that question. I've heard too much about what bands on tour do. I don't think I could take a description of gang bangs or male groupies. Of course, it's always possible that Aviva was celibate. Possible, but highly improbable.

I, on the other hand, have been celibate for ten months. But I've made up my mind. This weekend I'm going to tell John point-blank that, in celebration of his return from a triumphal tour it's time we consummated our relationship. Surely even angels let down their wings once in a while. And certainly he must be horny by now too. I doubt that any little groupie succeeded where his own woman hasn't. Come on, Saturday night!

John's absence has made things more chaste and Aviva's has made things somewhat quieter these past few months. Quieter, but surprisingly unboring. Jerry (who was fined by a judge for the amount the windows of the administration building cost to repair) kept calling me a lot about meetings of his police brutality committee. After I received Floyd's last letter, I agreed to go to a meeting. Ruth came with me. She was interested, she said. When I walked in, everyone cheered or slapped me on the back. I felt terribly embarrassed. But then people let me alone and we listened to several extremely cogent speakers who told such disturbing stories about their experiences with cops I actually found myself sweating. The one that really got to me was told by a Hispanic guy who one day was carrying a television from his father's repair shop to a customer's house when two cops grabbed him, threw him against a wall, pulled out their guns and demanded to know from where he stole the TV. They took him to the station, threw him in a cell and later beat him with cold towels and rubber hoses. It took his father a day and a half to find him and get him out. While I listened, I thought about Floyd the whole time. Then I suggested we take some action to help speed up his trial, such as bombarding the D.A. with letters about how Floyd was a good citizen and how he was framed. Jerry said that that was an excellent idea, so we spent the rest of the time working on the wording of the letters. I felt good about having gone to the meeting. Ruth was pleased she—and I—had gone too. We talked about it for weeks; I even discussed it with some of my students after class.

That brings me to the subject of teaching, which has certainly been ups and downs. The kids found out all about my escapade at Q.C.—except they too refused to believe I hadn't wanted to be there. So now I'm a big heroine to them. Our rapport is great and the lessons really crackle with energy. But I'm a big militant villain to Mr. Knoedler. He criticizes almost anything I do. The kids see it and they hate Knoedler's guts, which makes him hate me even more. Once, he got me so upset I practically ran out of the classroom, but I was saved by an interrupting P.A. announcement about some basketball game. Ruth listens to my ranting a lot, but that's all she can do. I sure as hell can't tell Bryant, the principal. He'd just take Knoedler's side. My parents probably would too. But fortunately, I haven't had to deal with them much—the bliss of having "my own" apartment for two months.

Except that lately it hasn't been my own. In May, Dorrie lost her bus-driving job for Happy Bunny. The woman who runs the school told Dorrie she was showing up late too often and she seemed "rather out of it" on the job. It's true Dorrie was late sometimes, but I know she was never stoned when she had to drive the bus. But she didn't protest. She didn't seem to care. However, she also didn't have any more money to pay her rent, so she lost her apartment, too. She said she was going to sleep in her car. I told her she'd better move in with me—at least until Aviva returned. So, for the past three weeks, I've had a roommate, and I must admit she's been getting on my nerves. She wakes up at four p.m.—just when I come back from teaching—lights a joint, eats everything in the fridge, returns to bed and goes back to sleep until nine at night when she gets up, lights another joint and watches TV when I'm trying to mark papers or plan my next lesson. A couple of times I tried to get her to talk, but she just kept watching the tube. Actually, I got so fed up a week ago, I wrote her a poem and left it where she couldn't fail to find it. It was called "Cloudance," and it went:

Dorrie,
   Dorrie,
Why are you high?
No one's insistin'
   that you fly.
You don't have to go
   Up
is not the only place

261

You know
Sideways is one way
    to travel
    if you must
Or even just
    straight ahead
    on a streak of dust
You can get there somehow
    if you try
No one's insistin' that you fly.

But Dorrie just said she found a poem of mine and liked the way it rhymed. I don't know what's the matter with her. Since February she's been going downhill—unable to work or talk or, now, even to get up. And I'm not really sure she's acting this way all because of Billy. It makes me sad and also angry. Well, maybe Aviva's return will help. I don't think Avi will stand for a roommate who sleeps all day long.

Speaking of Aviva's return—how do I feel about it? I'm not sure. I've missed her all right, but the joke she pulled still leaves a sour taste in my mouth. And, in a way, I've felt more my own person, clearer about my interests and involvements, since she's been gone. Also, I've felt more reckless and more like a leader. Like the leader of the Crew. One night, before Dorrie took to her bed, she, Nancy and I were hanging around with nothing to do. They both looked at me to come up with something. And I did. "Let's go to Max's Kansas City," I suggested.

"Without Aviva?" Nancy said.

"Why not? We're perfectly capable of ordering and paying for a meal ourselves, aren't we?"

"Yeah. But all the musicians hang out there and . . ."

"You *are* a musician. And Dorrie and I can hum a few

bars if necessary. Come on, don't be so uptight," I said, thinking I sounded rather like Aviva at that moment.

So, we dressed up and off to Max's we went. And when we got inside its red-and-black chintzy splendor, we discovered we only had enough dough between us for two hamburgers.

"Phooey," Dorrie said. "I'm hungry."

"Me too," Nancy said.

"God, you two sound like the kids you drive around, Dorrie. Just hold on." I glanced around the room as if it had an answer and caught the eye of a fat, pleasant-looking white man in his late thirties or so who seemed to have an odd entourage with him—a very tall Black girl in a tight red dress, a thin, pasty-faced guy with a hook instead of a hand and a tiny, wrinkled, old man who might have been Indian or Pakistani. On closer inspection, the girl in red turned out to be a boy. I tried to look away quickly, but I had caught the fat man's eye. He waddled over.

"Hello, I'm John Malone. Please excuse the breach of etiquette, but you look like three very hungry young ladies and I very much enjoy feeding the hungry. Please allow me to treat you to dinner."

Nancy giggled and Dorrie just stared, but, and God knows what possessed me, unless it was the spirit of Aviva, I said, "We'd be delighted, Mr. Malone," and I proceeded to introduce all of us.

Then, Mr. Malone introduced his crew—Ganesh, Tommy and Charlene—and asked us what we'd care to eat. "Hamburgers! Nonsense!" he said and insisted we order the excellent lobster.

"Hello, Mr. Malone, how's the stock market today?" the waiter asked and gave us a wink.

"It's had its ups and downs," Mr. Malone answered gravely, and then broke into a basso laugh, which threw us (and Charlene) into fits of giggles.

Throughout dinner, Mr. Malone regaled us with stories of previous guests he'd invited to dinner and of how he'd made his fortune by the age of twenty-three. Charlene looked appreciatively at him. Tommy nodded wisely. And Ganesh didn't say a word.

After dessert, we thanked him profusely, gave him our phone numbers and left. Outside Max's, we just looked at each other and grinned. Then Dorrie and Nancy gave a hoot and almost carried me down the street.

A week later, Mr. Malone called and invited me to travel to Boston on his private plane and play a hot game of Monopoly. I said I was flattered by his invitation, but I had a test to prepare. He hasn't called again.

Aviva probably would've accepted his invitation. At any rate, she should get a kick out of the finesse with which her protégé led the Crew into such a caper—even if she's annoyed at not having led us herself.

"Flight 304 from Chicago will be arriving on time at Gate 18," a voice squawks.

"Amazing," Nancy says. "A flight on time!"

And then the Group Ladies arrive.

"Wow, isn't this airport beautiful," Amelia Theresa says, hugging me.

I smile.

"Don't cry, Daddy's coming home," Lolly says to her baby.

Pat nods hello. "Miss John a lot?" she asks.

"Yes. You must've missed Murray plenty."

"Yeah. But I'm sort of used to his going and coming."

"But it's the coming part she really likes," Lolly says.

Pat snorts and laughs.

"Nina. Why haven't you been to see us?" Amelia Theresa says.

Surprised, I look at her and see a loneliness in her eyes

I've never seen before. Or maybe I just never really looked. She has always been just a wigged-out lady to me. "I'm sorry. I've been very busy," I say.

"Everyone's busy. No one takes time . . ." She stops. Her eyes fill with tears.

"Are you okay?" I ask.

"Don't mind her," Pat says. "She's always depressed the day after she trips."

"Oh Terry. That stuff is dangerous," Lolly says. "And bad for your future children."

Amelia Theresa just sighs and strokes back her hair.

Then we all tramp down to the gate and wait. Soon the passengers start to arrive. And then we see Murray's balding head, followed by the rest of the Foot. "Hi!" we shout. Everybody runs to everybody. I hug Aviva and look eagerly for John. He's not there.

"Avi. Where's John?" I ask, anxiously.

"Oh, didn't he write you?"

"No," I say. "Is he okay?"

"He's fine. Just tired like the rest of us. He went home to New Hampshire for a week to recuperate."

There goes Saturday night. Then I get irritated. Why *didn't* he write to me? Well, maybe the letter went astray. Or maybe he just figured I'd be loose about the whole thing—the way he always is. Or maybe he wants his halo to be fresh and bright for me. I resolve not to get too down. After all, it's only one more week.

We help fetch Aviva's luggage and take it to Dorrie's car. All this time Aviva's been noticeably quiet. Once inside the car, Dorrie lights up a jay. We pass it around, but Avi waves it away.

"No, I really want to go home and sleep. Grass keeps me awake."

Surprised silence.

Finally I can't stand it. "So tell us already—how was the tour?" I ask.

Aviva half laughs. Then she says, "The truth? It was an absolute, unmitigated flop. A real bummer."

Shocked silence.

"Oh no. You must be joking," Nancy says.

"I'm afraid I'm not. Oh the houses were full, all right. But never for us. Applause for us was polite. Record sales were—are—low. We fought constantly. In fact, I think the Foot may break up," Aviva says.

And then she starts to cry.

I'm speechless. Aviva never cries. So I just put my arms around her awkwardly and let her sob.

After a while, she stops crying. "Whoo, I must have jet lag or something."

"Never mind," I say.

"Things might get better," Nancy says.

"Sure. It takes a while to catch on," adds Dorrie.

"Thanks Crew, but in the rock world, it's here today, gone tomorrow. Or, for the Rabbit's Foot, perhaps I should say hare today, gone tomorrow."

We laugh. Too loudly.

Then we sit quietly the rest of the ride home.

At the apartment, Aviva dumps her bags, turns on the air conditioner and flops into bed.

I turn on a Traffic record.

Dear Mr. Fantasy
Play us a tune
Something to make us all happy.
Do anything
Take us out of this gloom.
Sing a song

266

Play guitar
Make it snappy.

"Jeez, how appropriate," Avi groans.

"Want me to change it?"

"Nah. Shit, I'm so tired I'm not going to be able to sleep. Let's do something."

"What?" Nancy asks.

Avi looks around the apartment. She notices Dorrie's sheepskin rug and an air mattress and other stuff.

"Hey, is that an air mattress?" she asks.

"Yes," I say.

"Whose is it?"

"Dorrie's."

"Great. Blow it up, Dorrie."

"Aviva, I have to talk with you," Dorrie says. "I . . . uh . . . lost my job and my apartment. I've been staying here . . ."

"Let's not talk about that now. Just blow up the mattress."

"What's going on?" I ask.

Aviva looks at me. I see that familiar devilish gleam in her eye.

"We're going to build a fetish bed."

"A what?" shrieks Nancy, loving it.

"A fetish bed. A fetish bed!" Aviva jumps out of her own bed and starts rummaging in her dresser. Out come silk scarves, lacy underwear. Into the closet she goes and emerges with the satin gown we gave her and two pairs of high-heeled shoes from God knows when.

"You're crazy!" Nancy yells.

"Oh, and somebody light me a joint," Avi says.

We all can't help grinning. Good old Aviva is back.

One half hour later, the fetish bed is complete. The rubbery mattress is covered with the sheepskin rug, then the satin gown, then the scarves. Littered carefully around it are the shoes and the underwear.

"Too bad we don't have a camera," Avi says.

"Too bad we don't have any men's stuff," I say.

"What do you mean?"

"Well, this is all women's stuff that men are supposed to dig. Don't women have fetishes?"

"For what? Jock straps?"

"Ugh," Nancy says.

"Personally, I think multicolored satin jock straps could be very appealing," I say.

Nancy giggles.

"It is missing something," Dorrie says.

"What?" Avi asks.

"A mirror."

"Brilliant. Help me get it down from the wall."

Dorrie and Avi take down her mirror and prop it alongside the bed.

"Perfect!" Avi says.

We admire our handiwork.

"Now what?" Dorrie asks.

"Now what? We enjoy it of course," Aviva says and immediately strips down to her underpants and begins rolling around on the bed.

"She really is crazy!" Nancy screams.

"Ooh, it's wonderful!" Avi says. "Come on, somebody else try it."

I laugh. "Oh what the hell." I take off my clothes and tell Aviva to get off. Then I sink into the bed. It is sort of nice.

Then Aviva crawls back on and we both roll around it for a while. Dorrie and Nancy decide to join us. There's not enough room and each of us keeps falling off onto the floor. After a while, we all just languorously lie where we've fallen.

"Hey, Nina," Avi says. "Have you ever had sex with a woman?"

"No. Have you?"

"No. It would be interesting. But I'm still too uptight."

"You are?"

"Aren't I allowed to be uptight?"

"Sure."

"I once masturbated with my cousin," Nancy says.

"Nancy!" Dorrie yells.

"For God's sake, I was only eight."

"Was it fun?" Aviva asks.

Nancy kicks her.

"Please, let's not talk about sex anymore," I groan.

"This is a fetish bed, my dear. How can we not talk about sex?" Avi says.

Then the doorbell rings.

We all spring to our feet and start throwing on our clothes.

"Who could that be? The doorman didn't buzz," Avi says.

"Must be someone he knows," I say.

"Or someone who sneaked past him."

"Don't be creepy."

"Only one way to find out. Who is it?" Aviva yells.

"Chip."

She goes to the door.

"Just a minute," Nancy says, buttoning her blouse.

"Don't be dumb. He's seen many naked broads," Avi says and opens the door.

"Hi honey," he says, handing her a huge bunch of flowers. "Long time, no see."

"Ha ha," Avi says, having just spent two months with the man. "Come in."

"Hi, girls," he says to us.

"Girls," I mutter.

269

Nancy giggles again.

Avi puts the flowers down. "What's up, Chip? You want something?"

"Gee, you really like to get right to the point. Aren't you going to offer me some grass?"

"To go with the flowers? Sure. You want some grass?"

"Yes, please."

Dorrie rolls a joint. "Hey, I'm really low. Got to get some more. Except . . ."

"Except you're broke," Aviva finishes.

"Oh listen. I don't want to smoke anyone's last jay," Chip says.

"It's not my last."

"Next-to-last." Chip smiles. "Here. Treat yourself." He hands her a twenty-dollar bill.

Dorrie stares at it and then at Aviva.

Avi just shrugs.

"Well, thanks," Dorrie says, pocketing the bill.

"I know a great dealer on West Tenth Street. Here, I'll write down his address."

Aviva taps her fingers against her hip. "Come on, Chip. Enough already. Why are you here with flowers and twenty-dollar bills?"

"Okay. Now, I know you just got home and you're dog tired. But Joe Wandemayer called and the band who was going to play tonight at Wheels had to cancel. So he asked if the Rabbit's Foot would be available. Just for tonight. I told him yes. Now I know John's away, but Chester has a friend who can fill in for tonight."

Aviva stares at him in disbelief.

"Look. It's going to be great publicity. Band on the Rise Returns to Old Haunt as Favor to Owner."

"The headline's too long," Aviva snaps. "And this band is more on the decline."

"Aviva, don't be ridiculous. Just because the album hasn't been a big seller . . ."

"And the concerts. And the press has ignored us."

"It will change. Now, at tonight's gig . . ."

"No."

"No what?"

"I'm not performing tonight. I am, as you so poetically put it, dog tired. I'm going to bed."

"Not alone, I hope," Chip says.

I wince.

Aviva turns livid. "Don't you try that on me. You did it once too often. I said I'm not singing tonight. And I mean it!"

Then Chip's face grows hard. "Listen, Miss Marcus. You will sing tonight. Because if you don't, you might as well say good-bye to your career."

"Are you threatening me?"

"Yes."

They glare at each other until Chip backs down. "For God's sake, Aviva. I've sunk a lot of money into the Foot. You cannot let them—and me—down."

"You and they don't give a damn about me."

"Untrue. We all give a damn."

"Right. Damn Aviva. That's what you give." Suddenly, she seems to deflate. "God, I'm so tired. . . . Oh, all right, I'll sing tonight."

"Great. I knew you'd consent," Chip says and goes to hug her.

"Don't touch me," she raps out.

He backs away. "Okay, okay. See you tonight at eight."

Then he hurries out.

"Goddamn," Avi says and throws a shoe across the room.

It bounces into the fetish bed and crashes into the mirror, cracking it into three big pieces.

271

"Seven years bad luck," Dorrie mutters.

"Yeah. The Rabbit's Foot Bad Lucks Out."

"What a shit," Nancy says.

"He really is," I agree. "Come on, Avi. It's nearly five. You'd better get some sleep."

Aviva looks like a rag doll someone pulled the stuffing out of. "Nina. Will you stick around and wake me in two hours?"

"Yes," I say.

"Thanks. You're a good friend."

After she tumbles into bed, Dorrie, Nancy and I shake our heads in dismay. Then we clean up the apartment. Afterward, I watch Aviva sleeping and think about Wheels, and the last poem of "On the Run," the one about Aviva, finally comes to me, complete, right there and then:

> *Putting Your Cold Shoulder to the Wheel*
> (For Aviva)
> You look so very small
> All curled up in a ball
> Not really there at all
> You want to run away
> But they insist you stay
> Chained to a tambourine
>
> You finish up your drink
> No time to stop and think
> Afraid that you will sink
> Down with those who wailed
> When broken voices failed
> Chained to a tambourine
>
> Words peeled off quickly
> Like bits of dead skin
> Casually tossed in the air
> Trampled into powder by dancers' feet
> And you're not really there

Sing so they can dance
Sing so they can dance
Sing it fast
Sing it slow
There's only one dance
That they know

The music's way too loud
It still attracts a crowd
They think it's time you bowed
You think it's time you bowed
Out

Their biscuit "improvise"
Is just one of the lies
They throw you
They know you
And you're still
Chained to a tambourine.

I read it once and wonder why I once thought the world
of rock music was so glamorous. I decide not to show the
poem to Aviva until she's feeling better.

Chapter 24

"Did you see this? There's going to be a three-day music festival at Woodstock," Nancy says.

"Yeah? Is that nearby?" I ask.

"Sure. It's less than two hours away."

"Who performing?"

"Jeez, everybody. Joplin. The Dead. The Airplane. Jimi Hendrix. Richie Havens. Crosby, Stills and Nash. Creedence Clearwater. Sly Stone. Everybody!"

"Holy shit! How much is it?"

"Eighteen dollars."

"That's all? Let's do it."

"Do what?" Aviva steps out of the bathroom.

"The Woodstock Music Festival."

"Yeah. I heard about it."

"You think the Foot will be performing?" Nancy asks.

"Are you kidding? We'll probably never leave Wheels."

I shake my head in commiseration. The Foot's "one-night-fill-in" has stretched out into nearly a week. John will be back tomorrow and they'll probably sucker him into playing at Wheels too. I only went there once this week. The atmosphere was even less pleasant than usual. Everyone in the group was snapping at one another and playing badly as well. And the crowd was kind of rowdy too. Maybe because of the heat. The audience talked so much through Aviva's "On an Island," Sam suggested they drop it from the next set. "It's not the song, it's the clientele!" Aviva snapped.

"Baby, no one's knocking your song. But you got to please your public."

"Please the public, my ass. All you know about is pleasing the pubic."

I thought it was going to escalate into a big fight, but then Murray laughed. And so did Sam. Then Aviva cracked up too.

"Man, we really need a vacation," Sam said. "I ain't working next week nohow."

"I second that," David put in.

But the air still zizzed with little tensions and I was happy to get out of there.

"Well, I'd like to go to Woodstock," Avi says. "Hey, Dorrie?"

A snore.

"Christ, is she sleeping again? We've got to do something about her."

"I know. But what? I've tried talking with her, but she doesn't want to listen. Should we tell her to go to a shrink?" I throw up my hands.

"I don't think she would go."

"Oh, why don't you guys leave her alone? She's upset about Billy," Nancy says.

"Sleeping all day isn't going to get him out of Vietnam. Come on, Dorrie. Get up." Aviva nudges her.

"Huh? What time is it?" Dorrie asks sleepily.

"Five o'clock."

"Wake me at six for dinner," she says and rolls back over.

"Shit."

Then the phone rings. Aviva picks it up. "Hello, Aviva Marcus speaking. Oh hello, Sam, what's up. What? . . . Now? . . . What about? . . . What does that mean? . . . Oh, all right. Where? . . . Okay, see you in half an hour." She hangs up and frowns.

"What's up?" I ask.

"I'm not sure. Sam says Chip wants to get together with us to discuss our future."

"It could be good . . ."

"Don't bet on it. Well, I'd better go. What are you both going to do?"

"I've got to go to that wedding I told you about," Nancy says. "In fact, I better leave now."

"I'll probably just hang around. It's too hot to do much else," I say.

"True. Okay then, I'll see you later."

Two hours later, Aviva returns. She has a queer look on her face. "Well, what are we going to do tonight?" she asks.

"What do you mean?" I ask. "You're playing at Wheels, right?"

"Nope. Not tonight."

"Oh great. The gig's finished."

"Oh, it's finished all right," she says sarcastically.

"Avi. What happened?" I ask.

"What do you think? I was fired. Hmmm, interesting term. Can the lead singer of a rock group be fired? Or watered? How about aired? Earthed? Oh, I like that one. I've been earthed."

"Stop it, Avi. You mean they got you there to tell you they didn't want you to sing with them anymore?"

"Chip told me. They all voted on it. Can you believe that?

They *voted* on it. Except for John, of course. He's not back yet. But then his vote wouldn't have mattered because the vote was otherwise unanimous. Aviva is out."

"You're kidding! Just like that?"

"Just like that."

"Sam and Murray voted against you?"

"Yes sirree. And David too, who so charmed my parents. And Chester, the darling. And Pete, of course."

"And Chip?"

"Oh no. He didn't vote. He diplomatically told the group it was *their* decision. The bastard!"

"Oh Jesus, Avi. That's awful!" I say. I'm afraid she's going to cry again.

But she doesn't. "Fuck it! I was going to quit anyway," she says. "Two-bit group going nowhere. Never thought they'd last."

"John's going to be upset," I say.

"He should be after what I've done for him. What I've done for all of them!"

"Yeah, you really made the group."

"Oh, I made them all right. I also contributed to their success." She snorts.

"I didn't mean the former."

"Never mind . . . Let's go have a highly fattening dinner. Then I'm going to do something I've been wanting to do for a while."

"What?"

"I'm going to trip."

"Avi, no," I say.

"Oh come on, Nina. Don't be such a dud."

"You're not in the best state to trip."

"Oh no? I think I'm in a great state. I'm free. Free of the Foot. I've been amputated. Hee hee."

277

"Aviva, if you expect me to trip with you, forget it. And if you encourage Dorrie to do it, I swear I'll never talk to you again."

"Don't worry. I'll just let Dorrie sleep. And as for you, I need you straight. Just in case anything goes wrong."

"If you're worried about that, don't do it."

"Look, Nina. I will do what *I* want to do. If you don't want to be around, then don't be."

I sigh. "You've made up your mind."

"Yes."

"Okay. I'll stay with you."

"Good. Now let's have that dinner."

Aviva holds the lavender capsule in her hand. "My passport," she says.

I shiver.

Then she swallows the pill.

"How long will it take?" I ask.

"I'm not sure. Half an hour. An hour. I'll let you know when it starts. If I know."

"What do you want to do now?"

"Listen to music." She puts on Mother Earth, Janis Joplin and The Airplane's *Crown of Creation*. We listen for a long time.

"Nothing yet?" I ask periodically.

"Nope," she answers.

When "Triad" comes on, Aviva starts to sing along:

*"You want to know how it will be
Me and him or you and me
You both stand there your long
    hair flowing
Your eyes alive, your mind still growing
Saying to me—'What can we do
    now that we both love you.'*

278

I love you too—I don't really see
Why can't we go on as three."

"Hey, what time is it?" Dorrie says.

"Time of departure," Aviva answers.

Dorrie gets up and comes over. "What are you talking about?"

"Dorrie. I didn't know you were green and pink," Aviva says. "She's a rainbow!"

"Huh?"

"Aviva, is it happening now?" I ask.

"Yes. Oh yes, yes, yes." She hugs herself.

"What's the hell's going on?" Dorrie fumes.

"Oh, the room is beautiful. I thought people were making up that stuff about things changing color, but it's true," Aviva says.

"She's tripping," I tell Dorrie.

"Wow!" Dorrie shouts. "You got any more?"

"No, she doesn't," I say.

"She can speak for herself."

"No, she doesn't," Aviva says and laughs. "Oh God, it's gorgeous. Look at the phone. It just turned blue."

"It is blue," I say.

"Not this shade of blue. Nina, hold out your hand. . . . There's a rainbow between your fingers."

"That's nice," I say.

"I wish you had some more acid," Dorrie says, lighting a joint.

Aviva gets up and goes over to the mirror. "Light. White light. I'm the moon. Look at my face. The face of the moon. Ooh. Craters. My God, I've got craters on my face. Ugh. They're horrible."

Oh God, she's going to freak, I think. "Avi. Avi. There are no craters on your face. Those are just your pores. Everything looks bigger because you're tripping," I say quickly.

She breathes deeply. "Oh, you're right. Just my pores and pimples. . . . Hey, let's go outside."

"I think it would be better if we didn't."

"Oh, come on. I want to see the rainbows in the street." She heads for the door.

I bolt after her, calling "Dorrie, you coming?"

"Not right now."

"Thanks a lot," I say.

We have been hitchhiking for the past two hours. Other than insisting on hiking and admiring the lights, Aviva hasn't been very odd. But keeping pace with her has been tiring.

"Why don't we go to a movie?" I finally suggested.

It turned out that *2001* was playing at midnight near Aviva's apartment, so we went to that. "A trip within a trip," Aviva kept whispering throughout the film.

It's now almost three in the morning. "You still feel it?" I ask.

"Yeah. It's not as strong, though."

We walk back to her apartment.

And there standing in front of the building is John. "Hi," he says.

"John!" I yell and embrace him. "What are you doing here?"

The streetlamp lights his hair, making him look more angelic than ever.

"Just got in. Hitched a ride."

"That's what we've been doing," I say. "Oh John, I missed you."

He smiles. We kiss.

Then Aviva says, "Hi lover," and kisses him on the lips.

"She's tripping," I say.

"Yeah? Having a good one?"

"Lovely."

"Me too," he says.

"What?" I yell again.

"Shhh," he hushes me.

"Are you kidding?"

"No. I've been tripping all the way down from New Hampshire. Mescaline."

"Oh Christ," I say. "Let's go upstairs."

"Oh no. I want to go somewhere."

"Avi, come on."

"Let's go to Calvary. I want to see those gates while I'm tripping."

"Aren't you tired? Haven't you had enough?" I ask.

"What's Calvary?" John asks.

"A cemetery."

"Hey, I'd like to see that too."

John. My John. What's happening here? "Listen Avi," I say. "If I take us there, you've got to promise that afterward we will retire for the evening."

"Okay. We will retire."

So we all get into the front seat of my old Chevy, John in the middle.

The gates of Calvary look eerie as ever with the gibbous moon shining on them.

"Wow!" John exclaims. "Creepy!"

"Beautiful," Aviva says. "Black and silver."

After a few minutes, I say, "Well, can we go now?"

"No. I'm going in."

"Stop clowning. It's three-thirty a.m. The gate's locked. And there's probably a night watchman."

She gets out of my car.

"Avi, you can't!" I protest.

"Shhh," she says and starts climbing the gate.

"John, stop her!"

"Why? Come on. Let's go inside."

I turn to him in disbelief. "You can't mean it."

He doesn't answer, just gets out of the car and begins to climb the gate too.

"Oh my God. How did I get into this one?" I say and go after them.

I practically rip my jeans on the wrought iron, but I make it over. Aviva is wandering ahead of me, looking like a ghost among the graves. John follows. Jesus walking again. Or maybe the archangel Gabriel about to wake the dead.

Aviva flits in and out among the tombstones. "Hey," I call in a loud whisper. "Don't walk so fast. Ouch!" A stone in my shoe. I have to stop to shake it out. When I look up, Aviva and John are gone.

I call their names.

No answer.

"Christ," I hiss and call again.

A glimmer of something. Maybe Aviva's watch. I start moving toward it.

Then I stumble and fall. It's only when I tug myself up that I realize I've fallen across the flowers on somebody's grave.

"Avi! John!" I yell. "Where are you?" I sob and start to run.

Then I hear a giggle. It's coming from behind the big mausoleum.

"Aviva?" I say more quietly. "John?" Breathing heavily, with my heart pounding, I make my way carefully over to the tomb.

"Aviva! John!" I call again. Almost there. Turn the corner. And I nearly stumble again, this time over two very living bodies, entwined about each other.

"Oh God!" I cry.

Aviva and John sit up. I see in the moonlight Aviva's bare breasts and John's unzipped fly.

"Oh God. What are you doing?"

282

"Isn't it obvious," Aviva says.

"How could you? Here. And with John!"

Aviva looks at me. "I guess it's time you knew . . ."

"Knew what?"

"Me and John. In California."

"What are you saying? You're tripping, Aviva. You don't know what you're saying."

"No, it's true. Isn't it John?"

"Yeah. It's true."

I stare at him. "You're tripping, too."

"Yeah. But it's still true."

"I can't believe this! Maybe I'm the one who's tripping. First Gwyn. Now you. Aviva, I trusted you. How could you do this to me?"

"Do what? I'm not doing anything to you. Remember that song: 'Sister lovers—water-brothers. And in time, maybe others. Why can't we go on as three?' "

"You . . ." I begin.

But then we hear a distant voice saying, "I think someone's there."

"Hide," Aviva commands.

We crouch down. The voice comes nearer. It swings a flashlight.

"Oh my God," I murmur.

Nearer.

Then we hear a patter somewhere to the left. Probably a cat. Or a ghost.

The voice takes off after it.

"Go," Aviva orders.

We go. Fast. Somehow we manage to scramble over the fence.

It's a long walk back to the car. Without saying a word, I drive back to Manhattan.

We get to Aviva's building.

"Aren't you coming up with us?" John asks.

"Yes. We're going to take a lovely bubble bath. Join us," Aviva invites.

"Get out," I say.

They do.

"Wait a minute," I say. "I want to ask John something. Alone."

Aviva walks inside. John faces me.

"We were going together for two months. We never had sex once. You told me you loved me. You went on tour and had sex with my best friend. Why?"

"She wanted to."

"I wanted to, too."

"You didn't . . . take charge."

I stare at him. "You mean she raped you?"

"No. But she was aggressive."

"And you loved it."

"Well, I liked it."

"And yet you said you love me."

"I do. I love Aviva too."

"You just love everybody, don't you," I sneer.

"Not everybody. But most people. Listen, if you want to have sex with me . . ."

"Not want. Wanted. The tense is past. I wouldn't have sex with you now if you flung yourself at my feet."

"Okay." He shrugs.

"You can go upstairs to your bubble bath now."

"Okay." He shrugs again, turns and walks into the building.

I stand still and stare at the lightening sky. I have no one, I say to myself. I never had anyone.

Then I get in my car and drive to the beach.

The ocean looks cool and calm. Pink gold in the rising sun. I remember sitting here months ago thinking about England, wishing I were in Gwyn's arms once again. Good-bye, Gwyn. Good-bye, John.

I take off my shoes and walk to the shore. It is cool. Foam eddies around my feet.

I take off the rest of my clothes and walk slowly into the water. It is not as calm as I thought. Waves buffet my legs and the undertow is strong. A big breaker gathers, bears down on me. I inhale deeply and plunge beneath it, then come up in a serene pool beyond the breakers. I think how wonderful it would be to swim straight out, to keep swimming until I reach some place, some island far away from here, to say good-bye to everyone and everything.

I begin to do the crawl. Long, clean strokes. To carry me to my island hung with jewels, where all are princes, none are fools. You always could write, Avi. Always. Thank you, fuck you and bye-bye. Say good-bye for me to Dorrie. Except she's gone already. And to Nancy. Poor Nancy. Well, nothing lasts forever.

I turn my head. The shore is far away. Never mind. Keep swimming, Nina. Keep swimming and you'll never have to see the Rabbit's Foot again. Or Mr. Knoedler. Or Mom and Dad. Or Queens College. Or Floyd.

Floyd. A panther arm stretches out before me, pulling me back from a whale. A strong arm that cradles me warm and caring. I forget where I am, inhale, get a mouthful, a windpipe-ful of salt water. I choke, sputter, flail about, then tread water.

Floyd. I don't want to say good-bye to Floyd. I want to see him get out of prison. I want to see him proud and strong again.

I don't want to say good-bye to Billy either. I want to see him come home safe and whole.

I don't want to say good-bye to Ruth. Nor to Jerry.

I don't want to say good-bye to myself.

And suddenly, everything is changed. Sea-changed. My

lungs, my head feel clear. I dive down, float up slowly, push my hair back from my eyes.

Then, I turn and swim back to shore, the sun coming up golden on my back, the air full of sandpiper songs.

July 15, 1969

Dear Nina,

Useless to sit and stir up memories, but I can't seem to help it. At least I'm still sane. Been thinking a lot about my granddaddy's farm and those peaches I once told you about. If I ever get out of here, I'd like to take you down there—and we can gorge ourselves 'til we never want to see another peach. Tell me, Nina, would you like to do that?

Floyd

July 23, 1969

Dear Floyd,
    Yes.
        Nina

PART THREE

August 1969

Chapter 25

QUEENS BOY TO GET MEDAL
William Klein, 21, of Flushing, New York, will
receive a Bronze Star for gallantry. While successfully rescuing a fellow soldier trapped by
a fallen tree, Klein was shot and seriously
wounded in the leg. Army doctors were able
to save the limb, but say that it is permanently
damaged. Klein returned home from Vietnam
to recuperate last week. He will be awarded
the medal at a ceremony in August.

The award ceremony is next week. I read it in the papers.
Just as I read the other article over a month ago.

It was late June and I had just returned from countercommencement. I had suddenly—or maybe gradually—decided I didn't want to shake the president's hand and be given
my mock diploma from Good Old Q.C. The president had
expelled Jerry, along with a lot of other people. He would
have expelled me too if Miss Burris of fencing fame and Dr.
Hewitt, one of my former English professors, hadn't spoken

up for me. So I was *allowed* to graduate. But I'd be damned if I was going to let the president pat himself on the back for doing so. So I decided to go to countercommencement, our alternative to regular commencement, arranged by the students for the students. I tried to convince Nancy to go to it too, but she said her parents would kill her if she didn't go to regular graduation.

My parents were appalled and hurt and they refused to go. They had already been dealt a low blow by the news that, thanks to Mr. Knoedler, Long Island City High School did not want me as a teacher in the fall. I wasn't too miffed—there are other schools that will require my services. "But not such good ones," Mom said, meaning ones that are mostly Black and Hispanic. Anyway, I explained that my real diploma would arrive by mail whether or not I went, and that they were welcome to frame it or use it for toilet paper, whichever suited their purposes. They yelled at me and shook their heads and said they didn't know me anymore, that I have changed.

Ruth, however, said she'd love to be my guest. She cheered when I called out my own name. We graduates shook each other's hands and railed against the war and the city university. I enjoyed it thoroughly.

When I got home, my parents weren't there. Ruth had had to leave early. I had no one I wanted to call. So I picked up the newspaper. Since May—the last time I got a letter from Billy—I've made it a point to look through it every day—especially the casualty lists. I was still feeling good from the ceremony and I wasn't prepared for bad news. Maybe that's why the little article hit me so hard. Billy. Wounded in the leg. My God, it had to be the leg. At least he was alive. But did he want to be?

I grabbed the phone and dialed frantically. Then I stopped and clattered down the receiver. I ran out of the house, jumped into my car and raced over to Billy's house. It looked more dingy than ever in the bright sun. I rang the bell.

Billy's father answered the door. He looked serene as ever, but paler and more drawn. "Yes," he said softly.

"Hello, Mr. Klein. I'm Nina. Remember me?"

"Yes, of course, Nina."

"I read . . . Billy . . . can I . . . is he okay?" I stammered.

"He is all right."

"His leg . . . can he dance . . . I mean . . . Will he . . . ?"

"The doctors say he probably will not be able to dance again."

"Oh no!" I clapped my hand to my mouth.

"It is sad," his father said. "But sometimes one can learn from adversity."

I was too upset to be angry at the facile remarks Mr. Klein made. "Can I see him?" I asked.

"He does not wish to see anyone. But since you are a good friend . . ."

Billy was sitting in a wheelchair staring out his window when I came in.

"Billy," I said softly.

He turned and looked at me for a long time. His eyes frightened me. They were no longer sparkling, or pained, or full of fear. They were cold and dead.

"I told him I didn't want to see anyone," he said.

"Billy, it's me. Nina. I'm not anyone."

"Go home," he said.

"Please. Don't send me away. I'm so happy you're back."

"Go home," he repeated.

"Billy, I'm your friend. I understand. Your leg. You might not be able . . ."

"You don't understand. No one understands who hasn't been there. Seen the bodies and parts of bodies all over the place. Seen people running with their skins on fire. And babies. Babies cut up like . . ."

"Stop it!" I yelled.

He stopped. "Now go home."

I turned and went.

Then I cried for hours. Afterward I thought of Dorrie. Did she know? Was she okay? But I couldn't bring myself to call Aviva's and find out. I wanted no part of Aviva anymore. Not after what she had done to me.

It was Dorrie who called me. Stoned and strangely calm. "Have you heard?" she asked.

"Yes."

"I tried to see him. His father wouldn't let me in."

"Dorrie . . . I saw him," I said.

"You did?"

"Yes. He's . . . he's bitter. He doesn't want anyone to comfort him. He won't be comforted."

"He never loved me."

"No," I said, "not the way you wanted him to."

"He loved you."

"No. We were friends." Then I got angry. "Dorrie, look at yourself. You used to be strong. At least, you seemed to be. I used to depend on your common sense. For God's sake, you can't live your life for Billy!"

"Why not? You lived yours for Gwyn. And then for John."

"No. No, I didn't. And if I did, I was stupid."

There was silence. Then, Dorrie said, "Avi's going to give up the apartment and move back home."

"What will you do?" I asked.

"I don't know . . . maybe I'll get married," she said, and laughed in a stilted voice.

I laughed too.

I shouldn't have. Less than one month later, when the first man walked on the moon, Dorrie was joined in holy matrimony

292

to an insurance agent friend of Carter's and moved to a house in the Boston suburbs.

I didn't go to the wedding.

Nancy was shocked by the whole thing. "Why did she do it? Why?" she asked over and over. "She hardly knows the guy!"

"I don't know," I said. "I guess she couldn't figure out what else to do with her life."

"The Crew is just falling apart. We used to be so together."

"Were we?"

"Of course we were," Nancy replied.

But I just shrugged.

June. July. August.

I wonder if Billy will pick up his medal.

Chapter 26

One year ago. Desperate hopes. Dangling dreams. The pain of leaving Gwyn. Sitting there, my ass hurting, wanting to turn the plane around. The Crew meeting me, kicking off a year that saw hopes wrecked and dreams broken. A bunch of middle-class girls confusing freedom with freakdom—and not even being very successful at the latter.

Yeah, I could look at it that way if I want to.

But it would only be half a truth.

Other things happened this year. Good, even glorious things. Things that maybe can't be mapped or charted or even written about. I've been thinking about this past year a lot. About the Crew. About Aviva. About Floyd. About myself. About why things turned out the way they did.

"Hey, you want some soda?" A girl in the car next to mine. Three other girls in the car smile.

All of us chugging along at five miles an hour. Bumper-to-bumper traffic. And nobody caring. Everyone singing. Smoking reefer. Getting tan on one arm.

"Yeah, I'd love some," I answer.

She hands me a can.

"Where you from?" she asks.

"Long Island. You?"

"Staten Island. You going up to Woodstock all by yourself?" she asks from the people-filled car.

"Yeah. By myself." Can't tell her that, like her, I too was supposed to have three companions. "Birds," Gwyn would have said. A nursery song comes into my head:

Four little chickadees
Sitting in a tree,
One got married and then there were three.
Three little chickadees
Wondering what to do,
One went to Europe and then there were two.
Two little chickadees
Sitting all alone,
Had a nasty fight and then there was one.
Chickadee, chickadee,
Fly away,
Chickadee, chickadee,
Fly today.

Yeah, Nancy went off to Europe with her parents—a graduation present, of course. Dorrie's still married. And Aviva . . . A fight? Could I call what happened between Aviva and myself anything as simple as a fight?

"There," the girl says.

"I'm sorry. I didn't hear what you said."

"I said, you won't have any trouble meeting people there."

"That looks true enough. At this rate, I don't even have to wait until I'm there."

She laughs.

The traffic eases a bit. As we roll past each other, she calls, "Let your light shine!"

I smile. "You too!" I say, and decide to pick up some hitch-hikers.

Eight hours on the road, but my four happy passengers and I are finally here. Well, almost. We're on the road that goes up to Yasgur's farm, where the festival is. It's lined with parked cars. "Hey, okay if I ditch the car and we walk?" I ask my passengers.

"Sure," they agree.

So off we go.

I've got to pee. "Catch you later," I tell my former passengers.

They wave.

Walk into a gas station. Tremendous line of prospective urinators. I laugh at my phrase.

Guy ahead of my laughs too, then asks what I'm laughing at.

I tell him.

He laughs again.

"You laugh," I say, "but you could just go behind a tree."

"Not I. I'm a prospective defecator," he says.

We crack up.

Finally get in. Toilet filled with paper. Won't flush. Oh well.

Hit the road. Feet, do your stuff. Lots of people with heavy packs. I'm traveling light. Have a motel reservation, booked months ago at Nancy's insistence.

"You from New York?" people asking people.

"Nah. Vermont."

"Pennsylvania."

"Yeah. Binghamton."

"No. New Jersey."

"Massachusetts."

"Utah."

Utah! And there are Texans, Californians, Coloradans, Georgians. Kids from Canada. Folks from France. Boys and girls from Brooklyn.

In jeans. In shorts. In spangles. In fringes. T-shirted. Bare chested. And even someone dressed in an American flag.

All walking up the hill.

God knows how many are already at the farm, hearing Arlo Guthrie or Jimi Hendrix or whoever is singing now.

But it doesn't seem to matter.

The air is glowing. Let your light shine.

At dusk I get to the entrance. Too late to go to the motel tonight. So what? Nobody's taking tickets. Nobody needs tickets. It doesn't seem to matter.

Thousands of people sitting, sprawling, dancing on a hill. At the bottom, tiny on a small stage, someone singing. "If I were a carpenter, And you were a lady . . ." Tim Hardin.

It's raining softly.

"Hey, want to come in our tent?" a girl asks me.

"Is there enough room?"

"Sure."

Five people already inside. Packed like sardines. "The more the merrier," one says.

I squeeze in.

"Isn't this incredible?" a boy asks. He looks about fourteen.

"Yeah. Incredible."

And it is. "Harmony and understanding. Sympathy and trust abounding . . ." Maybe this really is the dawning of the Age of Aquarius.

Later, we sit outside in the damp field and listen to Ravi Shankar play the sitar. Timmy—the young-looking boy—massages my neck, then kisses the nape softly. "Beautiful lady," he says. I smile and roll a jay. Suddenly, a crack of lightning and the rain really comes. People are running all over the stage doing something to the equipment. We watch a minute.

Then, giggling and slipping, we dive into the tent.

The storm doesn't last long and soon there's more music. One by one, we fall asleep, arms around each other, while Joan Baez sings a lullaby and the rain patters softly.

The next morning, stiff and happy, I wake up. Got to walk. Find some food. My hosts are all out. Want to feed them. Do something for them.

Vendors are running out. Someone says this commune called The Hog Farm is cooking up batches of rice and stuff for everyone.

"You know how many people are here, man?" a guy says to me.

"How many?"

"Half a million."

"You're kidding."

"No, man. They said it on the radio." He waves a transistor.

It's hot and humid. Everything is muddy and squishy. Toilets are useless. There's no running water. The governor has declared us a disaster area. Nobody minds.

I find the Hog Farm's booth. Feed myself. Take some back to the tent. Ask where my motel is. Too far away. "Stay with us," my hosts say.

"Don't want to impose," I say and decide to find somebody else to impose on tonight or sleep in the mud. Which doesn't seem like such a bad idea.

Strange. Fussy, cautious Nina. What's happening to her? Maybe more of the sea-change. Or a mud-change. Whatever it is is good.

"Nina!" Voice hits me like a whipcrack.

I turn. Her eyes are sharp as always. Insolent, maybe. She's mud-stained too. Half a million people seem to disappear.

"Aviva," I say. "Half a million people, and here we meet."

"Does it surprise you?"

"No, not really."

"You alone?"

"Yes."

"Having fun?"

"Yes."

"I dropped John, you know," she says.

"Oh."

"Don't you want to know why?"

"No. I don't."

"Sure you do. He was a bore. An absolute dimwit. You didn't need him, Nina. You're much too smart for him."

I say nothing.

"It was stupid for us to fight over him. Good riddance, I say. So you can stop being angry . . ."

"Aviva," I interrupt, "what happened wasn't about John."

"What do you mean?" She looks confused.

"I saw John as someone he never was. I did the same thing with Gwyn. Our fight wasn't about either of them. It was about how we used—misused—each other. For months, years even, you led. You gathered us all around you—me, Dorrie, Nancy, Billy—because you needed us to be there. But only on your terms. You didn't like any of us to have anything you didn't supply or stamp your seal of approval on. I think you didn't want any of us to be happy without you, independent of you. But it wasn't all your fault. Somehow, I went along with it. Maybe I felt I had to keep up with you—to compete with you even. I didn't know why it was so important to do that. I still don't. But I did it. And you encouraged it. Yeah, I know, there were times we loved each other. But we weren't good at loving."

"Whew, what a mouthful. I've known you to get pompous, but not to sound like a goddamn shrink."

299

"I haven't shrunk. I've grown."

She snorts. "So you think we've been fiends, instead of friends."

I shake my head. "No, not fiends. Opponents. But not fiends." I turn to go.

"Nina. Wait."

I look at her. She seems small now. Eyes sort of troubled. "You don't think we can be friends?"

"I don't know. Maybe we can. But not now. Not until we learn more about ourselves."

"You think that's possible?"

"I don't know that either. But if half a million people singing and loving in one place are possible, anything's possible."

"Oh come on, Nina. You don't believe this can last . . . this Age of Aquarius crap? By next summer, we'll all forget it. Nothing lasts forever."

I pause and look out over the crowd, remembering how I once said that same thing. "You're right. Nothing lasts forever. Things change. That's something I've had to learn. The worst thing is to cling to what was, to fight the changes and possibilities for change. And those possibilities always exist. No matter what happens next summer or the next decade, I will have changed. Because I want to."

Then, I walk away, and, as if on some crazy macrocosmic cue, a blessed breeze blows across the hill. And through the air, across the crowd, a lone voice sings:

"It's been a long time comin'
It's going to be a long time gone."

300

Chapter 27

I've never been in a courtroom before, but I knew it would look like this: paneled walls, hard wooden benches, a gate separating us spectators from defendant and counsel, judge and jury. My stomach feels terrible and I've been biting my nails.

The day after I returned from Woodstock, Jimi Hendrix's knockout early-morning rendition of "The Star-Spangled Banner" still throbbing in my head, Aggie called. "The trial date's been set. Ten days from today."

"Thank God!"

"Yeah. Let's hope the jury gives us a reason to."

"Will I be able to watch?"

"I think so."

"Okay. Give me the details. . . ."

So here I am. Half an hour early. When Floyd's family comes in, I recognize them right away. Tall, handsome father; tall, beautiful mother; and tall, beautiful Aggie, who looks just like Floyd. Only Floyd's brother is a surprise—short and slim; but also handsome.

Aggie comes over. "You must be Nina," she says.

I nod and hold out my hand. She gives it a squeeze.

"Come sit with us," she offers.

I thank her and accept.

We try to talk, but we're all tense. Other friends arrive—Jerry, who waves; Arnie the flautist; Jimmy, Aggie's boyfriend; and the whole "Police Brutality" committee. But no one from the Rabbit's Foot. Soon the lawyers arrive. The slim white woman in the green suit is Floyd's. The burly white man in blue pinstripes must be from the D.A.'s office. Then the judge and court stenographer. Other people—witnesses?—fill the seats. Finally, Floyd is brought in by two policemen.

He looks haggard—sort of gray under his dark brown skin. And his fine big Afro has been shorn—it was impossible to take proper care of it, he wrote me. I have a flash of Billy at the train station, wan, hair clipped, mustache gone—another man going to another battle. A man stripped of his soul along with his hair.

Floyd turns his head and sees us. And he smiles, smiles so his face is no longer haggard, but radiant, full of strength. His eyes rest on me and I see a light in them I never saw before. And I know then that no matter what happens, Floyd will never lose his soul.

Then the jury files in. Floyd turns his head to see them. The judge raps his gavel. And the trial begins.

Charges. Plea—"Not guilty, your honor." Procedure to the jury.

Prosecution's case. First witness. Cop who claims on January tenth Floyd was at Jamaica Avenue and Sutphin Boulevard selling dope. D.A. tries to establish that January tenth was just two days after Floyd's previous trial for not carrying his draft card.

Counsel for the defense objects.

Objection overruled.

Witness says he and partner gave chase, but suspect got

away. But they caught the junkie who identified the pusher as Floyd.

Second cop testifies.

Counsel for the defense cross-examines. Could either cop identify Floyd himself? Cop waffles.

Junkie is next witness. He looks doped. Contends it was Floyd.

"They made him testify," Aggie whispers. "Told him they'd let him off if he said it was Floyd. Had to be."

Defense counsel asks if Floyd was junkie's regular pusher.

Junkie sniffles, wipes nose and finally says, "No. I never bought from Floyd before."

"Thank you, no more questions," counsel says, surprising everyone.

And finally, the judge recesses for lunch.

I go for a walk by myself.

Back from recess. More cops on the stand. This one claims he found dope in Floyd's apartment. Exhibit A.

I am incensed. This is an unbelievable frame-up.

Cross-examination by defense. Where was dope found? Was the dope necessarily Floyd's just because it was in his apartment? Is it possible someone dropped it there?

"Why isn't she exposing the frame-up?" I hiss.

"Because there's no proof," Aggie whispers. "She's working to make the jury believe someone could have left it there— but she can't finger the cops."

Then the judge adjourns for the day. Floyd's family invites me to dinner. I thank them, but tell them not tonight. I know it's not the right time yet.

Next day. Defense introduces character witnesses who attest to Floyd's abilities as a student and as a musician, and his tough antidrug stance. Prosecution tries to get them to talk about Floyd's militancy. "Militants are antidrug," they say.

Then defense introduces two new witnesses. Musicians who

say Floyd was jamming with them all that night in Manhattan. The prosecution is visibly stunned. Audible murmurs in the courtroom.

The D.A. musters forces and tries to shake the witnesses. They use dope, he implies.

Defense objects.

Sustained.

We all sigh.

D.A. tries a new tack. Floyd could have slipped off for an hour, sold dope and come back.

Ridiculous.

Much argument over timetables of subways. Prosecution making like Monsieur Poirot or someone.

We recess for lunch.

Back again. Defense and prosecution are asked to sum up. Prosecution delivers a scathing attack on drug pushers and anti-American militants. Defense says the issue here is not politics (which of course it is), but drug dealing. The dope could have been left in the apartment by anyone. The junkie is frightened and mistaken. Perhaps he heard Floyd's name and used it. In any event, he is not a reliable witness. But the two musicians are. It is clear from their evidence and the evidence of others that Floyd Cooke is not and never has been a pusher.

The jury goes out.

A half hour, an hour passes. My nails are bitten to the quick. "They can't convict him. It's obvious the cops, the junkie are all lying," I say.

But Floyd's brother shrugs. "That jury is five-sixths Good Upstanding White Americans. They don't like militants no-how."

"Be quiet, Paul," Mrs. Cooke says.

Another hour.

I feel I'm going to faint.

Finally, a signal and in they file.

"Have you reached a verdict?" the judge asks the foreman.

"We have, your honor," he says, like out of some movie. "We find the defendant Not Guilty."

Floyd and his lawyer embrace. I bolt out of my seat and don't even realize I'm yelling until I reach Floyd. So many arms are trying to grab him I don't know whose I'm holding.

This time I do accept the dinner invitation.

Dinner at the Cookes' turns out to be funny, sort of awkward, but nice too. Floyd showers and shaves and changes his clothes, while his parents show me family scrapbooks. Then Floyd comes in and groans at the old photos. During the meal, Mr. and Mrs. Cooke ask me about my upcoming teaching career. Paul seems aloof, maybe suspicious. Aggie and her boyfriend kid Floyd about the long vacation he's had and how it's time to get back to work.

"Got a lot of work to do," Floyd says. "More organizing than ever."

And across the table, he and I smile at each other.

Finally, Floyd and I leave his parents' house and go to his apartment. We sit in his kitchen.

"Aggie won't be back tonight," he says.

"Shall I borrow her nightgown again?" I ask.

"It's too warm for a nightgown."

We look feelingly at each other.

"A lot's happened since New Year's Eve," I say.

"Yes, I know."

"I didn't write you all of it."

"You'll have plenty of time to tell me about it, if you want to."

"I want to."

"But not tonight."

"No, not tonight."

And then we both stand up, I so swiftly I knock over a chair.

"Clumsy," I say.

"No. Never."

And we embrace, kiss. An aching kiss, telling months of denial, frustration, changes and joy.

"Floyd, I haven't made love with anyone in a year."

"It's something you don't forget how to do—like driving a car." He grins.

I laugh.

Then, arms around each other's waists, we walk to Floyd's bedroom.

I lie on the bed.

"Let me be naked for you first," he says.

"You've seen me naked before," I say.

"Yes. But that doesn't count," he says gently. He takes off his clothes and lies beside me.

I look at him for a long time, learning the curves of his body, the gleam of his skin. "You are so beautiful," I say at last, running my hand down his side.

He draws me to him, kissing my mouth, my ears, my neck as he slides me out of my clothes.

"Oh woman, woman, you feel so good," he moans.

"Oh man, so do you," I answer, pressing tightly against him.

And slowly, passionately, we make love all night long.

===== **Chapter 28** =====

"I am not much of a speaker. But I was once a good dancer. The Army got my leg. It almost got my mind, too. But I saved it."

In Bryant Park, Floyd and I stand right in front of the platform listening to Billy Klein.

In August, Billy showed up at the awards ceremony, made an impassioned speech against U.S. involvement in the war and refused his medal. The media went wild. Articles in the papers. Stuff on TV. Then Billy joined Vietnam Veterans Against the War. Today, at the Moratorium, he is their key speaker.

"But I want to say that if we don't fight to end this hellish war, we'll all lose our minds, our hearts and our souls too. Because this war is truly evil itself."

"Not much of a speaker indeed. He's like a preacher," Ruth says.

"You can say that again," Floyd agrees.

In September, he and I went down to his grandfather's farm in Georgia. It was glorious. The sun. The fields. Both idyllic and down-home. Over the past year, we'd seen each other desperate, hurt, crazed, frightened, angry and loving too much and too often to fool with preliminaries. The earth was solidly under our feet. We skinny-dipped in a swimming hole, went fishing, milked cows, fed pigs, lay naked under a peach tree while Floyd licked the peach juice from my lips and chin. At night, his tough, taciturn grandmother turned a blind eye when Floyd and I slept together in a single, narrow bed, holding each other tight and feeling so strong. One night I awoke, moonlight streaming on my face, to find Floyd looking at me, tears running down his cheeks.

"What's wrong?" I asked, startled.

"Nothing," he answered quietly. "For once, something be right." Then, he pulled me on top of him. "Love me up, woman. Nobody can love me up the way you do," he said huskily. "Come on. Give it here."

And I gave it, all the while silently singing "You Make Me Feel Like a Natural Woman."

Afterward, he said, "I ain't no courtier, Nina. No prince. You know that?"

"Thank God!" I exclaimed.

And we both laughed.

"You're my lover," I said proudly, "and my friend."

"And a friendly lover?"

"That too."

We smiled at each other and cuddled closer in the tiny bed.

When we returned to New York, I decided to rent an apartment with Ruth on the Upper West Side of Manhattan, not far from where I'm teaching. Floyd was not happy. He wanted us to live together.

"Is that why you won't live with me?" he said.

Holding hands. Lying in bed. Listening to Rahsaan Roland Kirk.

"All those things I once said about Black men balling white women?"

I smiled. "No. It's just . . . Well, I seem to have lived my whole life competing with women and acting for men. If we're going to work out, I have to try a different way."

"Oh Lordy," he said. "Not only do I have to fall for a white woman, but a feminist, yet." Then he grinned and kissed me softly.

"You understand?" I asked.

"Yo comprendo," he said. "But my God, Nina, things ain't never gonna be easy."

"No," I agreed. "Never."

Billy finishes his speech and the crowd roars. Then he limps down off the dais and sees me. "Nina," he says softly. "My God. It's been a long time." We hug.

"You're okay now," I say.

"Yes." He turns. "Floyd . . . I'm glad to see you. I've been wanting to apologize for a long time for when I jumped you after *Hair*. It was macho, racist crap."

Floyd is a little taken aback. He just nods.

I introduce Ruth. But then she moves quietly apart from us, letting us talk, get to know each other a little again. We grope for words, three survivors from three very different wars with a lot more battles ahead of us.

The crowd is moving out of the park, marching down 42nd Street.

Tonight we will carry candles for the dead and for the living.

Now, singing "Give Peace a Chance," we join the marchers. Walking side by side. Holding hands. I marvel at how different we are, how different some of us have become. Ruth, Billy, Floyd and me.

My first new friends.